The Jazz Phillips Mystery Series
(in order of publication)**

Murder in the Choir*

Murder by the Board*

Murder in the Kirk*

Murder was a Blast*

Murder by the Queen*

Murder on the Run*

Jazz in the Cross-hair*

Jazz in the Golden Light*

Jazz Plays the Big Easy Blues*

Jazz Draws a Wild Card*

Jazz and the Black Widow*

Jazz and the Last one Left*

*Available in print

** See page 258 for a case chronology

Jazz and the Last One Left

a jazz phillips mystery

by

Joel B Reed

White Turtle Books LLC
Canby, Minnesota

This is an original work of fiction. No character presented here represents any flesh and blood person, living or dead. The events reported never happened except any major historical events mentioned in passing. The same is true of any places mentioned. These exist only in the author's imagination. Yet, these could have been real people living out real events in the real world as we know it, and this is what makes the storyteller's craft.

The quotation from William Shakespeare on page 143 is from the opening lines of *Richard III*. The quotation on page 197 comes from *Amazing Grace* by John Newton, first published in 1779. The last line in the Note from the Author is the closing line of "The Night Before Christmas" by Clement Clark Moore and was first published in 1882. All these works reside in the common domain.

ISBN 978-1-933482-28-6 (1-933482-28-1)

White Turtle Books, LLC
Canby, Minnesota, USA
WhiteTurtleBooks.com

An Odd Call

1 It was the strangest case. Nicole and I were both working mostly for Sam McKee by then, living in the national capitol during the school year and spending our summers at our place in Wyoming. The kids loved it and we did, too. It gave us time to be a family, three months to enjoy each other's company as we did all the things most people try to cram into a two week vacation. There were horses to ride, varmints to hunt, canoes to paddle and some of the best trout fishing in the state. When we felt the need of company there were plenty of friends to visit, and at least once a month there was a gathering at the McKee ranch near Casper. Siblings get tired of one another and this gave ours lots of honorary cousins to see.

We had been back in Washington a couple of months when the call came. I was working on something Sam wanted me to look at and was surprised when my personal phone rang. Nicole had helped me set it up so I could tell who was calling by the ring tone and I was surprised to hear the annoying sound of an old style telephone bell. It took me a moment to remember that this was the sound reserved for the general public.

I started to let the call go to voice mail but changed my mind. I still do training seminars for police departments and other law enforcement agencies, and I really enjoyed presenting seminars. It gave me a chance to get away by myself and gave us all a break from being together too much. It also helped me expand my professional network.

Then, too, there are occasional calls for help catching a serial killer. While I hand most of those calls over to Dee these days, I still like the occasional opportunity to do real police work for a change. That's especially true if Dee and I can work the case together and that day I felt the need of a break from sifting through an avalanche of spreadsheets.

So I picked up the phone. "This is Jazz Phillips," I said. The man I found myself talking to told me his name was Thomas Smith. His voice was a pleasant baritone but I knew from the get-go that his real name was something else. I can't explain how I know this but I do. Dee calls it my lie-dar. He claims it's as accurate as my hunches, which average ninety-four percent or better according to his reckoning.

Unlike a lot of the people who call me for help, this caller sounded very relaxed and seemed to be in no hurry. Yet he wasted no time getting to the point, either. "I appreciate your talking my call, Dr. Phillips. Just to make sure I have the right person, weren't you once the head of the Arkansas State Police CID?"

"Guilty as charged," I answered and the alleged Thomas Smith chuckled politely. "I go mostly by Jazz these days," I added. "I think Dr. Phillips sounds too much like foot powder."

Smith chuckled again, this time with a little more feeling. I got the impression he was enjoying our repartee. "That's exactly what I was told you might say. I just spoke with a gentleman named Steven DiRado in Mountain Home, Arkansas. He gave me your number and suggested I get in touch with you in person."

The fact that Dee had referred the call directly to me surprised me. Normally he would screen an inquiry and get in touch with me himself. So something about this didn't seem quite right to him.

"Yes, we were partners for more than twenty years. He was my second in command when I was head of CID and took over when I retired." What I didn't say that Dee was no gentleman, though he knew how to act like one in a pinch. Like many policemen he was more comfortable when he could spit and scratch and talk like a mule skinner without giving offense. "How can I help you?" I asked.

"I am calling because the company I work for has a rather delicate problem," he told me. "It's something I cannot discuss over the phone. Is there somewhere quiet that we could meet and discuss it face to face?"

I thought about this. The problem is that there is a price on my head. It is the result of working for Sam McKee, who carries a bounty of five million dollars. The reason is that the two of us have cost a major drug consortium over eighty million dollars in the last few years. Sam has a nose for a dirty company and when he smells one, he asks me to take a look and tell him what stinks. Our last major venture together took down a huge conglomerate called Kwan Tea Company. It was a major force in the Cadre, the drug consortium that wants us dead. Since the Agency ended up owning the company for all practical purposes, I got saddled with general oversight of their diverse operations. What I do mostly is to look at spreadsheets and make sure the company stays on track. What I am paid to do this seems outrageous, but Sam tells me I am one of the few people in the world who can do the job.

"I could meet you this afternoon," I told Smith. "Do you know where the National Cathedral is?"

"I can find it," he replied. "I understand it's a big place," he added dryly.

"Yes, it is, but they have maps. If you go in the western visitor's entrance you will find an information booth near the George Washington bay. It's a good place to meet. Do you know what I look like?"

"I'm afraid not."

"Well, I'll have on a blue blazer with a red paisley tie and gray slacks. I'm told I look like a monk dressed like a high school guidance counselor."

Smith chuckled. "Well, I'll have on a bright teal tie and will be wearing a black suit. I'm something of a bean pole, too."

"Then we'll look like Mutt and Jeff," I replied. "How does three o'clock sound?"

Smith agreed and rang off. When he did I looked for the number of the phone he used to call me. The number was blank but I got out my Agency phone and requested a caller identification for the last call to my personal phone. The agent who took my call didn't even bother to put me on hold. She read off a number to me and then added, "It's a number for a law office in Silver Springs, Maryland. It apparently is a general number. Do you want us to check their calling log and find out who placed it?"

The voice was one I knew but I couldn't place it. What she was asking is if I wanted the Agency to hack the law office's phone system and get the information. "I guess you better," I told her. "It was a call out of the blue."

"Out of the blue?" she chuckled. "I haven't heard that expression in a while."

"Careful. You're admitting you know dinosaur-speak."

"I love dinosaur-speak," the lady replied with a deep South drawl. "That's why I married one. Someone will call you with the information in the next half hour. Have a good afternoon, Jazz."

"Liz, is that you?" I asked. "I thought the voice sounded familiar. How are things with the Dills?"

"Why don't you come over Sunday afternoon and find out in person?" she asked. "I'll give Nicole a call."

I had to laugh. It was a not so subtle reminder of how absent minded I can be. After I hung up I went back to work and was surprised when the agency phone rang. I thought that was fast and glanced at the clock. It told me that twenty-three minutes had passed since I rang off with Liz.

The clerk who called back went through the standard ID dialogue before he gave me a name. I learned that the caller had been lying about his name, indeed. He was one Willard Isaac Nordwald, a senior partner in a law firm that carried his name within its own. This told me that whatever he wanted to discuss was very important and I wondered if he would give me his real name when we met.

The cathedral is not far from our offices. I took off my tie – I have no idea why – and left for the church a few minutes early. I arrived exactly seven minutes before the hour and stationed myself where I could watch the hallway leading to the information booth. There were the usual assortment of tourists wandering through the place even at that hour but none of them looked like a high powered lawyer to me. Nor were there any beanpoles near the booth.

Then I saw a tall figure in a black suit walk through the main entry and I got up and turned so it appeared I was looking at one of the marvelous stained glass windows that line the nave. Yet I was watching the man in the black suit out of the corner of my eye, too. He looked harmless enough, although he could have been carrying a pistol under the raincoat draped over one arm. So I gave a hand signal to my guardian angels, the security people Sam insists I take with me when I go to the cathedral. Nor can I really argue with this policy. I damned near got murdered there by a suspect once, as had he.

I didn't look directly at the tall man, but both my angels did. He looked out of place dressed the way he was. After a moment he spotted me and walked over to where I was standing. I gave another signal to my angels just in case they had not seen the first and they closed in on either side. This was a potential client and I didn't want to embarrass him being confronted, and possibly decked, on the flagstone floors of the Cathedral. Security is priority one with the angels and I'm glad it is.

"Dr. Phillips, I presume," the tall man said, smiling and offering a hand. When he did, both angels were zeroed in and both had a hand inside their jackets. "My name is Willard Nordwald. I apologize for the subterfuge over the phone. We seem to be living in the Orwellian world of 1984 and I didn't know who might be listening."

"I understand completely," I replied. "You picked me out pretty quickly, even without the tie. How did you know who I was?"

"Your description was pretty accurate," Nordwald told me. "Besides, you were the one person here who looked the least like a policeman. That's how Steven DiRado described you. Not at all like those two folk." He nodded at my angels who were watching him like a hawk.

"You're pretty observant," I told him. "You, on the other hand, look exactly like a corporate lawyer."

"Well, I wasn't always a lawyer and I'm really the black sheep of the firm. I'm the one they use to handle the criminal cases we catch every once in a while. I also handle any and all investigations we need to do." He draped his raincoat over his other arm and took a business card from his shirt pocket. I tensed, ready to move if he pulled a gun. He saw this and paused and blinked before handing me the card.

"Which is why you're the one talking to me," I said, looking at the card. Willard nodded and I gave the angels the stand down signal. "So is this about corporate or personal crime?"

"This is about busting a beast we *may* have. Not our firm, but one of our clients."

I was intrigued. *Busting the Beast* was the title of my first book, the popular version of a textbook about tracking down serial killers. Nor did I think Nordwald had used the phrase by accident. "So is this client an individual or a corporation?"

"It's a corporation. I can't tell you more than that until you have agreed to do at least an initial consultation. We would require a non-disclosure agreement first."

I shook my head. "Sorry. I can't sign a non-disclosure release. I work as a government contractor and the agency I contract with most works in national security. What I can do is to take a dollar from you as a retainer. That should protect you and your client under attorney privilege. If I am after a beast in the corporation, there should not be any conflict of interest. Can you and your client live with that?"

Nordwald thought for a moment and nodded. "I think so but I'll have to get consent from my client. The problem is if word got out they were looking for a beast at their bosom, so to speak, it could create havoc with their business. Even if there is no beast found it could be quite devastating. Just the rumor they were looking might bring down one of their main sources of revenue."

"Which is why they don't want to go to the police," I observed.

Nordwald nodded. "With things as they are these days, it might generate even more interest in their events, but they don't want to take the risk. What complicates things even more is that there may be multiple jurisdictions involved, international jurisdictions."

I thought for a moment. "I need to be very blunt," I said. "What happens if there is a beast, one that needs to be taken down and stopped? What will be done with the information in that case? I cannot sanction vigilante justice or turning a blind eye."

Nordwald nodded. "Neither can we, which is why we are being so careful even looking into this. The client is one of our big accounts but we would have to risk losing the client over breaking the law. Integrity is what we offer our clients. I think that's something our firm has in common with you."

I nodded. "You do understand that I will need to let the head of my agency know what I'm doing. We operate on a strict need to know and no one else will be informed. The other side of that coin is that this gives me access to sources of sensitive information not many people have."

Nordwald nodded. "I think we can accept that. Let me have until noon tomorrow to work things out with our client. I will call you one way or another."

I told him that would be fine but he seemed reluctant to leave. "Is there something else?" I asked.

"Just personal curiosity. Those two people who I said look like police, are they with you?"

I nodded. "They're my security detail."

"You need a security detail? May I ask why?"

I nodded. "I was one of the main players when we took down Kwan Tea. This cost them a lot of money and angered certain people. So there's a price on my head."

"Goodness. I thought dealing with our criminal clients was bad enough. How do you live with that?"

I figured he was asking about the constant presence of security people in our lives. I shrugged. "The choice is to live with having the detail or to die without it. I have young children. They need me to help them grow up."

Brass Tacks

2   Willard Nordwald called early the next morning to let me
     know his client had approved our arrangement. We had
a late lunch at a little cafe with private booths to iron out the
details. The cafe is one the Agency uses when we need to talk to
people we don't want to bring to the office. Michael Angelino,
McKee's executive assistant, has it swept for electronic bugs every
few days. So it is a secure place to talk about sensitive topics. The
only bugs allowed there are ours.

There are also small sweepers about the size of a small cell
phone that we can bring with us to make sure the people we
are talking with are not wearing a wire. While I didn't sense any
threat from Nordwald, I took one along just to make sure. He
might be a great guy but he was a lawyer, and legal eagles march
to a different drum. I was glad to learn that he was not using a
bug.

When we sat down, I explained to Willard that I preferred to
enjoy my food first and deal with business over coffee. He thought
this was an excellent idea and we talked about other things until
we were done. He was interested in my work as a detective and
we talked for almost an hour about that. "You've had a fascinating
career, Jazz," he told me. "I was approached by the FBI my last
year in law school. I've often wondered how things might have
turned out if I'd done that. Law is a very lucrative career but there
isn't much adventure." He looked sad when he said this.

"What held you back?" I asked, having a good idea what he
would tell me. I was right.

Willard chuckled. "It was actually J. Edgar Hoover himself, the
character of the man. I had a very bad feeling about him right off

when I met him and the agents I met seemed cast in the same mold. Since then I've kept track through a few friends who ended up there. The whole culture of the Bureau seems to have been warped by Hoover's rather twisted character. A good example is his vicious campaign against the Black Panthers. His agents were told to do anything they thought useful to bring the Panthers down, but they were also instructed to never let anything they did come back on the Bureau."

"Sounds like you dodged a bullet," I pointed out. "I do a lot of consulting and training work for them and I can still see the imprint Hoover made in the agency. That's been what, twenty-something years?"

"More like thirty. I was just out of law school when he died. I must have been one of the last prospects he interviewed."

Our coffee arrived about then and neither of us wanted any dessert. "So how can I help you, Willard?"

"Well, before we get down to brass tacks, let me do this." He handed me a crisp new hundred dollar bill. "That's a retainer from our firm and I'd like a receipt, if you don't mind." He handed me another document. "That establishes you as an investigator for us and covers you under our client confidentiality with the people we represent. You can bill us for any additional hours at your customary rates." Then he smiled. "Lunch is on us, too."

I read through the simple receipt and signed it. Then I picked up the hundred dollar bill and made a note to myself before I tucked both in my shirt pocket. "That's my low tech filing system. What can I do for you and your firm?"

"I'm going to keep things anonymous for this first visit," he told me. "When, and if, you verbally agree to continue, I will fill in the blanks. What we require is absolute secrecy. I assume you are not recording this, are you?"

"No, I am not." I took out my bug sweeper and explained what it was. "I will be using this for every interview, and if we need to meet elsewhere it will protect us both."

"Excellent," he answered.

"There is one caveat, however. I agree to your terms, assuming your client is not up to something illegal. If I discover that the client appears to be criminal, I will inform you in detail and the consultation will end. I will also turn over any evidence I may have for you to use as you see fit. Am I to assume I will report directly to you?"

"Yes. The situation is this. Our client is a company in the entertainment industry. They put on competitive events and use the competition as the structure for television shows. It boils down to a group of people competing for a large cash prize and the competition takes place all over the world. The corporate offices of the company are not in the United States but a lot of their subcontractors are. So it involves a rather complex problem of jurisdiction. Any questions?"

I shook my head and he continued. "These competitions have been going on for a number of years and there have been a large number of winners. Where your expertise comes to bear is assessing whether or not some of our winners are being murdered. There seems to be a higher death rate for the winners than there is for the general pool of competitors. It may be that the competitive character of the winners is the culprit since they tend to be extreme risk takers. What we need is your professional opinion on what is going on. Then, if you think winners are being murdered, we would want you to do an investigation that discovers who is behind it."

Something clicked in my mind. "I don't suppose this involves a million-dollar winner having an alleged accident in along a scenic shoreline, does it?"

Willard blinked and looked at me in surprise. "May I ask why you ask that?"

"Just a hunch," I said. "I remembered reading about it in the newspaper a while back."

Nordwald nodded. "DiRado mentioned your hunches, too. He told me your accuracy with those is about ninety-three percent."

I shrugged. "It's just intuition," I told him. "It's like being left handed or having perfect pitch hearing."

Willard smiled and leaned back in his chair. "DiRado told me you'd say that, too. Do you think you might be interested? There will be some travel involved."

"Yes, but I will need some help. You've talked to Dee – Steve DiRado – and I would like to have him as my wing man, literally. He is as discreet as I am. I may need to hire one or two others but that would be down the line and only if there is a full investigation."

"Why do you need a wing man?" Willard asked. Nor was this framed as a challenge. It was a simple request for information.

"It's a basic principle of police work. Going after a killer is dangerous so you don't go after one alone or unarmed. With a serial killer, the danger increases tenfold. It's even more dangerous with a multiple killer or a professional."

"A serial killer, Jazz? Do you really think that's what lies behind these deaths, a psychopath?"

"I don't have enough information yet to say one way or the other. Or even if you're right about the unusual number of deaths. Assuming the deaths are tied together, it might not be an ordinary serial killer at work, either. We may be after a hit man or some other multiple killer. There's a lot of money involved and this may well be the common link between all the deaths. Isn't this what you think it might be, murder for profit? Otherwise, why hire me and not some other investigator? Am I wrong?"

Nordwald grimaced. "No, but I thought it was a remote possibility. Your spelling it out makes it real and maybe even probable." He sighed. "All right, I'll authorize hiring Steve DiRado at his usual rates. We can talk about more help later if you need it. Are you in?"

"I'm in and Dee probably is, too. He misses police work." I handed him a list of my standard fees. He glanced at it and nodded. "I'll call Dee today and keep you in the loop. I'll also try to update you every few days, but it may be longer. Why don't I fly him up here and you can brief both of us together?"

Nordwald agreed and Dee was as enthusiastic as I thought he might be. Since it was mid October, most of his resort business was done for the year and he was facing four months of boredom. While an occasional regular customer might show up for a weekend, Karin or the caretaker would be there to unlock the cabin and set up one of the boats if someone wanted to go fishing.

I knew the money would be welcome, too. The resort and Dee's CID pension provided a basic living with little to spare. Dee once told me the money he brought in from consulting with me and McKee paid for the fun stuff. It was part of what he did to make amends to his wife for all the ugly years of his drinking career. He tells me that AA calls this living amends.

As things turned out, it was a week before I could clear my desk and Dee could meet with us in the district. I was surprised when Karin came with him but she had never been able to spend any time in the capitol. She and Nicole had become friends and over the years and we had plenty of room at our place. Nor was there anything urgent on Nicole's calendar so she and Sam's wife, Megan, took Karin in hand and gave her the Queen's tour.

Our briefing took place at Willard Nordwald's office in Silver Springs, Maryland. Since we were outward bound, the traffic wasn't bad at all and we were on the way when Willard called to say he was running late. So Dee and I fell off the wagon with a huge breakfast at an IHOP we discovered nearby. It's one of the perks we give ourselves when we work out of town. Silver Springs isn't exactly out of town, but we were glad of a chance to sneak off the reservation. Both our wives keep us on a pretty rigorous regimen when we're home.

I was just as glad for the delay because it gave Dee and me more time to play catch-up. We stay in touch by phone and email, but it had been a while since we had seen one another in person. Face to face visits are important because so much is conveyed by all the subtle nonverbal signals we give one another, often without knowing we do. The more intimate the relations, the more important these little tells become and Dee once told me he could write a dictionary of mine. When he said this I knew he was right. We have been known to carry on complex conversations without using more than a dozen words. People at the CID used to say we were psychic but it's only verbal shorthand developed over the years we were partners. Couples long married often do the same.

Willard Nordwald's office was exactly what one would expect a senior partner's lair to be. There was nothing but a closed laptop on his desk and a small leather cup for three pens and two pencils. The swivel chair behind the massive walnut surface looked more like a throne, and all the usual appointments were a combination of dark leather and brass.

There was also a wide window behind the desk, forcing those who sat in the small chairs opposite the throne to look directly into the light unless the drapes were drawn. This window was flanked by large walnut book cases filled with hefty leather bound volumes that heightened the contrast and conveyed majestic power. The unstated irony was that there was probably more legal information available on the laptop than in all the leather bound volumes combined a hundred times over.

Even so, Willard did not receive us at his desk. He took us to a well lighted conversation area in a corner far from his desk. This had several comfortable easy chairs around a low walnut coffee table. To one side of the area was a rack full of folding side tables about the size of a TV tray, and next to this was a walnut credenza with a silver coffee service and simple mugs. Three of the chairs each had a folding table beside it.

After offering us coffee and serving us himself, Willard got down to business. "I assume you both are familiar with the reality show The Last One Left." Dee and I both nodded and the lawyer continued. "What you may or may not know is that is that the show is a subsidiary of a British production company called Jolly Good Times. The parent company is headquartered in the Cayman Islands though for practical reasons it has its major production offices in Los Angeles. That's where most of the staff on Last One Left live. The home office is in Newark, New Jersey.

"As you know, if you have seen the show, Last One Left has some very simple rules. Contestants are each given the same number of specific challenges and a certain amount of game money, and they are allowed to work as teams or on their own. They are not allowed to physically harm one another, although other physical contact is allowed. Any contestant is allowed to challenge any other contestant or team of contestants to a duel, but these do not involve direct physical contact. The duel may take the form of a tree climb, for example, or a foot race over an unknown course, wagering a limited amount of game cash. And the number of challenges is limited. There are other rules designed to level the field as much as possible, but that gives you the general idea. Any questions?"

Dee and I looked at each other and shook hour heads. Nordwald went on. "The whole game is set up to eliminate contestants. The goal is to win other players' game cash and a visible record of each one's account is kept on the scoreboard. When a contestant loses all of his or her game cash, they "fall" out of the game. They return home and only come back for the Grand Finale among the last three contestants still left."

"What got your attention about the number dying?" Dee asked.

"I don't know. The death of James Spradley, I suppose, though I must have been aware of this on some level before he died. He was one of our million dollar winners and I knew him personally. The awful way he died really hit me hard and I realized he was not the only one."

"Wasn't he killed in a rather bad car crash?" Dee asked.

"Yes, a rather fiery one, too. What was left of his body was burned beyond recognition and his head was never recovered."

"So how was he identified?" I wanted to know. "DNA?"

"There was not enough unburnt tissue to recover DNA from his torso and his limbs were literally ripped off his body. When his car went off the curve it landed upside down on some very sharp rocks and most of what was left of him after the car bounced the last time was thrown into the ocean. Then the wreckage burned up the rest. That's a very dangerous part of the coast, you know, with multiple currents and rugged shoreline. It's called the Devil's Cauldron and I've seen it. Anything in the water could be ground to bits in minutes. Most of the blood and tissue around the car body was washed away by the tide coming in, and it was very lucky that anything was recovered at all. The fire fighters could not get to the wreckage until the fire burned out. Then it took several days before the car could be removed. They had to bring in a crane."

"So he's not dead for sure?" Dee asked.

"No, but given the circumstances he was declared dead. It *was* his car, or what was left of it, and he was seen driving it less than ten minutes before the wreck happened. Oddly enough, the exact time was recorded by the dash camera on a state patrol car, as was the fact that Jim was not wearing a seat belt. Somehow the trooper missed that, but when the fuel tank exploded in the crash, he had a window down and actually heard it. He turned around and came back to investigate but there was nothing he could do. From what I've seen of the photos the officer took, it's a wonder the wreck didn't wash away with the tide. The shore is very steep there."

"That doesn't sound like nearly enough to declare him dead," I pointed out.

"They had more. Jim was a veteran and he was still wearing his dog-tags. One of them was driven into his chest and was still there when they found what was left of his torso. That was under the body of the car and was burnt into bone fragments. It's a wonder the remaining dog tag didn't melt or wash away in the sea. There was also a lethal amount of blood on the rocks high above the water that did test out with Jim's DNA. So there really is not much question that he died in the crash."

Dee and I looked at each other and I knew what he was thinking. He and I have worked several cases where a man declared dead was later discovered alive. "Even so," I said, but Willard interrupted me before I could finish.

"His family is prominent, Jazz, and Jim had a certain amount of notoriety from winning the prize. So there was a bit of pressure to wind up the investigation. There didn't seem to be any evidence of foul play, so the police closed the case two days after the accident."

"But you weren't convinced," Dee pointed out.

"Well, I was at first. Then I began thinking of the other deaths among our winners and I began to wonder."

"Was the car examined by the state police?" Dee asked.

"Yes, what was left of it. The case had been closed by then but they wanted to make sure. I didn't see the wreckage myself but in the police photos I have seen, it looks like a beer can that's been crumpled up and tossed in the fire."

"Getting back to the contestants," I said, "how are they chosen?"

"It's a pretty simple process," Willard told me. "There is a button they can use on the contest web site to volunteer. Those who meet the age and residence requirements are asked to present a video of themselves and selfie photos. These are previewed by staff at the production office in Los Angeles and a certain number are selected. Those who make the cut are given a telephone interview, and whoever is left are each given a screen test. At some point, there is a rigorous physical exam and a background check, but these are late in the process." Nordwald thought a moment. "That's about it."

"There's no psychological screening?" I asked.

Willard looked surprised by the question but shook his head. "Not as far as I know. I think the physical may test for things like depression and there may be a medication assessment, but nothing like the MMPI."

I smiled, thinking of Willie Dill. "A friend of mine tells me the MMPI is almost useless," I said. "He holds an advanced degree in psychometrics and claims it can be played like a fiddle by any good method actor."

"That surprises me. A lot of psychologists swear by it."

"Yeah, well a lot of people used to swear the world is flat, too," Dee pointed out with a shrug.

"It sounds like the process is more like television or movie casting than physical or psychological screening," I observed. "It's easy to see how a psychopath might slip by and become one of the contestants."

"So you do think it might be a psychopath after all?" Willard asked. He looked confused.

"No, all I'm saying is that we can't eliminate that possibility. I have given it some thought since we last met and the problem

I'm having is seeing any other motive. Who else might benefit from James Spradley's death? The only other motives I can see to the distorted reasoning of a psychopath is murder for profit. Or that the killer or killers might be trying to cover up the murder of someone else they want dead."

"Killer or killers?" Willard asked. "Do you think more that one killer is likely?"

I shook my head. "Only if it is murder for profit or convenience, but I can't see how that would work. It's way too early to narrow things down too much. We will have a lot of digging to do, so this may take a while."

I looked at Dee, who nodded, and then back at Willard Nordwald. "What we need from you to get started is a list of the other winners who have died. Since we will be dealing with a lot of local police, I think Dee needs to take point on local investigations and I need to work in the background and with the production company."

"Why do you say that?" Willard asked.

"Two reasons. One is the price of success. I'm simply too well known in cop-world. My books and my seminars have made it impossible to keep a low profile. Dee is not as well known and can be just another investigator. He's also much better dealing with local police."

"Don't let him fool you, sir," Dee replied. "Jazz is damned good with locals, particularly pathologists and departmental brass. He's particularly good at cutting through red tape with the feds, too."

I ignored Dee's comments. "The point is that if I show up looking around, local people will think it's a big case. I believe we need to be as covert as possible. So I think we need to present our investigation as something like an insurance company inquiry. I don't like being deceptive but insurance people are always poking around. No one thinks much about them asking questions."

"Actually, that's not far from the truth," Willard said. "Our firm has a lot of insurance companies for clients and I use free lance investigators all the time. I think it would be better to tell anyone who asks that you are working for a law firm. Of course, we would prefer that you not reveal who we are unless it's absolutely necessary."

"That will work," I told him. "Legal investigators are pretty common, too. My biggest concern is keeping the circle of people who know what we're actually doing as small as we can. God help us if the media get hold of it."

"Yeah, talk about a three-ring circus," Dee grumbled.

"That must not happen," Willard said. His face was grave.

"You know, we could always fly the research flag," I said, looking at Dee. "We could be gathering material for a book or even a movie."

Dee laughed. "Yeah and I've got the perfect title: *Live Fast, Die Young, and Leave a Beautiful Memory*. We could dedicate it to the memory of James Dean."

"Assuming anyone remembers him," I pointed out. "The point is, it would give us a good fall-back if word gets out."

"Word must not get out!" Willard Nordwald said severely.

"We'll do everything humanly possible to make sure it doesn't," I replied. "However, you need to understand that once we start asking questions it's pretty much out of our control. The media seem to have a built in sensor for any hint of conspiracy or cover-up. I think we need to assume word will get out at some point and it's better to have an alternate story in place when it does."

Willard didn't like it but he saw the wisdom in what we were telling him. I decided to push it a bit. "What I would recommend is that we keep what we're really doing on a need-to-know basis. That means the three of us and only the top management of Jolly Good Times. That will need to include their head of security."

"That's actually who raised the nondisclosure issue with me," our host told us. "The thought was that an outside inquiry might be more productive."

"Then Dee and I will need to talk to him," I said. "In person."

Willard smiled. "It's actually her," he told us, "and she had the very same thought. She will be here tomorrow."

Daniella Cooper completely surprised me. I expected the

head of security to be a mature, no nonsense woman in at least her middle forties, if not older. Yet when Dee and I arrived at Willard Nordwald's office the next morning he was standing at the credenza in his conversation area talking to a beautiful young woman in her mid thirties. She was very serious, almost severe, and at first I thought she was an administrative assistant. Then as we drew closer I revised my estimate upward to mid forties. I was quite surprised to learn later that she was actually well past fifty.

Even so, I sensed immediately that Daniella, as she preferred to be called, was no fool. She projected an air of quiet competence and was quick on the uptake. Yet she was easy on the eyes, too. She was tall and lanky with a dark Scandinavian complexion and black hair, and as far as I could tell, wore almost no makeup. She certainly didn't need it. Her skin was tan, unblemished with any signs of cosmetic surgery.

Even so, it was her bright blue eyes that caught my attention. Their gaze was open and direct, just short of intimidating, and they revealed nothing. I was curious what passions might lie behind the austere barrier of the persona that insulated her from the world. The only softness I saw lay in the hint of humor I detected in the wrinkles around her eyes. Yet this was not that evident at first.

When we were introduced, Daniella was the first to extend a hand. I found her grip warm and firm, and very business-like. Then, when she was introduced to Dee, I saw a hint of an odd smile flit across her face. Glancing at Dee, I understood why. His face was a mask and his handshake, brusque. It was clear to me that he would sooner offer his hand to a rattlesnake and Daniella was amused. While he didn't actually glare, his hackles were up. There was no question Daniella had captured his undivided antipathy.

Once we all had coffee, Willard summed up our discussion the day before. When he was done, Daniella turned to me. "My only reservations are the lack of a non-disclosure agreement and your need to inform the head of your agency what you will be doing. I understand that you are an independent contractor."

"Well, first of all, Dee and I are sworn law enforcement officers in Arkansas. We are not spooks, although our work is covert. What we do falls under the umbrella of homeland security, and that is why the head of our agency needs to know what we are up to. He is a lawyer himself and is licensed to practice at the federal bar."

"What is it you do for him?" Dan asked, her tone more severe than necessary.

"I'm primarily a financial analyst," I told her, refusing to do the intimidation game. "My real passion is financial crime. What I do is to help take down dirty corporations."

"He's got a nose for it," Dee interjected. "He can look at a set of books and see things nobody else can."

"Oh, I thought you were an expert on homicide. Aren't you the one who wrote *Busting the Beast?*"

"Yes, and I'm still trying to live that down," I answered and was rewarded with a smile from Willard Nordwald. Daniella Cooper was not amused.

"The original title was *The Mind of a Serial Killer,*" I added. "The thing is, there's far more harm done in corrupt board rooms and that's how I first got involved with multiple killers. We were looking for three million dollars of missing public funds."

Dan looked at Willard. It was clear to me she was far from sold on team Jazz and wondered why I had been sought out. At that point I was beginning to wonder, myself.

"My understanding of what you need is an assessment of the deaths of several winning contestants," I said and Dan nodded. "Dee and I have a lot of experience doing just that," I told her. "So do a lot of other investigators," I added. "You seem to have some reservations and I'd be happy to give you a few referrals if you have a problem working with us."

"It's nothing personal, Dr. Phillips," she began.

"It never is, Ms Cooper," Dee interjected. His tone was a harsh back country rasp. "Jazz is a lot more polite than I am. Why did you drag us all the way down here if you weren't serious about hiring us?"

"I can think of one reason," I answered, looking at Dee. "She may be involved."

"You can't be serious!" Daniella declared, almost snarling. She was clearly indignant. Yet there was an edge of fear in her voice, too, and this intrigued me.

"Why not?" Dee replied with a shrug. "Getting involved in the investigation is a classic tactic of serial killers."

"We run into it more often than not," I added. Daniella couldn't see it but Willard was having trouble hiding a smile. Nor was what I said completely true but she didn't know that. "Do you have anything to do with these deaths, Ms Cooper?" Willard told me later I looked like a cat watching a mouse.

"No, of course not!" she declared and I sensed she was telling the truth.

"Good," I said. "I didn't think so but I needed to know. Please don't take it personally." Turning to Willard, I asked, "What do you think? Do you still want us to look into this?"

"Not for a minute!" Daniella Cooper snarled.

"That's not your call, Daniella," Nordwald told her gently. "Jazz is working for the firm, not your company. Besides, Nigel is very enthusiastic about us hiring him. He asked for Jazz by name. So it might be best for us to negotiate a way of working together."

"I'm good with that," I answered. I looked at Dee and he nodded. "We both are."

Willard looked at Dan but she was studying the carpet. "For now we can communicate through me," he added. "I assume you will want to talk with our CEO and I know he wants to meet you. I believe he will be in New York this next week. What is your schedule like for next Thursday?"

"She's hiding something," Dee told me as we were driving home. "I don't know what it is, but she is."

"That's what I thought, too," I answered. "Are you still cleared to visit Sam's office?" For some reason I couldn't remember if he was or not.

"I think so," he responded, grinning. "I still have that magic

Homeland Security card he gave me. Man, do the airport cops jump when they see it."

"Let me make a call," I told him. Then I changed my mind. "No, that's out of the way. Wasn't there a frozen yogurt place on the way here?"

The Head Shed

3   Since our meeting with the CEO of Jolly Good Times was late the next week, Karin and Dee decided to stay over. She had never really seen New York except from the air and the four of us decided to make it an expedition. It had been a good while since I had been to Philadelphia and Nicole had never seen the Liberty Bell, so I rented a Crown Victoria. It was only a couple of hundred miles from where we lived, almost next door by Wyoming standards.

Even so, the drive to Manhattan was challenging. We don't have East Coast drivers in Wyoming, or the volume of traffic. We don't waste time getting from here to there out west, but we don't rush along bumper to bumper fifteen miles an hour over the speed limit, either. Nor do we indulge road rage. Out there chances are good the other driver is armed and doesn't suffer fools gladly. So I had to devote most of my attention to avoiding crashes.

I also set the cruise control five miles an hour slower than the herd and maintained a four second spacing between us and the car ahead. This annoyed those following to no end, but it gave the lane swoopers a chance to do their thing. It also provided high stress entertainment watching when drivers from both sides decided to swoop into the gap ahead of us at the same time. By the time we reached our destination we were all ready to be out of the car.

Fortunately, the East Coast office of Jolly Good Times was across the river in Newark, New Jersey and the building had its own parking lot in the basement. This meant we had to stop for a security scrutiny before we were allowed to enter, but it did mean we didn't have to find a spot on the street. Since we were only going to be there an hour or so, the ladies decided to wait for us in the Italian bakery and café on the ground floor.

"I tell you what," I said, seeing the pastry display. "Why don't you ladies take the meeting while Dee and I hold the fort here?" Dee grinned but both of the women ignored me.

The Newark office of Jolly Good Times lived up to the company name. It must have been designed with a children's playscape in mind because it certainly didn't look like the normal corporate suite. The walls were painted with bright primary colors and the floor was covered with a bright checkerboard of tiles. At one end of a large open area, one undefiled by cubicles, a cartoon mural showed the infamous red triplane of the Red Baron fighting it out with a beagle flying a Sopwith Camel. Here and there around this vast common office people worked at oddly designed desks with large surfaces and huge computer screens, and mellow jazz played softly in the background. The interesting thing was that while a few workers stood around in clusters looking at layout displays, no one seemed to be goofing off.

The only standard office area I could see was along the wide wall opposite the aerial dogfight. This consisted of what looked like a business office to one side and a big executive office on the other. Sandwiched between was a spacious conference room with a folding work table in the center. The walls were glass with a wooden railing at waist height to prevent someone from walking through clear glass and I noticed bright drapes that could be pulled for privacy.

Daniella Cooper met us at the elevator and led us into the office next to the conference room. Her countenance was about two degrees below glacial and she didn't say a word as she led the way to the executive office. When we reached the door, she opened it and stood aside motioning us to enter.

I noticed the executive office had privacy curtains on its two glass walls, and as we entered these were closing. When the opaque glass door shut, the ambient sound from the main area ceased abruptly. I glanced back when it did and was surprised to see that Daniella had not joined us.

Nigel Pleyer, the CEO, turned out to be a pleasant round fellow who looked like Santa Claus in mufti. He wore rimless octagon eyeglasses and sported a bushy beard that matched his bright white hair. He was dressed in hunter green slacks held up by a cordovan belt that matched his wingtips. As he rose to greet us I caught a flash of red socks and the sports blazer I saw hanging on a rack behind his desk was deep maroon. Yet what my eyes noticed right off was his red and white candy cane tie. It was striped like a barber's pole and neatly knotted over a silk shirt in Carolina blue.

Nigel rose from his desk and greeted us warmly. "I really appreciate your looking into this, Jazz," he told me. "Please don't take Daniella's attitude personally. She's something of what you Americans call a junk yard dog. She is very effective at what she does to protect us, inside the company and out, but we limit her contact with our clients. We have other people for that."

Turning to Dee, Nigel said, "You must be Steven DiRado. You look every inch a policeman. Had Jazz not been described to me, I would have thought you were the beast buster."

"Oh, he is," I assured him. "Dee has actually taken down more bad guys than I have."

"Yeah, but Jazz told me who to bust," Dee assured him, smiling. I was surprised how quickly he warmed to Nigel Pleyer. Normally, it takes him a while to be easy with people.

"So do you prefer to be called Steve or Steven?" Nigel asked.

"Why don't you call me Dee," my partner responded, surprising me. Normally he prefers to be called DiRado. Only a very few souls are privileged to call him Dee and he is very quick to correct those who transgress.

Nigel ushered us to a sitting area at the back of his office. It was screened from the door by an ornate folding divider painted with simple daisies, but I noticed that he could see the door from where he sat. The others could not and, unlike the conference room, the comfortable chairs were set around an elegant circular table.

"I took the liberty of ordering coffee," he told us once we were seated. "I hope you don't object. I'm a caffeine junkie."

Turning to me, Nigel added, "Again, I apologize for Danny. She is my human Rottweiler. She tends to be a bit overprotective at times and that's a good thing. I tend to walk around with my head in the clouds and she keeps me from walking in front of busses. Here in the States that's a possibility. I'm used to looking to the right for traffic, not the left. A lot of American tourists are lost by that small mistake in London."

As Nigel spoke he struck me as a gabby guy for the CEO of a major company. Even so, he had sharp blue eyes that I thought missed very little. His head was not so much in the clouds as he might lead us to believe, and I wondered why he did that. I didn't get the sense he was nervous or that he was hiding something. Yet there seemed a deep reserve behind his outgoing manner.

"No problem, Nigel," Dee answered, smiling. I was surprised once more. It was Dee's warm, charming smile, the one I most often see when he talks about his friends in AA. Seeing it, I wondered if Nigel was a friend of Bill and Dr. Bob. "We're used to living with characters with plenty of attitude."

"Yes, I imagine you are," Nigel responded. "Which is why you are here. I take it Willard outlined the situation."

"He did, but we'd like your take on it, too," I answered.

"Well, I was aware of the fatalities of course," Nigel said. "We insure all of our players for several years after the events and the insurance company wanted to examine their files. I was even more aware of this after James Spradley passed. He was such a pleasant fellow. Yet, I was surprised when Willard called and advised me to postpone a media interview because of the number of winners who have died. I was floored when he suggested the possibility there might be a killer at work. I'm still not convinced, but it is a possibility we cannot afford to ignore. If word got out it could be a disaster. It would taint every thing we do."

"Yes, it could," I told him. "On the other hand, Oscar Wilde was right, too. The only thing worse than being talked about is not being talked about. I don't know what your primary market is but I imagine the US is a large segment, and the American public is well known for its short memory."

Nigel nodded. "Yes, I understand that. Richard Nixon is a good example. On the other hand, I'd rather err on the side of caution. It's better not to risk it."

"I understand and I agree completely. On the other hand, once we start digging there is a real possibility someone will catch wind of what we're doing. No matter how careful we may be, there are a great many things beyond our control. The deaths are a matter of public record, for example. Some bright fan might put it together."

Nigel nodded. "I realize that, only too well. On the other hand, I don't think it is a possibility we can ignore."

"No, it isn't," Dee replied. "Sooner or later someone's going to turn over the right rock. If you ignore it, you risk it being an even bigger story. Maybe even a scandal."

"That was what Danny – Daniella – thought."

"So who else in the company knows about this?" I asked.

"Just Danny and me, and, of course, Willard."

"Possibly one more," Dee observed. Seeing Nigel's surprise, he added, "The killer could be someone inside the company."

Nigel nodded. "I thought of that, too. But why would someone do it? We treat our employees very well."

I nodded. "Yes, but multiple killers have a different mindset. It might be someone like a subcontractor, too. To be thorough we'll need a list of those, particularly subcontractors you have used over a long time – as far back as several months before the first death."

Nigel nodded and made a note on the pad in front of him. Just then I heard the door to the main office open and Daniella appeared with a stainless steel service cart loaded with two coffee carafes and a box of pastries from the first floor bakery. Once she had parked the cart against the wall she looked at Nigel and raised an eyebrow. He smiled and nodded and she left without a word.

This struck me as being rather strange. I couldn't understand why Nigel would not include his head of security in our meeting. I was just as happy she wasn't there. The room warmed considerably once she left, but I thought it odd. Then I realized she was probably listening in on our conversation from another room. Casually slipping my small scanner out of my pocket I glanced at it and put it back. The display showed two bright red diodes. This meant we were being monitored or recorded, or both.

"Who has access to the recordings?" I asked.

Nigel blinked and I saw a flicker of something in his eyes. I saw him make a decision and he smiled. "Just Daniella and myself to the conversations here," he told me. "Recordings from the conference room are available to area leaders. Everyone in the office knows we tape those."

"Video, too?" Dee asked pleasantly.

"Yes, but we don't let those out of the building. We use them to make sure nothing drops through the cracks. May I ask how you knew?"

I nodded. "It's what I would do in your place," I told him. "The reason I ask is that could be a source of word getting out. Where else do you record?"

Nigel looked embarrassed. "We do audio recording in the rest rooms and lounge areas. The staff canteen and stairwells are full loop video with daily downloads to permanent storage. We don't make a big deal of it, as you say here, but the staff know we record the workplace."

"What does this office do compared to the one in Los Angeles?" Dee asked. "Why do you need so much security here?"

"This is where the important decisions are made," Nigel replied, nodding toward the conference room. "This is where most of our basic creative work begins, where we brainstorm new ideas and where we refine concepts for program use. Aside from a good track record and basic real estate, intellectual property is all we really have. It's our product and this is where it's produced. This is also where our board meets quarterly to take care of company business. Part of that is approving projects such as Last One Left but it's not a rubber stamp. Once we develop a project we have to convince the board that it's viable. Since they are our major investors, it's their money at risk." He smiled like a kid who has successfully read to the class.

"Why don't you take us through the process from concept to being on the air?" I suggested.

"Very well. One of our resident geniuses comes up with an idea and brings it directly to me. If I like it, I assign three to five people to develop the concept and give them a deadline, usually a month to six weeks. They pitch the idea to me and I decide whether to give it some careful thought for a week or two, or to scrap it. If I decide to give it some thought, the team is asked to work with a facilitator and come up with a general production plan by another target date. Assuming the plan is workable, I give it to a couple of specialists to work up an estimated cost-ROI analysis."

"An arrow-eye?" Dee interjected.

"Sorry, that's an R-O-I. It means...."

"The return on investment," Dee said nodding. "Grandpa must be getting deef."

"No, it's probably my accent," Nigel chuckled. "I grew up Bow-Bell Cockney and it still comes out when I get to talking too fast. Anyway that's the first stage of development. Jazz, I see you taking notes. Are there any questions before we go on?"

I nodded. "Yes, is there a bonus for the folk who come up with the idea?"

"Yes and no," Nigel answered. "We give a team bonus that's divided up according to a formula our employees developed. So there is a bonus but not one personal to the idea person alone. Why? Were you thinking of jealousy?"

"That's exactly what I was thinking about. It's a powerful motive, especially if there is a rivalry. How is the idea brought to you, in person?"

"No, actually. It comes in the intraoffice mail and if the same idea comes independently from someone else here, we split the credit between them."

"How well is the idea spelled out at first?" I asked.

"It's not that well detailed," Nigel answered. "I limit idea notes to a couple of pages in summary."

"Are we talking about ideas for specific games or a whole new program?" Dee asked.

"Either, actually. If it's an idea for a challenge or a game for an established show, the process is much simpler. Then, too, at times there's a suggestion for a whole new show but all we use are bits and pieces of the concept."

I looked at Dee and he nodded. "We're going to need to look at your people in this office, Nigel," I told him. "We both spotted at least one item that could generate rivalry and resentment."

"Surely it's nothing worth killing for!" Nigel protested.

"Welcome to the dark side, Nigel," Dee said gently. "You might be surprised to know how little it takes for some folk to kill."

"The reason doesn't have to be rational, either," I added. "It can easily be something imagined."

"You're frightening me," Nigel told us. He looked like he'd been kicked in the belly, like a jolly old Santa Claus who's come down a chimney only to find hot coals and an angry guard dog awaiting him.

"That's not our intent," I answered. "More than likely the killer, if there is one, is not among your staff. However, we need to check and make sure."

"How in the world am I going to break this to my people?"

"We'll think of something if, and when, it's needed. Right now, why don't you continue telling us the process. We may see a more likely vector."

"Where was I? Oh, yes. After I look at the analysis I present it to the board at their monthly meeting. Assuming they agree, we go to the second stage. We present the concept to the production group in Los Angeles and they assess what it will take to make this happen. Their report, including an accurate estimate of cost and time-line, comes back to me within six weeks. If I like it, I run it by the board. If I do not, I ask the original team for a refinement of concept and send it to production for a second analysis."

Nigel stopped and took a sip of water. "Once we get acceptable concept and production reports the board takes a final look at the proposal. Assuming it is acceptable, and most are at this point, we set up a countdown calendar and production begins pulling it all together. There are the inevitable glitches along the way, of course, but our time-lines are designed with this in mind. More often than not, we come in well ahead of the deadline."

Nigel stopped and looked at us. "All right," I told him. "I think the best way to approach this is to start with your victims list and then move on to your staff here. That includes any staff members no longer with you. Then we'll look at the production side, particularly any subcontractors involved."

Nigel opened a folder and handed me a three page summary. "Willard said you would need this. It's a list of those who have passed on. I've arranged them in the order in which they passed and included a some details of the episodes they performed."

I looked at the list. There was a date to the left of each name and the cause of death was given after. There was also a date for each episode they played, as well as a list of all contestants on that show. One thing that was missing was a list of the support staff for each episode and I mentioned this to Nigel. "This will probably be listed with the outside contractors, but we will need the names of any of the extras, too. This includes the drivers, pilots, lifeguards, housekeeping staff, cooks – anyone who was compensated."

Nigel looked at me in disbelief. "That's hundreds of people. Are you going to investigate them all?"

Dee grinned. "No, we're not. What we're going to do is sift out the names that appear most often. That's who we're going to take a close look at first."

Nigel frowned. "I suppose that will include the people closest to them, too."

"Only if they are connected in some way with other victims," I answered. Then I had another thought. "Do any of your staff here any tie to any of the contestants?"

Nigel shook his head. "No, not really. We critique the episodes before they are broadcast but there are no direct ties that come to mind. Sometimes I occasionally slip in incognito as an extra to get a feel for the show and sometimes I take office staff along, but we avoid direct contact with the players. Our policy is no fraternizing and any violators are dismissed immediately."

Dee and I looked at each other. "We need to look at those

people, too, the ones you have had to fire. Right away. One of them may be trying to sabotage the series."

"What about your security arrangements?" I asked. "Who oversees those?"

"Daniella, of course. She is the head of security but she has no direct contact with players, either. No, I'll take that back. She sometimes keeps an eye on the production people on site, particularly the locals. Sometimes she runs into the players but doesn't fraternize."

"How about background checks on the contestants?" Dee asked. "Does she handle those herself?"

"Yes, but she does most of that from here. It's mostly electronic these days."

"Does she screen them all herself?" I asked.

"Yes, of course, but that's late in the process. She does the final background check just after the medical and right before the screen test. She's quite thorough, too."

"I imagine she is," I replied. "Dee and I will need to talk to her about this at some point and we may need you to referee. Do you live here in the city?"

"Oh, yes. England is far too dreary. New York is alive!"

Dee looked at me. "What about groupies, Jazz? It could be a stalker."

I shook my head. "I don't think so, but we can't write it off." I turned to Nigel. "Have you had any problems with stalkers or over-zealous fans?"

He shook his head. "Not that I'm aware but I'm not really the one to ask. Daniella is who would take care of that but she hasn't said anything to me. On the other hand, that's not something I'd need to know unless it became a problem." He smiled. "I try not to joggle my department managers' elbows. I prefer to be a team player, not a micro-manager. My department heads are instructed to remind me of that."

I nodded. "We can save that for later if nothing else turns. I think we have more than enough to get started. Dee?"

Dee picked up the list of victims. "I notice you didn't list their street address and phone numbers," he said. "I will need those to check them out."

"Of course," Nigel said. He picked up a cell phone and punched in a number. He listened for a minute, then punched in something else before hanging up.

"Do you use cell phones for interoffice communication?" Dee asked.

"No," Nigel said, shaking his head. "They're far too vulnerable to hacking. We only use them to locate where someone is and for coded messages. I just called Daniella's number and put in the code letting her know I needed to see her."

"How do you use them to locate people?" I asked.

Dee rolled his eyes and Nigel blinked. "Jazz is a Luddite," Dee explained. "He finds anything more complicated than a number two pencil confusing."

"All our personal phones come with a GPS," Nigel told me, looking puzzled. "Don't you use a computer?"

"My partner has been known to exaggerate," I replied dryly. "What he forgets is that by today's standard, he and I are both dinosaurs." What I did *not* tell Nigel was that the phones Dee and I always had with us were Agency issue and had capabilities far beyond a normal GPS. Not only could they show our GPS location within a couple of feet, but they could also show our elevation above ground level. Don't ask me how.

Daniella Cooper appeared within half a minute. So wherever she had been listening was not far away. Once again, she never said a word, answering Nigel with a brisk nod when he explained what we needed.

"Doesn't waste words, does she?" Dee murmured when she was gone.

Nigel laughed. "She makes up for it in efficiency."

Cooper was back within three minutes and handed Nigel a single sheet of copy paper. I took the opportunity to ask her about groupies. She replied with a terse negative. "Not a problem."

"What about stalkers?" I persisted. "Any problems with those?"

"No," she replied, looking at me like I was an ugly bug she'd like to stomp.

"Really?" I asked, determined to get more out of her than that. "That's surprising given how long the show has been on the air. How do you account for that?"

"I don't," she told me. She glanced at Nigel, who was giving her a surprisingly stern eye, and shrugged. "Tight security."

"Yes, but even the very best security has some vulnerabilities," I pointed out. "Even the Secret Service. John Hinkley almost killed the President."

"I wasn't in charge," she replied, giving me a cold smile and Dee laughed. When he did, Copper gave him a smile that was forty degrees warmer. Even Nigel was grinning.

"Point well taken," I allowed, trying not to smile myself. Yet even this didn't break the ice. When she looked back at me Cooper had a bug stomper's look in her eye again. I decided to kill her with kindness. "Thank you, Daniella," I said gently.

"I think we have what we need to get started," I told Nigel. "I will need to come back up here in a couple of days and take a look at your contestant and subcontractor files. Dee will begin checking out those who have died. He will need to check in with local police but his cover will be that he's working for a lawyer checking out double indemnity or some other insurance issue."

Nigel looked puzzled. "Double indemnity?" he asked.

I nodded. "A lot of life insurance policies over here have an accidental death rider that pays double indemnity. Since only about five percent of deaths in the US are declared accidental, it's a good money-maker. Homicide is considered to be accidental death under certain conditions. Since such large sums of money are involved, insurance companies like to make sure they are obligated to pay. So they send investigators. With James Spradley, for example, they might save a bundle proving he had a heart attack that caused the crash."

"Wouldn't that apply only to those who are insured for it?" Nigel wanted to know.

"Yes, but it's a good cover story even if the dead aren't insured for it," Dee explained. "Survivors rattling the cage over insurance issues is a motive us cops understand. Particularly if relatives are involved. Death seems to bring out the greed in people."

Nigel looked at me and then back at Dee. "Goodness, you must work in a very dark world," he said. Daniella nodded.

"We do," I answered. "However, death can bring out the best in people, too."

"Yeah," Dee added, "it does, especially in the dearly departed. At least, it does in the eulogy." When he said this, I saw Daniella grin for the first time and I wish I had not. For just a moment I beheld a dark abyss open wide behind her eyes and I felt a malevolent presence staring out at me.

I mentioned this to Dee as we drove out of the city. "Did you catch the look in her eye? There's a lot of darkness there. It put me in mind of Jubal Mullen Stone."

He nodded. "Yeah, I saw it, all right," he told me. "Hell hath no fury like a woman."

"You mean a woman scorned," Karin suggested. Dee just shrugged but out of the corner of my eye I saw my beloved Nicole nod. She knew exactly who Jubal Mullen Stone was and what Dee meant. She had stood too often on the threshold herself, staring into the abyss, far more than I.

The First Sweep

4 Neither Dee nor I were very good company that afternoon on the trip home. This was not unusual for us. Over the years we had worked out our own way of working through a case and sometimes we said very little until we'd had time to mull through things on our own. This was one of those times and I was glad Karin had Nicole for company for the long drive.

We did stop in Boston, arriving with plenty of time to spend visiting the Liberty Bell. I had seen it the first time as a child and remember being told that the crack in the bell happened when it rang at the announcement of the Declaration of Independence. Now we were informed this was not so.

Over the years since my earlier visit historical truth had prevailed and we learned that the bell cracked the very first time it was rung in the early 1750s. This was twenty-some years before the Declaration, and the bell was plagued by cracks during its early history. It had been recast twice and the final crack occurred in the early nineteenth century.

As we looked at the bell that afternoon and listened to the guide, I realized something. There is a cruel historical irony behind the name of the bell. The truth is that the Liberty Bell got its name from abolitionists who adopted it for their symbol. This was some seventy years after it was first cast. The irony is that had the colonies remained British, American slavery would have been abolished in 1833, thirty years before it was.

Even so, I said nothing about this that afternoon. I didn't want to rain on our parade. Yet I couldn't seem to get it out of my mind, and both Nicole and Dee asked me about it later. When I explained to Nicole, she simply nodded and then snuggled closer offering the comfort of her presence.

It was Dee who helped me find some perspective, as he often has. "Well, old partner," he pointed out. "I guess you could drive yourself crazy over this. You could even get drunk over it, too, if you were so inclined. About all that would gain you would be a hangover. For me this falls into the category of the things we cannot change. The best thing I've found to do is pray to accept these things with serenity."

I spent the next day in the District, clearing my desk and letting Sam McKee know I'd be gone for a while. When I told him about the investigation, he said, "You pull the damnedest cases, don't you? Well, you and Dee have fun. Let me know if you need anything."

I was back in the Jolly Good Times offices the following Monday afternoon. Dee and I had spent the Friday before mapping out a plan for working the case, and the next day we all had joined the McKees for an extended family gathering on Chesapeake Bay. Jack and Martha were there, too, and Jack asked me to test out the latest Agency laptop he had supercharged. Since I seem to have a talent for messing up electronic devices Jack uses me to test out his beta units. If a device can survive my bumbling attentions, and best intentions, it is truly fool proof.

Then on Sunday, Dee and Karin flew back to Little Rock. Just before they took off Dee drew me aside. "Thanks for having us stay over, Jazz. I haven't seen Karin this happy in a long time. It meant a lot to her seeing the sights here and in New York. Please tell Nicole I really appreciate it."

I started to ask Dee why he didn't tell her himself, but then I knew. Dee is a cop's cop. He would never be rude to Nicole because she is my wife. He is also deeply grateful to her for saving my life more than once. Yet he is still a bit ambivalent. On the one hand, he thinks she deserves a medal of honor for what she did on the dark side, finding serial killers no one knew were there. What sticks in his craw is her taking the next step, becoming the angel of a severe mercy to those whom the law could not bring to justice.

"Dee knows, doesn't he?" my bride asked as we watched their cab drive away.

"I think so, but we haven't ever talked about it. Nor will we. You have nothing to worry about from Dee."

"I know," she murmured, touching my cheek in that wonderful way she has. "Sam and Megan know, and probably Willie Dill, I think." Then she sighed and gave me a look I know well. "We're lucky, husband. The thing is, our friends are gone and the kids are next door watching Gene Autry. What do you think?"

With two children in school, I was acutely aware how few and far between were the golden hours we could spend together. So I took Nicole in my arms and kissed her. "I think, sweet wife, that we're about to get lucky again."

The next morning I arose quite early, hoping to get a jump start on the Monday morning traffic. Nicole fixed me my favorite breakfast and we lingered over coffee. Then the kids were up and it was time for me to go. After I had said my goodbyes to them my bride walked me to the door. "Be careful, Jazz-beau," she murmured in my ear as we said goodbye, using the pet name she gave me the first time we spent the night together. Then she gave me a long, lingering kiss that left no doubt how she felt about me. As I drove away I wondered for the ten-thousandth time why this beautiful, intelligent woman had chosen me to be the father of her children.

The trip to the Big Apple was fast and frenetic. I continued my practice of driving the speed limit and the only incident was when I got pulled over for going too slow. Nor could I blame the officer, not really. Drunk drivers often drive slowly, though I didn't consider driving the speed limit as going that slowly.

Even so, I remained calm and polite and I was surprised to see the reaction of the officer when I handed him my driver's license. He didn't salute or come to attention but his whole manner changed. "Sorry to bother you, Dr. Fudd," he said after a careful comparison of my face to the picture on the Homeland Security

ID card I had given him by mistake. This is the card I use when I am on Agency business and I think someone in Sam's office was having a little fun issuing me the card for Elmo D. Fudd, PhD.

I have never been able to figure out just where this card places us in the Homeland Security hierarchy. I do know that senior FBI people defer to us and the rank and file of various agencies grow nervous when we're around. This is great when it comes to getting through airport security but it troubles me that Sam encourages Dee and me to use the ID for personal travel, too. He also tells us to pick our flights at random or to book them under an assumed name and to bump business passengers at the last minute if need be. The sad truth is that we're simply too well known to the multinational underworld. The people we are after would not hesitate taking out a whole planeload of civilians to get one of us.

I thanked the officer and wished him a good day. Yet, I think he must have passed the word. I must have gone by a half dozen patrol cars as I drove north, still at the speed limit, but none of them gave me a second look.

It was almost two o'clock when I walked into the offices of Jolly Good Times in Newark. The garage attendant must have called upstairs because when I got off the elevator, Daniella Cooper was there to meet me. She greeted me with a curt nod and without a word led me into a small room just off the executive office where a work station had been set up. I was surprised to know the room was there and I was grateful that whoever had designed the office had placed it on an outside wall that gave a nice view of the city.

I glanced around the room and turned back to ask Daniella how to turn on the computer. Yet she had disappeared and in her place was a middle-aged woman with a pleasant smile. "Hello, Dr. Phillips," she said and I found her voice very pleasant. "I am Trudy Howard, the head of Human Services for Jolly Good Times."

"As opposed to inhuman services?" I asked, giving unintended voice to the thought.

"We call those Cyber Operations, Dr. Phillips," she answered, smiling sweetly.

"I beg your pardon, Ms Howard. Please call me Jazz. I'm afraid I'm a pun junkie."

"That's a character flaw I'm afraid we share," she answered. "Please call me Trudy. We normally use given names around here." She pointed to a three-ring notebook on a shelf by the workstation. "That's the manual for our computer system. Would you prefer to read that or have someone show you the ropes? That's a lot simpler than reading the manual."

"That sounds good but it needs to be someone who speaks plain English. I seem to have a talent for doing exactly the wrong thing."

Trudy smiled. "Another trait we share. They won't let me near the mainframe, wherever that is."

What followed was a comedy of errors. The man Trudy called to join us looked very much the part of a systems wonk. Yet he was reasonably fluent in Normal Speak, too. "What did you do?" he asked when I laid my hands on the keyboard he set up and the system went crazy. "I set this up myself and tested it this morning."

"He's like me, Dom," Trudy explained.

"Two of you here at once?" Dominic asked, aghast.

"I get along all right with my own laptop," I said. "Is there any way I could use that?" I picked up my briefcase and took out the new Macbook Pro that Jack McKee had tuned up for me. It used a used a combination of biometric tests to make sure it was me at the keyboard.

Dom glanced at the laptop and started to blow me off. Then he took a second look at the machine when I took out a sensing pad and plugged it into one of the USB ports. I pushed the power button and laid my hand on the pad, and the machine booted itself immediately. "Hello, Jazz," the speaker greeted me. "What's up?"

"Death and taxes," I said and Trudy chuckled.

"You're verified, Jazz, all levels," the machine reported and then was silent.

"Cool!" Dom said. "Biometric authentication along with a password. Hard to hack. Too bad you didn't get it all in one unit."

"Oh, it works without the pad, too," I said. "Shut down and reboot! Stat!" The computer went dark. I turned it toward Dom, unplugging the pad. I wrote a note asking him to do the reboot sequence. Ten seconds later it came to life again and greeted me again. When Dom responded, the computer informed him he was not Jazz. Then I took Dom's place and went through the process. It worked like a charm.

"How did you do that?" Dom wanted to know.

Before I could answer, Trudy brought us back on track. "As pleasant as it may be to play with new toys, fellows, we need to move on. Can Jazz use his computer with our system, Dom?"

"Yes, but it would take a lot of time developing. Maybe we need to have someone operate our system for him."

"We probably need to talk, you and I," I told Trudy. Dom nodded and left the room. "Do you know why I'm here?" I asked.

Trudy nodded. "Nigel told me you're doing security evaluations on our staff here. I assume that includes the West Coast office, too. Or will at some point. What I don't understand is why this needs to be done, but Nigel wouldn't tell me this."

"I'm afraid that's my fault. I'm a security specialist these days."

"These days. And before?"

"I started out as a policeman for the Navy but that was a long time ago."

"In a land far away?" Trudy asked and I chuckled. "You don't come across as a policeman."

I nodded. "I find it useful to come across as a befuddled high school guidance counselor most of the time," I told her. "It throws the bad guys off their game."

Trudy gave me an appraising look and nodded. "You and Nigel have that in common," she told me. "He cultivates the image of a sweet Santa Claus until it comes time to negotiate a contract. Then he turns into a real Torquemada. I bet you do bad cop well."

I lapsed into Pike County patios. "Well, if you cain't catch flies with honey, try stank."

Trudy thought this was funny. "You do Oakie from Muskogee well, too," she laughed. "Is that where you grew up?"

The casual way Trudy said this threw up a bright yellow caution flag in my mind. I realized I was being subtly lulled into intimacy and gently interrogated by an expert. I wondered why. Trudy came across as a sympathetic older sister and it would be very easy to let down my guard with her. Yet had Nigel wanted her to know what was going on, I thought he would surely have mentioned this at our first meeting. I made myself a note to ask him. Then it occurred to me this might be Nigel's way of testing my discretion. I noted this, too. Assumptions can be deadly.

"Close enough," I said. "What I wanted to ask you was about Dom. Where does he fit in the company operations?"

"Oh, sorry, I meant to tell you earlier. He's a CPA and his first job started out as production auditor. Now he's evolved into the one who also keeps all our computers going, too."

"Does he cover your West Coast operations, too?"

"Yes, though he has an assistant in Los Angeles who audits most of the production expenses. Lane Birdsall is her name and she also takes care of a lot of the routine computer stuff."

"Does Dom cover your office in the Caymans, as well?" I posed the question mostly to muddy the waters. I hoped I wasn't being too obvious.

"You know, I'm not altogether sure about that. I'm not sure how that office operates. I don't do any of the human resources work for them. Their staff is independent of our operations here."

"Who handles cyber security?" I asked. "Dom?"

Trudy nodded. "Yes. Nigel and Dom go way back, even before Nigel began Jolly Good Times. I think they may have grown up in the same place. Nigel really trusts him."

Dom seems so much younger, I thought. I was surprised when Trudy responded. "I didn't quite get that, Jazz."

"Oh, I was talking to myself again," I told her. "It goes along with galloping senility."

Trudy smiled and I told her what I'd said. "A lot of people think Nigel is much older than he is, Jazz. It's the white hair and his Santa outfits. He's only a few years older than Dom, and Dom looks a lot younger than he is."

"Well, let's get Dom back in here. It sounds like he knows how to keep his mouth shut. Does he know about the security check?"

"I'm not sure," Trudy answered. "You will need to ask Nigel that." She took out a cell phone and offered it to me. "I have him on direct dial."

I shook my head. "No, thank you. I'll ask him later. Why don't you send Dom back in here? Give us a minute before you come back in, if you wouldn't mind."

When Dom came back in, he looked puzzled. "What did Nigel tell you about why I'm here?" I asked.

"Said you were a security wonk. Here to review staff. Some kind of security clearances. Didn't tell me why and I didn't ask."

"Why not?"

Dom shrugged. "We operate on need-to-know. Had he wanted me to know he would have told me."

I nodded and got up and asked Trudy back in. "Sorry for the need to be so hush-hush," I told the two of them. "We're all singing from the same page but what we say needs to stay among the three of us. Nigel wants to keep things quiet until we're done."

Trudy and Dom nodded in unison. "All right, then, let's get to it. Dom, you can run Trudy and me through the process until we can do it on our own. Who has the longest time working with the company?"

"That would be me," Dom said. "Nigel brought me with him when he started the company."

"All right, let's see if I can call up your record." I very carefully typed in my password and hit the return button. The computer sat there a moment and then and then went crazy.

Dom sighed. "This is going to be a long day." He took out his cell phone and pressed speed dial. "Nance, it looks like I'm going to be a while.... Yeah, I've got a double Trudy situation.... No, I'll explain later." Then he looked at me. "Maybe we should try to use your laptop, Jazz."

Two hours later, Trudy and I were in business. I knew Dom was itching to get his hands on my laptop but there was no way I could explain how it did what it did so easily under my hands. "I think of it as black magic," I assured him. "I think it has something to do with killing a white chicken at midnight in a crossroad cemetery."

Trudy thought this was funny, but Dom was not amused. He just shook his head and left the room, telling us to call him if we ran into an issue. "Mark one up for us Luddites," I told Trudy.

"Kind of hard on the chickens," she quipped and for some reason this struck us as hilarious. We had to work so hard to keep from laughing we finally gave up and went to lunch.

Having lunch with Trudy was fun. As a matter of fact, I enjoyed it so much another yellow flag went up. There was a lot of frisson between us and I wondered why. I am long married to the most beautiful woman I know and we work hard making sure there is enough private time just for us. At first I was concerned that this would take the spontaneity out of our love-making, but it had the opposite effect. We enjoyed being conspirators and we were not at all hesitant to grab a random opportunity. So why did I have these attractions with certain other women?

I knew what Forster would say. He's the cranky old priest I talk to now and them when I need rock bottom reality. He would tell me I was like a kid in a candy shop who wanted to taste it all. "You always choose the best of the best, too," he assured me.

"They seem to choose me," I declared.

"That's my point, exactly. I don't know how you do it."

Nicole and I have talked about this, too. Nor was it I who brought up the subject. "You created quite a stir in the henhouse, husband," she said with a laugh one day as we left the bookstore. "I thought that sales clerk was going to rip off her clothes and have you right there on the cash register."

"Well, I certainly didn't encourage her," I grumped and this made her laugh. "Couldn't she see I wasn't interested?"

"That only fanned her fires all the more," my bride replied. "I thought she was about to self-ignite and burn down the store."

I held up my left hand. "Couldn't she see I'm married? And I was with my wife, too."

"She didn't know we were together," Nicole answered sweetly. "If she did, she probably thought I was your daughter." She gave me a measured look. "Seriously, Jazz-beau," she said using the pet name she knows I love best. "I know you're attractive to other women. I don't even mind sharing you with them up to a point. You have superb taste when it comes to us girls."

"The way she was coming on to me was way over the top," I replied, ignoring the implications of what she was telling me. "It really put me off completely."

"You are carefully overlooking what I'm trying to tell you, husband," Nicole told me sweetly. "So I'll be perfectly blunt. You're free to gather whatever rosebuds may come your way. Do I need to be graphic?"

"I would never risk ruining what we have," I told her.

Nicole sighed. "You can be such a sweet, dumb, asshole, Jazz," she said. Her tone was like she was telling me I had spinach on my teeth. "I meant it when I said I will never willingly leave you. Nor will I hold a grudge. There are only three things I ask. One is that you be very careful not to bring home more than you left with. That would piss me off. The second is that I don't think it would be a good idea for you to have a long term mistress. Maybe a sex buddy you run into at random times, but not a mistress."

I was having a hard time believing I was hearing this from my bride, the mother of my children. Her tone told me she had given this a lot of thought. "I'm having a lot of trouble getting my head around this, Nicole," I told her. "I don't understand why you're telling me this."

"I know," she replied, nodding and giving me the smile she knows I love best. "This is new to you but I've been thinking about it for some time. And these things are different for women."

My chest felt tight and I felt light headed. "Are you telling me you want to take a lover?" I asked. I don't panic easily, but the thought of her with another man floored me. Luckily there was a bus bench right there and I slumped down onto it.

"Not for a moment," she told me gravely, sitting down beside me and taking my hand. "You are all the man I could ever want."

I thought about this for a moment, trying to figure it out. Then I gave up. I needed to talk to either Forster or Sofya, the Agency's in-house mental health monitor. This was one time I knew I needed help with understanding and acceptance. I sighed and looked into my bride's eyes. There are times she let the guards down totally and allows me to see the depths of her soul and this was one of them. There was nothing in her eyes but compassion. "You mentioned something else, too." I reminded her.

"Yes, that brings me to my third request. I am sure you've heard Dee say we're only as sick as our secrets, and he's right. I don't want there to be any secrets between us, so I ask that you share any experiences you may have with me as fully as you can." She smiled. "Being a woman, of course, I'll want to know details."

She paused and I knew she was not done, so I waited. After a moment, she nodded, almost as if to herself, and looked at me. "I may get a little green-eyed but I can deal with that. Your best strategy would be to ignore it. Unless, of course, it becomes a problem. Then we'll need to do something about it." She smiled sweetly, as if she'd just told me we were having ribs for supper.

That conversation had taken place several months before and I had talked with both Sofya and Forster. Sofya was very careful in choosing her words and asked if I was all right with her talking with Nicole about this. I assured her that I was and asked for her assessment once she had. When she got back to me Sofya told me I was married to a very wise woman. "So listen to her, already!" she told me.

Forster, on the other hand, was quite blunt from the get-go. "Good Lord, man!" he laughed. "Most fellows would look at this like a bird's nest on the ground. You, being the suspicious soul that you are, are not even sure that the conversation really took place. You believe you dreamed it. Sometimes I wonder if you appreciate what a pearl beyond price you have for a wife."

The old padre also told me once that there cannot be any virtue where there is no temptation. Now here I was, having lunch with this delightful lady who was obviously as attracted to me as I was to her. Nor was there any question in my mind that she was just as aware as I exactly what was going on between us.

I carefully cleaned my plate and finished the mouthful of food I was chewing. Then I sighed and set my knife down by my place. When I looked up to thank Trudy for such an enjoyable meal, our eyes met and I saw fear in hers. Yet she held my gaze and I saw the fear pushed back, almost like a curtain. Nor was I prepared for the depth of suffering and longing I saw there. It was like being kicked in the chest, so intense I felt totally overwhelmed. I was tempted to pull back. Yet I did not. Even though I had no idea how to respond, I stood fast in my own sense of being.

Then Trudy reached out and took my left hand, lightly touching the simple golden band I wore. The connection in our eyes faded gently and once again we were simply who we normally were. I smiled. "I need to ask you an intimate question..." I said and stopped. I meant to say a personal question and opened my mouth to correct myself.

"The answer is yes," Trudy replied before I could clarify. "Now it's my turn. I need to ask you the same question."

"Same question, same answer," I said, surprising myself. "What I meant to say was 'personal' but 'intimate' is good."

"Are we playing word games, Jazz?" she asked. Her voice was carefully neutral.

"I am not playing any kind of games," I told her. "That was a Freudian slip. I really did mean to say 'personal' but you have no way of knowing that. I am truly sorry. Can we start over?"

"No, but we can go on," she answered, smiling. "There is no need to toss away anything that's happened. Let's just let it be." She patted my hand and took a drink of her tea. "So what was the personal question?"

"I was wondering if Trudy is a given name or a nickname," I told her.

"It is a given name, a family name. It comes from Gertrude and I believe it has something to do with the strength of a spear."

"Or the power of having a spear," I said without thinking as the memory of a men's retreat came to mind. We had made our own spears and learned how to cast them. Nor will I will never forget the thrill of power that moved up my arm when I first hefted mine.

Trudy's left eyebrow went higher than I would have imagined. "Yes, especially of having a spear to shake if you're a poet," she chuckled. There was a sultry inflection in her voice, one she certainly knew I wouldn't miss.

I tried to be obtuse. "Now there's an odd name," I replied. "Shakespeare. I wonder where it comes from."

"Men shaking spears at each other," she quipped.

"Well, I'm glad we shake hands these days."

"It may be more sanitary. Or maybe not. It's much less intimate than shaking spears."

"You're not going to let me forget any of this, are you?" I asked.

"Not for a minute," she answered. "I'm not going to let you forget your answer, either."

"Maybe we need to talk about that."

"Maybe we do." There was challenge in her eyes.

"You're shaking your spear at me," I told her.

"Better than you shaking your...." Trudy broke off, blushing.

"Why don't we take a walk and get some air?" I suggested. "Is there a park around here somewhere?"

"Not close by. I have a roof garden. Would that do? It's not that far that we couldn't walk there. On the way you can tell me why they call you Jazz. Are you a drummer?"

Uncharted Waters

5 Trudy lived about eight blocks from Jolly Good Times and it didn't take that long to explain my sobriquet. "To make a long story short, my first name is John. The same is true of my dad and my grandpa. To keep things straight, grandpa was called John, my dad was Jack, and my grandpa called me by my first two initials, J.S. Then I had a football coach in seventh grade who was from the Mississippi delta and talked like he had a mouth full of mud. What he called me sounded liked 'jayuzz' and the name stuck. All the girls thought it was cute and so did my parents, so Jazz I became."

"So you're not a musician?"

"I play a pretty mean stereo," I told her and she thought this was hilarious. I didn't know if she was being polite or if she had never heard that shaggy old dog before. Nor did I care. The sound of her laughter was delightful.

"So is jazz your favorite music?"

"Yes, mellow jazz, especially the old guys. But my very favorite music is Pachelbel's Canon in D played by a tuba and strings."

"You've got to be kidding."

"No, I found it on one of those Lifescapes CDs they have at the discount store. I have it on my iPod if you'd like to hear it."

When we arrived at the apartment building where Trudy lived the doorman greeted her warmly. The place was very large, big enough for a family of four, and a ten foot strip all the way across the southern square footage was devoted to the roof garden. "We get lots of sunshine but there is plenty of shade for things like the Astilbe hybrids," she told me. Seeing the blank look on my face she pointed to a photograph near the fireplace. What I saw was a grouping of plants with lush, small leaves and lots of delicate pink flowers.

"I recognize that," I said, pointing toward another photograph. "That's a copper plant, isn't it?"

"Very good," Trudy said. "I take it you are not into flowers?"

"No, I love flowers but I don't know much about growing them. My late wife, Nellie, was a master gardener and I loved to photograph her work."

"Your late wife? So you're not married?"

"No, I remarried and we have small children." I fished out my family pictures and showed them to Trudy.

"This looks like a very recent photo." She looked closer. "Yes, there's the date in the bottom right corner. Why, that's just this summer."

Seeing the question in her eyes, I laughed. "No, those aren't my grandkids," I said. "That is my wife, Nicole, and those little imps are certainly mine. How about your family?"

"My children are all grown and they all live in Seattle. My husband is in a long term nursing facility here. He was diagnosed five years ago with early onset Parkinson's and it's progressed quickly. He doesn't recognize me these days." There were tears in her eyes when she said this. "Let's sit inside, shall we? It's a little cold in the garden. We get lots of breeze." She pointed to a comfortable couch and I took a seat in the middle. "Coffee?"

I told her I was fine and she asked if she could take my jacket. She laid it across the back of a chair and took a seat beside me. "I don't think I want to talk any more," she said softly, taking my hand in both of hers. "Let's just sit here quietly. Take off your shoes if you'd be more comfortable."

I did so and when I sat up again, she took my arm and snuggled close to me. I could feel the softness of her breast and found myself responding. Then she laid her hand high on my thigh. "Are you comfortable cheating on your wife, Jazz?

"She wouldn't consider it cheating." I told her about my talk with Nicole. "The odd thing is, Nicole is the one who brought it up. We also talked with a good friend of ours who is a psychiatrist.

She told me to listen to my wife." I shrugged. "I don't even pretend to understand."

Trudy turned so she was looking directly into my eyes. Her face was only inches from mine. "So what's stopping us?" she asked softly. "Nigel doesn't like employees dating but he doesn't raise an issue if it doesn't interfere with work. And you're not exactly an employee."

I thought about that for a long moment. Looking at Trudy's generous lips I wondered how it would be to kiss them. "I don't know," I answered. "Habit?"

"Now there's an idea," she said, grinning. "We could put on bathrobes and pretend you're a monk and I'm a nun."

"Or we could just start the old fashioned way, with a kiss."

"What a radical concept. Let's try it." When first our lips met, hers were warm and sensuous and our kiss, long and lingering.

"Nice," I said. My voice was husky. "Let's try it again."

I awoke to the smell of pizza. The light through the bedroom window told me that the afternoon was gone. Still half asleep, I got up and wandered into the bathroom. After answering the call of nature I washed my face and returned to the bedroom. Trudy was there, sitting on the side of the bed dressed in a smile. My response was immediate.

"Oh, my," Trudy chuckled. "Someone seems to like me." She stood up and walked over to me.

"You're beautiful!" I told her and she blushed and moved into my arms for a wonderful hug.

"Hmmm," she murmured. "The thing is, Trudy will stay hot. Our pizza will not." She pulled back, smiling as she looked into my eyes. "Would you like a robe to wear while we eat, kind sir?"

"Only if you do, fair lady."

We ate quietly, attacking the pizza like we had not eaten for weeks. It was excellent and when we were done we cleaned up the mess. Then Trudy came into my arms. "I seem to be insatiable, Jazz. It's been a long time. Would you mind?" She kissed my neck gently and began to work her way down. Then she giggled. "I'll take that as a 'yes.'" A moment later she kissed me again and the sensation was almost more than I could bear.

"I've never done that before," she murmured as we lay quietly entangled an hour later.

"You could never prove it by me," I told her. "You seemed quite good at it."

"So did you," she said blushing. "But that wasn't what I meant. I've never played hookey from work for a whole afternoon. Not like this."

"Oh. I have to admit that's a first for me, too, but my schedule is pretty flexible. I hope we didn't get you in trouble with Nigel."

"No, we didn't, but I do need to stop back by the office this evening and check my desk. I may need to spend a little time clearing it, too."

I nodded, looking at the clock. "I probably need to check into a hotel. I hope I can find one with a room left."

"We have a room you can use. I meant to tell you earlier. We keep a small efficiency booked for clients all year round." She paused. "Or you can stay here if you like. It would be wonderful to sleep together. Assuming I could keep my hands off you."

I thought about this for a moment. This was not something I had anticipated. "Sure," I heard myself agreeing. "That would be very nice. Thank you."

It was well past eleven that evening before we were able to leave Jolly Good Times and head back to Trudy's. Something had come up that needed her immediate attention and I decided to keep going through the employee records on my computer. The interesting thing was that there was nary a glitch using my machine and I was able to get through the records of most of the New Jersey people fairly quickly.

As I worked I kept a running series of notes of things I needed to ask Trudy or Nigel. I was surprised when Trudy stuck her head in and said Nigel would like a word with me. "He must be a real night owl," I said, glancing at my watch. "What is it, three in the morning in London?"

Trudy chuckled. "He's calling from Honolulu," she told me. "It's about supper time there."

"Jazz!" Nigel greeted me warmly. "You're really burning the midnight oil. Couldn't you sleep?"

"No, I just got caught up in the project and lost track of time. How are you?"

"Fantastic! We just tied up another large contract in Japan. I know it's early days but how's our special project going?"

"It's going very well. Dom and Trudy have been very helpful. I wonder, though. Is there any reason not to fill them in on the full scope of what you want?"

"Not really. I was just trying to keep the circle of those in the know as small as we can. Why do you ask?"

"Well, my cop sense tells me neither of them is who we're looking for. They're also a lot better informed of the ins and outs of your operations. It occurred to me they might be able to make suggestions Dee and I might never see. I think it might help if they could kick ideas around with us."

Nigel chuckled. "That's interesting. I almost suggested that very thing the last time we talked but I didn't want to jostle your elbow. Dom is one of the smartest people I know and no one knows our people better than Trudy." He paused. "How are things going with Daniella?"

"To tell you the truth, I haven't seen much of her. I expected that she would be working with us."

"Yes, that was the original plan. However something came up that I need her to look into. I can bring her back in once she's done with the project she's on, if you wish. To be frank, I thought it might be better if your paths didn't cross that much."

"You're probably right but I don't want to shut her out. She's the head of your security department and I certainly don't want to step on her toes. Maybe I need to keep her in the loop."

"You Yanks have a wonderful saying," Nigel responded. "Don't fix it if it ain't broke. Did I get it right?

"I couldn't have said it better myself," I assured him. Nigel had told me, without explicitly telling me, to leave well enough alone.

We visited for a couple of minutes more and Nigel rang off. As I shut down my computer and put it away Trudy came in. "How do you feel about takeout Thai?" she asked. "There's a place we can get takeout on the way home. I'm too beat to eat out."

"Sounds good," I told her. Yet I felt some dissonance in my soul and wondered if I was making a mistake staying at her place. No, I wasn't cheating but for me home was with Nicole and my children. Yet I knew it would be strange to wake up with someone else.

Something of what I was feeling must have found itself into my voice because Trudy looked at me sharply. "What?" she asked.

I shook my head and lied. "Nothing. It's been a busy day and it just hit me how tired I am." I gave Trudy a hug to reassure her. "In Arkansas we call it old-fartitis."

"Please don't lie to me, Jazz." Trudy's face was troubled.

"I'm not. This whole situation just feels strange to me."

"It's strange to me, too," Trudy told me. "I've never, ever done anything like this before."

"Then we'll just have to help each other take delight in it. Now, I believe there was something said about takeout Thai."

Despite what Nigel had told me, Daniella Cooper was there to greet me when I came in the next morning with Trudy. Her eyes narrowed when she saw us arrive together but said nothing. I decided it was best to be polite and I greeted her warmly. "Good morning, Daniella." I told her. "I wasn't expecting to see you. Nigel told me you are on another project."

"Just passing through," Daniella replied curtly. "Checking in. Need anything?"

"Not really. I expect it will take me another day or two to finish up on the HR files. I don't have much to report on those yet. Trudy and Dom have been very helpful."

Daniella nodded once and turned on her heel and walked away. "I guess I really offended her," I told.

"She's pretty territorial," Trudy murmured so quietly I could barely hear.

"I'd like to get together with you and Dom when you both can get away for a half hour. Nigel wanted me to brief you on what I'm doing here. I wonder if I should include her."

"You did a pretty good job of debriefing me last night," Trudy said in the same soft voice. Then in a normal voice she said, "What did Nigel tell you?"

"He didn't mention her, just you and Dom."

"There you go, Jazz. Do what the boss wants." Then she frowned. "You do know she's not your problem, don't you?"

"Yes, but I don't want her sabotaging my work." I shrugged. "Oh, well, it's her issue. Would you mind finding Dom for me? I'm going to finish what I was doing last night."

"That might take you quite a while," Trudy said. Then she added, "Sorry. I'll try to keep things straight around the office."

"Well, you won't have much trouble doing that," I replied and she flushed. As I turned to head for my work area I saw Daniella on the other side of the office. She was watching us intently.

"Bugger!" Dom declared. "What a bloody mess!" I had just finished bringing him up to date.

Trudy's response surprised me. "I knew something was going on and I almost went to Nigel."

"Why didn't you?" I asked.

"It was only a feeling," she told us, "not even a real hunch. I just knew things didn't feel quite right but I couldn't figure why I felt that way. Even Nigel seemed different but I thought it was just me. There was nothing I could point to."

"How long back?" I asked.

"Two months, maybe three. It wasn't a sudden flash, either. It was more of a growing awareness I couldn't quite identify."

"So this is why you're going through employment records," Dom said, nodding. "Do you really think it might be someone in the company?"

I shook my head. "Chances are it probably isn't, but this is a good place to start. From a policeman's point of views it's an obvious place to look. So it's important to eliminate that possibility first and then move on."

"Like looking at the family of a murder victim first," Dom said. "Well, you need to look but I don't think you'll find anything. We vet our people very carefully."

"I imagine Daniella is very efficient in doing that," I agreed.

"Efficient, that's a polite way of putting it. She's downright ruthless as far as I'm concerned," Trudy said. "On the other hand, she gets the job done quickly and with impressive results."

"Yes, there was that one fellow," Dom nodded. "He looked very good on paper and quite impressive in person. Nigel was just about to hire him when Dan smelt something off and dug deeper. The man was a bloody disaster looking for a place to happen. He had a criminal record a yard long."

"Did you turn him in to the police?"

Trudy nodded. "Yes, as a matter of fact, we did. Daniella told us there were outstanding warrants and Nigel told her to notify the police. She told us the police bungled the arrest and he got away."

I found myself getting excited. "Do you still have the paperwork on him?" I asked.

"Does a squirrel hide nuts?" Dom laughed. "We put together a paper trail going all the way back to when and where his great grandfather was born."

"We may not have it now," Trudy told us. "We had a serious fire here about that time and things got shuffled in storage. Some of the paper files got wet and had to be thrown out."

"What about your computer files?" I asked.

"We hadn't entered his information into our employee database since we hadn't hired him. So his information might have been thrown out. Fortunately our vital employee and operations files were backed up on computer, thanks to Dom. So what might have been a disaster has only been a continuing inconvenience."

"I'd like to see what you have, anyway." I sighed. "Well it's time for me to get back at it. Do either of you have anything else we need to talk over?" Trudy and Dom shook their heads. "Well, you know where I'll be."

When I fired up my computer, the first employee record I

asked for was Daniella Cooper. I couldn't remember asking how long she had been with the company so I took a look. I was not surprised to see she had been a security consultant for Nigel when the company was first established. I wrote myself a note to ask Nigel about this the next time we talked.

Fifteen minutes later I was in the middle of another record when Trudy looked in and said Nigel was on the phone if I needed to talk with him. I said I did and she showed me which button to push on my desk phone.

I greeted Nigel and told him I had a question. "When you first got Jolly Good times going, what company did you hire to set up your security system?"

Nigel gave me a company name, one I didn't recognize. "I'd be very surprised if you ever heard of them," he added. "They were in business less than a year and I'm not surprised they went under. We were one of their first clients and they simply didn't do the job we contracted. They were long on good references and short on their performance. They ended up wasting a lot of time we didn't have. So I ended up hiring Daniella and haven't regretted it a moment."

"How did you find her?"

"She was actually the assistant to the account executive who was assigned our company. She was the only one who got anything accomplished and the board and I were impressed. She was far from happy where she was, too, and we hired her."

"Well, I'm impressed, too. Trudy took me through your hiring process and it's quite thorough. It's very similar to what we tried to set up in Arkansas."

"You tried? What happened?"

"Corn pone politics and endemic nepotism. It's one of the main reasons I'm a consultant these days."

Nigel laughed. "Well, it's our gain. Do you have everything you need?"

"Yes, Dom has been quite helpful and Trudy has been, too. You have an incredibly good staff from what I've seen."

"Yes, they are. The market hasn't much room for deadwood

these days, I'm afraid. That's why we take great pains in hiring and keeping good people. Like yourself."

"Careful, Nigel, my hat won't fit."

He laughed. "That's why I never wear one."

The rest of the morning went quickly and I was surprised when I discovered I was done with the employee files for the New Jersey operation. That left the West Coast office which involved more than twice as many employees, not counting part time folks and contractors. Nor did I expect the employee screening there to be as rigorous as it was at the home office. When I asked Trudy about this over lunch, she told me I was absolutely right. I made a note to myself to ask Nigel or Daniella about this. Among other things, I needed to ask Nigel how deep he wanted us to dig. Daniella could do it, too, but I wasn't sure how well she would cooperate.

"So are you done here?" Trudy asked. She seemed a little sad when she did and I hoped she was not falling in love with me. From all I have read on the subject, this is the primary danger in having an affair. At least it is for Americans. A couple may start out both agreeing it is a casual thing but that has very little to do with what happens within the human soul when human beings grow intimate. Despite their best intentions deep attachments develop, and with attachment, the potential – even certainty – for hurt from losing someone we have come to care for deeply.

Is it worth it? Now at this season of life, having lost a beloved wife and someone else whom I would gladly have married, both to killers I was after, I have to say it is. Life without intimate love is less than really living, and the total acceptance of inevitable loss opens the door to the incredible gift of joy. As I see it, we are created for joy and allowing fear to keep us from embracing it with every breath is a mortal sin.

Now, hearing the sadness in Trudy's voice, I reached out to squeeze her hand. "Don't let me forget," I said. "There's something important I need to tell you." Seeing the question in her eyes I added, "This is not the time or place. It's about the gift of joy and living in the moment."

Since the mid-day break was flexible there were several people in the dining area when Trudy and I took a table. Trudy had packed us a lunch and when we came in, Dominic picked up his tray and came over. "May I join you?"

"Of course," I replied, waving him to a chair. "I do have one rule I try to follow. Eat first and enjoy the food, and then talk business."

"Sounds good to me," he said. "So what do we talk about?"

"Well, what do you do for fun?" I asked.

"I run," he said, smiling. "And I like museums, too. Whenever I can I take in a show at Birdland."

"Birdland?" I said. "I've never been there. Who do you like to hear?" What followed was a wonderful discussion of jazz and New York jazz clubs. Trudy seemed to prefer listening to us rather than contributing to the conversation and we had all finished eating when someone from her office came to fetch her. It was apparently something she had to do herself and she left.

Once she was out of earshot I asked Dom, "How long has Trudy been with Jolly Good Times?"

"Pretty much from the beginning," he told me. "Nigel and I had found this place and were going crazy trying get organized. We had hired Daniella but she was tied up with permits and the legal stuff and we needed someone to set up our personnel department. John Howard, her husband, was doing our legal work and he suggested we hire her to set things up."

"That surprises me," I replied. Then I remembered Nicole and I both work in the Agency and it works well. Sam and Megan McKee were a good example, too, as were Willie and Liz Dill.

Dom nodded. "Nigel was a little leery of having both a husband and wife involved, but they were in different areas. They were good together, no overt conflict and a stable marriage. So he turned her loose on the job. Two weeks later Trudy told him she would be finished within another two weeks and that he needed to hire a HR director so she could get the new director on board and start recruiting the talent. So Nigel hired her. It was one of the best decisions he ever made."

This confirmed what I had learned and inferred from everything I had read and seen. I was mulling this over trying to decide what I needed to do next when I realized Dom had asked me a question. "Sorry," I told him. "I was gathering wool. What did you ask?"

"I asked what's next for you?"

"I think I need to touch base with my partner," I told him. "After that it's back to the mines with subcontractors and the West Coast roster."

"You should be able to do most of that from here," he pointed out.

"Yes, but I'm a policeman at heart," I reminded him. "I need to look people in the eye. A lot of times I see stuff that doesn't appear on paper."

"That's almost scary," he replied. He looked rather uneasy and I wondered what was behind it.

"Only if you have something to hide."

"That's just it. Everyone I know does."

"That's why we're *here* but don't worry. We're after a killer, not jaywalkers." Dom chuckled when I said this but he still seemed unsettled. I wondered if he had a joint in his pocket but I didn't ask.

Conversations

6 Actually I had two partners I needed to talk with. To be honest, I was dreading calling home so I called Dee first. Even though I had Nicole's *imprimatur*, I felt terrible about having spent the night with Trudy. Nor could I figure why I had done so though I knew what Forster would say. It would be something like '*Hogamus, higamus* man is polygamous." I tried to run that saying down once but discovered it had been in general use long before someone famous used it.

Dee didn't have much to tell me. He had not made it to the West Coast until that morning and had just arrived at the district headquarters of the Oregon Highway Patrol. "I talked to the state commander yesterday and I'm waiting for the district supervisor to come in," he told me. "The supervisor knows you from one of your seminars, the one in Seattle a few years back. His name is Hamilton, Donald Hamilton."

"I remember him. Please give him my warm regards."

I brought Dee up to date quickly, hitting only the high points except for the conversation with Dom. Like me Dee thought we needed to follow up with the man not hired. "It sounds like he might be another Ted Bundy," Dee said. "Any luck finding out more about him?"

"No, Daniella Cooper could probably fill us in but she isn't in the office and neither is Nigel. I'm not sure she'd tell me much unless he was there, either. On the other hand, I think she might have a crush on you. Otherwise, I'm going to have to put on a hazmat suit and dig through a storage unit. Maybe more than one."

Dee ignored my jest. "They couldn't even remember the guy's

name?" The way Dee asked told me he was having a hard time believing this. "Not even Nigel?"

"I just came across this. I haven't had time to call him yet, but I'm not expecting much. It's been years ago. That's my next call."

Dee picked up something in my voice. "You seem a little reluctant, partner. What's going on?"

"Well, that's been a long time ago and all I have is a gut feeling. I hate to waste our time running down a dead end. I've got a shit load of other files to check."

"Correction. You have two gut feelings about this guy. I like him, too."

"Yeah, but your gut feeling is last night's burritos," I replied and he laughed. When we were on highway patrol together back in the day I had to threaten to ask for another partner if he didn't lay off the beans. Even with bodies which have been in the water for weeks, I have never smelt anything quite as vile as Steve Dirado's burrito fumes.

When I hung up I was not surprised how much better I felt. Talking to Dee does that, even when he's raking me over the coals. He tells me that's the way AA works, too, and the cranky old padre I see says the same. "It's soul poison, Jazz! When you keep things bottled up inside it's like a festering spiritual lesion that only gets worse."

He had glared at me, his bushy eyebrows twitching. It struck me as funny but I didn't dare laugh or even smile. "You understand, I'm not telling you anything new. This is exactly what damned near killed you and forced you to take medical retirement. Let someone else share your burden."

"Everyone I know is burdened enough as it is," I tried to protest, knowing it would be useless.

"Horse apples, and you know it! Serving others lightens the load and letting someone else help you find your way lets them set aside their own troubles for a while. It's one of the greatest gifts you can give a fellow traveler."

"Fellow traveler? Shades of Joe McCarthy." The padre's answer had been a snort.

Nor did I doubt Dee's assessment of the GNH, our verbal shorthand for "guy not hired." Since both of us had the same sense of the man, he was definitely a person of interest. So it was time to dig through the files, literally.

I picked up the phone, intending to call home, but I put it back in the cradle. I told myself I needed to stay focused on the investigation. Talking to Nicole would be a distraction, particularly with what we needed to discuss. So I put away my cell phone and headed for the Human Services office.

"Oh, here he is," Trudy said as I stuck my head in her office. She handed me the phone. "Nigel," she whispered.

Nigel got right to the point. "Trudy tells me you want to rummage through our storage files."

"Actually I dread it, Nigel, but it looks like the only way to get the information we need about the guy you almost hired."

"You think he might be the one?"

"Based on what I've been told, he's the leading contender right now. I just got off the phone with Dee. He agrees."

"What makes him so attractive as a suspect? Or is it a 'person of interest'?"

"All the lies. From what I have been told, his whole *curriculum vitae* was phony. One of the main traits of a sociopath is that they lie like rugs. Ted Bundy is a case in point. It was almost as if he couldn't tell the simple truth unless he could use it to manipulate his victims. There are a number of other traits of the pathology but that one raises a red flag."

Nigel was quiet and I waited for a response. After a long pause he said, "I hate for you to have to do this. I tried to dig something out myself one time but couldn't. Even with a respirator mask the smell of mold and mildew was overpowering."

"I thought about that," I replied. "I was actually thinking of wearing a medical hazmat suit."

"Seriously?"

"Absolutely. You would find it hard to believe how many times I've had to wear one. It's not fun."

"Would it help if I put together a list of what I remember

about the man?"

"That would be a great help," I told him. "It might save us a great deal of time."

"And time is money." He chuckled. "My money. Well, let me check my planner and my personal files and see what I have. I may have noted his name in my work diary. None of those were damaged in the fire. Can you wait until I get back there? I'll be in on Friday, or Monday at the latest."

"Couldn't Trudy or Dom look through them if they had the approximate date?"

"I don't know, Jazz. My planner has personal things as well as very sensitive business information of a proprietary nature. It's double encrypted and I don't want to release the code. I really don't like anyone else rummaging around my desk, either."

"Isn't there some general digital work journal Trudy could look at? All she needs is a general idea of the date."

"That's just it. I am going to have to do some looking to find anything like that. I simply can't remember. It's been quite a while."

Nigel's reluctance to allow anyone else to go into his desk or planner told me he had something to hide recorded there. I wondered what it was but I reminded myself that the man was not a suspect. He was the boss and had to be treated with all due respect. So I decided to back off and change subjects.

"Well, I've got plenty to keep me busy the rest of the week looking at subcontractors and the West Coast files. Do you think there's any reason to think it might be someone from your Cayman office?"

"Not really. I'd say look elsewhere first. That office is purely financial."

Then something else occurred to me. "I don't suppose you have anything on the guy recorded on video, do you? The guy not hired. Even parking lot video. I have access to some pretty sophisticated facial recognition people."

"Oh, so do we if you need them."

"This is one of those extras I bring to the table, Nigel. The services I'm talking about are not commercially available. It's state of the art."

Again Nigel was silent for a moment. "Well, I hope you're talking about legitimate services," he said. "I don't want us involved in anything remotely illegal."

"If there were, Nigel, I wouldn't suggest it. A couple of friends of mine are people who develop this stuff. We swap services."

When I hung up I sat there and thought about the conversation I just had with Nigel. He had not answered my question about video storage. So I picked up the phone and called Dee back. He didn't answer and I sent him a text message. "Not urgent. LBBN obfg. Glass eye. 93%." Read in our working code, not urgent meant something important or a red flag. Glass eye meant keep an eye out, and LBB is Little Boy Blue, generic for main suspect or head honcho. Obfg is our shorthand for obfuscating. Ninety-three percent refers to Dee's batting average for my hunches being right and I had no doubt Dee would know LBBN meant Nigel. So what I was telling my partner was, "Red Flag, I have a hunch Nigel is hiding something important so keep looking for it."

All this may sound silly, even paranoid, but keep in mind that Dee and I have spent most of our career together chasing serial killers. These guys may be crazy but they are not stupid and they have very well tuned antennae for potential danger. I have been in their cross-hair, literally, as has Dee. I have almost been killed by one of these people at least seven times. So call it silly if you wish. I call it careful. There's nothing like getting shot at to put things in perspective.

I sat there for a while after I called Dee. Nigel's reticence bothered me and I wondered what lay behind it. Was it simple embarrassment over a personal secret, something we could safely ignore? Or was it a factor of substantial bearing in the case? Either way it was an impediment to our work until it was brought to light. I made myself a note to talk to Dee as soon as I could.

"What next?" I asked myself softly. Then my eyes fell on the phone and I looked at my watch. It was time to call my bride. The longer I put it off the harder it would be and this was a good time for me to call.

Nicole answered on the second ring. "Hello, stranger," she said. "I was just thinking about you. How are things in the Big Apple?"

"Oh, work is going well," I told her. "I should be able to wind up what I need to do here by the end of next week. Maybe. Things keep popping up that need to be run down. I'm planning to fly home Friday morning. I really miss you."

"What's going on, Jazz-beau? You sound a little strange."

"I ran into one of those situations."

"What situations?" she asked innocently. I knew she was teasing and was glad she was felling mellow.

"Those situations you talked to me about," I said ruefully.

"Can you be a little more helpful?" she asked, deliberately obtuse.

"One of those birds and bees situations," I replied. I was sure she new exactly what I was talking about.

"I see. That sounds interesting. So what did Dr. Jazz do about it?"

"Do I have to draw you a picture?" I asked and Nicole laughed. I felt myself getting exasperated. "I did exactly what Soyfya told me to do. I minded my wife."

"Oh? Help me remember. What was that?"

I was really getting irritated but I tried not to growl. "Look, I need your help, Nicole. That's why I called."

"You need suggestions for what to do? You never had trouble like that with me, not that I noticed."

"I'm about to hang up," I told her. It was something neither of us had ever done in all the years we'd been married.

"I'm sorry, Jazz-beau," she said gently. "It's not often I get you on the run like that. I'll be good. Or do you want me to be bad? You seem to like it either way. I'm sorry. Truly. What do you need from me?"

Nicole is rarely glib and I realized she was having a hard time with this, too. I felt like a heel even though I had done exactly what she told me.

"I need you to hold me. I need you to make love to me. And I need to forget about murder. You know what I mean." That last was not a question.

There was a long silence. "Yes, Jazz-beau, I do know what you mean and you know I do," she answered softly. "I wish you were here so I could hold you right this minute. I didn't realize how upset you were."

"Neither did I until just now. I'm really uncomfortable with this. It doesn't feel right."

"That's very good. At least, it is as far as I'm concerned." There was no hint of levity in Nicole's voice.

"It's very good as far as I'm concerned, too. How are you doing with this?"

"Oh, I'm a little green-eyed at the moment. I'll get over it. After all, I'm the one who put you up to it. We'll talk when you get home. Then I'll show you why you hang around."

"I know why I hang around. You're even more beautiful on the inside than you are on the out."

"Keep talking like that and I may fly to New York. So what's she like?"

"Well, if you can get past the glass eye and the wooden leg and the missing teeth, she ain't bad," I said, trying to match her earlier mood.

"Be serious!" she said in a tone she rarely uses with me.

"Now who's got whom on the run?"

"Touché. Are you going to sleep with her again?"

"Only if you insist," I replied lightly.

"Is that a dare, Jazz?"

"Of course not. I don't do dares, not with you. I'm too scared you'd take them," I added and she knew I meant it. My wonderful bride is not someone to mess with. A number of violent sociopaths have learned that a bit late.

"Well, I'm going to insist, anyway. Just remember, you'll have to tell me about it in detail." There was no question in my mind she was serious.

I tried a paradoxical response. "How about I use a tape recorder? Then we can listen to it together."

It worked. "You're bad!" she laughed. "Rotten to the core."

"And you love it," I reminded her.

"I sure do. Just don't you forget it."

"I wouldn't dare," I confessed. "Seriously, I'd rather not sleep with her again."

"Well, that's too damned bad, Red Ryder. Those are your marching orders." She paused and I waited. "Does she know I told you to gather what rosebuds came your way?"

"Yes, I told her about our conversation."

"Smart woman. She struck while the iron was hot. Still, I don't want you to hurt her feelings. Is she married?"

"She told me her husband's been in a nursing home for several years. Early onset Parkinson's."

"So she's older then?"

"Yes, she's roughly my age."

"So she's rough, is she?" I was glad we were teasing again.

"It's hard not to be with snag teeth."

We talked a long time after that, mostly about the kids and our friends at work. When Nicole picked them up from school I talked with them until they got home. Then I talked to my bride again while she fixed supper. It came as no surprise that my cell phone battery was seriously depleted when I rang off and looked at the clock. It was after six-thirty and I was surprised at how good I felt.

Just then Trudy stuck her head in. "Well, it looks like someone's cheered up," she said. "You seemed to be a little down earlier."

"Talking to my family does that," I answered. "Nicole told me to treat you right. So you can choose between my cooking and take-out. Or we can eat out."

"You told her about me?" Trudy asked, surprised.

"Of course. That was part of our original agreement."

She nodded but I could see she was still not completely convinced. "So you're staying over with me again?"

"Only if you want me to. I suppose I can get a hotel if you prefer."

"Are you kidding? I don't even want to waste time dining out.

I have plans for you, Mister."

Our evening together was delightful. I insisted that we set work aside and simply enjoy the gift of this special time. We had both worked hard all day long and it was time to play, and the only intrusion of work came with a call on my phone as we were putting away the dishes.

I looked at the caller ID and told Trudy it was Daniella and I'd better take the call. "Good evening, Daniella," I said in an effort to be cordial.

Daniella wasn't buying. "Nigel told me to call. The name is Mills, James Mills."

"Whose name?" I asked. I thought I knew who she was referring to but I wanted to be sure.

"The name you wanted," she said, quite terse. "The guy Nigel almost hired."

"Thank you," I replied. "I appreciate it. Could we talk about this at the office in the morning?"

"Huh!" Daniel ejected. It sounded like a zebra's bark. Then I realized it was a laugh. "Not in town. Back next week. No point talking. Phoney name."

"Yes, but I understand you were the one who warned Nigel. I'd like to talk about that. What made you suspicious."

"K," Daniella barked and I was listening a dead line.

"That was strange," I told Trudy. "She actually uttered eleven words in a row. Have you ever heard her laugh?"

Trudy nodded. "I think so. She makes sort of a barking sound at odd times. If that's laughing, she's got a strange sense of humor."

"Does she always talk like that?"

Trudy nodded. "Most of the time she does. The only time I've heard her speak normally was when I overheard her once talking to Nigel. I wondered who he had in his office but it was just the two of them." She started to add something else but shook her head instead.

"What were you going to tell me?" I asked. She shook her head again I looked at her fiercely, spreading my fingers extended like talons. Faking Schwartzeneger I said, "Vee half our vaze. Am I going to half to tickle it out of you, Fraulein?"

Trudy laughed. "That sounds like fun, Herr Doktor. When you're ready." She turned and walked into the bedroom with a definite hitch to her get-along. Later, as I was drifting off into a wonderfully peaceful sleep, she whispered, "She's had a hard life. That's what I was going to say."

A terrible play on words came to mind but I was too faded away make my lips work properly. What I heard myself reply sounded like, "Anghkkah." Then I was gone.

First Leads

7 I was at my desk early the next afternoon when Dee called. Looking at the clock I saw I had worked through the lunch hour and was ready for a break. I was surprised that Trudy had not looked in to remind me but I was just as glad. It felt like we were getting a little too domestic.

I shut the door to my workspace and leaned back. I knew Nigel probably had this workspace wired for sound. Yet I could at least avoid casual eavesdropping if someone came in. Even so, no one else had a reason to be there, not so far as I knew.

As I had expected, Dee had covered the waterfront looking at the James Spradley crash. The first thing he did was to talk with the district Highway Patrol supervisor. Don Hamilton vouched for the officer and told Dee that Sergeant Lee Dunmire was one of his very best troopers.

"I don't see Lee around here as much as I'd liked to," Hamilton said. "The Patrol uses him for a training officer and he's loaned out to other districts to break in rookies. The guys sent in to cover for him are good officers, but not in the same league as Dunmire. It was a fluke that he was the first officer to the crash site."

Lieutenant Hamilton also noted that there was a discrepancy between the official report and Dunmire's observations. "The official crash report shows Dunmire's response time as 4.68 minutes. Lee told me that it seemed much longer, as much as twelve to fourteen minutes, maybe more."

The problem was that there was no safe place to turn around and Dunmire had to go an extra four miles before he could do so. This was consistent with Oregon departmental policy which puts safety first. Dunmire told Hamilton that he called in his response only after turning around and getting up to speed. He reported it could have been as much as six or eight minutes before he actually called in the response. He said he was looking at the road, not his watch, so he couldn't give an exact time.

When Dee asked to speak directly with Dunmire, he was told the officer would not be available for two weeks. He had left just two days earlier on a remote fishing trip in Alaska. The supervisor was hesitant to try to track him down. "He really needed a vacation," Hamilton told Dee. "This doesn't seem like an emergency."

Dee assured him it was not and said he would call back later. He asked for a copy of the coroner's report and looked it over carefully. He told me that nothing caught his attention there, so he moved on to the crash site. There he lucked out again. The local fire and rescue supervisor was interested in the case and offered to show Dee the scene of the crash. "It seems he had some questions about the so-called accident, too. He told me it's hard to see how remains washed away and the blood did not, given where it was found."

Dee paused for a moment. "To tell you the truth, Jazz, I have to take his word for it. I'm surprised that the whole wreck didn't wash off the rock before they pulled it out with a winch truck. I'd hate to fall in the drink anywhere near there. Looks like the sea would tear you to pieces." There was an odd note of fear in his voice and I wondered what had spooked him. Nor did he leave me wondering. "I've never, ever seen surf like that. It scared the shit out of me. It felt like it could reach up and grab me if I got too close."

Dee also reported he had talked by phone with the State Medical Examiner. The ME knew the crash scene technician very well. She was new and had just finished her six month hire probation the week before the crash, and she had served this probation in his office. The ME went on to say that there had been no complaints about her work. While she might have made a mistake, he thought it was very unlikely.

There was actually very little forensic evidence from the crash except for the DNA testing of the blood samples. When they recovered the torso later, what was left of it was too burnt to give a reliable sample for DNA. Since the crash was considered a straight-forward car crash, there was no rigorous testing done. It could have been ordered but the technician's supervisor was running on a tight budget and considered it an unnecessary expense.

"What about the skull?" I asked.

"It didn't come in with the body bag. The tech told me they searched all over both sides of the highway and the Highway Patrol sent a couple of officers to help look. They came up empty. The assumption is that it was lost at sea. If that's the case, there won't be much left by now big enough to see. You would not believe that surf." Again there was that odd note of fear in Dee's voice.

"That's probably a reasonable assumption," I replied. "It's strange but it doesn't sound like there was any reason to assume foul play. Or do you think there was?"

"That's just it. I can't see how in the hell someone could set something like that up to look like an accident and not be seen. Not in the time window we got."

"Well, let's go at it from the other direction. Assuming the dead guy is the killer, how was being considered dead an advantage? With that much work there would have to be a pretty good payoff."

"Aside from getting off on being a real asshole, I can't see it. Maybe it was a power thing, being able to get away with it. Fool the stupid police." What Dee left unsaid was that we'd both seen this many times before.

"I don't know," I told him. "Right now it makes more sense to me to look at Spradley as a homicide or crash victim. I had a feeling he might be our man, but I think I'm wrong. We do need to keep him in mind as a possible Unsub, but we need to look elsewhere, too."

"As our Unsub? When did you start talking like a Fat Boy, Jazz?"

Dee has very little use for the Bureau and its Special Agents, and his feelings are based in personal experience. The Natural State has unfortunately been used as a punitive assignment by the Bureau and this means we get more than our share of culls who like to lord it over local officers. Then, too, both Dee and I can remember a time when Special Agents were sent down to Arkansas infiltrate the Ku Klux Klan and were converted into full blown Aryan racists.

I ignored Dee's jibe. I still couldn't quite write off James Spradley as a suspect, but I couldn't see why someone besides Spradley would go to such ridiculous lengths to stage a death like this. So Spradley was either the victim of a very strange accident or a twisted master of illusion. Even if he was an illusionist, this should have turned up in the background check Daniella ran. Illusionists like to show off their skills and I thought surely someone would have mentioned this. I shared this thought with Dee and made a note to myself to check it out.

"Sounds about right to me," he responded. "So where do we go from here?"

"I still have all the West Coast files to go through," I told him. "Depending on what I learn from Nigel and Daniella, I may set those aside and run down the guy not hired. I also have a bunch of East Coast subcontractors to look through. How about you?"

"I'm off to Los Angeles this evening and then on to Las Vegas when I'm done here. There was a death in both places and another one in Yuma, Arizona."

"Well, if it's not too much out of the way, why don't you scope out the West Coast operations center, while you're there?" I asked.

"Why would I be doing that, Jazz? What's the cover story?"

"You could be doing background checks on some of their subcontractors," I said. "I can have Nigel call and let them know you're going to be around. He can tell you who you need to talk with. And if I come across something in the files you could check that out, too."

"What are you after, Jazz?" Dee said. He sounded confused. "I mean other than a serial killer?"

"I'm after your impression of their operations people. I'd like you to specifically talk to the people who work directly with the subcontractors. It doesn't matter what you talk to them about, they'll know you're a cop. I'm sure you'll pick up on it if anyone has something to hide."

"Yeah, I could do that," Dee agreed but I could tell he wasn't too enthusiastic. "The only thing is, this is the Left Coast and we're dealing with entertainment types. Everybody will have a joint or two tucked away and possession is still a crime, even if it's not enforced that much. They pick up on the fact I'm the fuzz and it's going to torque their sphincters. They're going to be sending off vibes we don't care about like crazy. Unlike me, you come across like a guidance counselor. So you can get away with all kinds of stuff I can't. That's the long and short of it."

The man had a good point. I am told I play bad cop well when I get wound up. It is such a contrast to my normal mild manner that even hard core officers like Dee find it scary. I have been told more than once by a tough observer that they were glad it wasn't them I was focused on when I let the wild Jazzbeast out to rumble. Dee once called this side of me Jazzilla. He told me the only man he's seen do this better is Jubal Mullen Stone. While I know he meant it as a compliment I'm not sure I like the comparison.

There was a knock on the door and I turned to see Trudy smiling at me. "Have you eaten yet?" she asked when she came in. "I got tied up in a tedious meeting." She rolled her eyes and shook her head.

"I know what you mean. Sometimes people think it will make stupidity true if they repeat it ten times or more. Loudly. And, no, I got tied up in what I was doing and lost track of the time."

"So you found something of interest?"

"Nothing that panned out. Mostly I was chasing rabbits that popped up." I showed her the hand written log I use when I'm researching on the computer. There were more than a dozen questions in the notebook I was using and they were all crossed through.

I looked at my watch and saw it was almost two. "What would

you like to do?" Trudy's answer was a raised eyebrow and I had to laugh. "Let me rephrase that. What would you like to do about lunch?"

"I'd like to go home. I made us a tuna salad last night and it should be perfect by now. I also made lime Jello with pineapple for desert."

"A tuna salad and Jello? When did you find time for that?"

She gave me a saucy grin. "While you were napping in between...sessions."

"So will I be allowed to eat first?"

"It depends on...." Trudy broke off and turned bright red.

I moved around her and locked the door. Then I pulled the drapes, hiding us from the main office. "There's something I always wanted to try," I said, sweeping everything off the desk and lifting Trudy onto it. Then I gently laid her back, feeling the heat of her pressed against me. I bent over to kiss her and felt her open to me.

I should have closed my eyes. When I looked out the glass wall that my desk abutted I was staring straight down and my acrophobia kicked in. I felt my head spinning and my knees buckle. A moment later I was on the floor.

The attack didn't last long. When I came to I was looking into the worried eyes of Trudy. "Jazz. Can you hear me?"

I nodded "Yes, I hear you fine,"

"Do I need to call an ambulance?" she asked.

"No," I answered. "It's only vertigo. I've had it before. If you open the door and let some air in I'll be fine."

Fortunately, no one was in the outer office. "Let's go have lunch," I suggested. "I'll be fine."

Trudy was very subdued at lunch. "I'm sorry," she told me. "That really scared me. I thought you had a heart attack."

"I'm sorry, too," I told her with a smile. "I'm sorry it didn't work. I wish I'd kept my eyes shut but I wanted to look into your eyes as we...." I shrugged. "It probably wasn't a very good idea in the first place. Not at the office."

"No, it wasn't but I was terribly excited. If you couldn't tell."

"Really?"

"Yes, Jazz, that's how I made it through that long, tedious meeting. I daydreamed of us making love." She smiled and I saw mischief in her eyes. "Do you want me to tell you what I daydreamed of us doing?" She blushed.

"Why don't you show me?" I said, laying aside my fork and pulling her to her feet.

I was late getting back from lunch. The bedroom clock told me it was a quarter of seven and it had been tempting to quit for the day and play hooky with Trudy. She had brought along some material she needed to get read but we had filled two hours with our attention to one another. As pleasant as this was, I felt a need to stretch my legs and finish up what I had been doing at the office. So I walked around Trudy's block a couple of times and headed for Jolly Times. Solitude is something I seem to need as much as I do good company.

It was well past seven when I got there. Most of the lights were out in the main work area and the glass walls of Trudy's office and the conference room were dark. Even so, there was enough light to navigate my way to my work area and I was surprised to find Nigel's office door unlocked. I wondered about this apparent lapse in security and made a mental note to myself to ask Trudy about it. I had been given a numbered key to use.

After looking around the office and finding Nigel's inner sanctum door locked, I locked the door to the main area. I still felt uneasy and quite vulnerable being unarmed. So I took the stairs down to the garage where my car was parked and got out my Glock and shoulder holster. As I climbed the stairs to the office I wondered if I was being silly. It was possible the cleaning crew had left the door open. On the other hand, we were after a serial killer.

When I got back upstairs the main door was locked but the door to Nigel's office area was not. Letting myself in quietly, I drew my pistol and moved to the open door to my work area. The light in the work area was on but I could have sworn I had turned it off when I sent downstairs. When I looked into my work space what I saw was Daniella Cooper seated in my chair and trying to find her way into my computer.

"Can I help you?" I asked and Daniella jumped up and turned to face me. Seeing my pistol her eyes widened even wider. Seeing her fright, I holstered my weapon.

"You're not supposed to have that in here!" she snapped, nodding toward my pistol. It was the longest complete sentence I'd heard her say.

"Two things," I told her. "One, I am a sworn federal law enforcement officer. So I can carry. Two, the office door was unlocked and I thought there had been a break-in." I shrugged.

"Nigel hates guns," she responded.

"I respect that. I regret the necessity."

We looked at each other, unblinking for several long moments. I decided to take the initiative. "I thought you were out of town."

"Passing through," she told me. "Needed something here."

"Fair enough," I said. "Do you have a few minutes for a couple of questions?"

Daniella shook her head. "Short layover. Taxi waiting." When she said this I realized how shaken she was by my appearance. She was so scattered she couldn't even come up with a plausible lie.

"Then I won't hold you up," I responded, moving to one side. "The questions can wait 'til later."

Daniella moved out of my work area, staying as far from me as possible. "Daniella!" I said as she was about to leave the office area. Nellie calls it my General's voice. Daniella flinched and turned to look at me.

"Got off wrong foot. Need to fix it. Work together," I said in the same clipped style she used.

Daniella blinked, then barked, again sounding like a zebra. I'll be damned if she didn't smile.

"OK. Next week," she replied. Then she was gone. I locked the door behind her and fired up my computer.

"I must be making progress," I said to Trudy later when I told her about what had happened. I ended up working until almost midnight and we were going to bed. "Daniella gave me a full OK, a bark, and a smile. I'm not sure what to make of it."

"I wouldn't put much stock in it," Trudy replied. "I've never known her to change her mind about someone." When she said this she was mumbling and looked like she could barely keep her eyes open.

I nodded and slipped into bed beside her. It didn't seem as strange as it had and I realized this didn't trouble me the way it had. It seemed almost normal and *that* troubled me. "Maybe she was embarrassed getting caught snooping at my computer."

There was no answer from Trudy. She was fast asleep and I lay there for a few moments thinking about how Daniella had responded. I wondered if it wasn't something else, something like the way I spoke to her. Just before I fell asleep I figured it out but when I awoke the next morning I couldn't recall what it was.

The next day was Thursday and I got to work early. I worked through the morning without a break and only took a half hour for lunch. By half past three that afternoon I finished going through the last file and stuffed all my notes into a box. I locked this in the trunk of my car along with my computer, initially intending to work on these at home. Then I drove to Trudy's to pick up my travel bag.

Our farewell was as melancholy as it was sweet. "I am going to miss you, Jazz," she told me and there were tears in her eyes. "This has been wonderful and I hope you know you are always welcome here when you're in town."

"This *has* been wonderful, Trudy," I agreed. "But I need to get home to my family. I hope to be back on Monday or Tuesday but it depends on how the case develops. I need to see both Nigel and Daniella in person."

When I kissed Trudy goodbye it was very tender and lingering. "I don't suppose...?" she murmured softly and I kissed her again.

This time tenderness quickly turned to passion though our lovemaking was gentle and a little sad.

"Your wife is a very lucky woman, Jazz," Trudy told me as we lay holding one another quietly. "I am very grateful for our time together though I don't suppose it would be appropriate for me to tell her so."

"Probably not," I agreed. I kissed her tenderly and got up to shower. "I need to be going," I said when I was done. "I'll see you next week, God willing and the creek don't rise."

"What does that mean?" She asked.

"It means life is full of surprises." She nodded and I kissed her once more and let myself out. What surprised me was how relieved I felt to be on my way.

I was very late getting home that night. I called Nicole to let her know I was leaving and normally I would have been able to make the trip in four hours. For some reason the southbound traffic was heavy that evening and three different wrecks slowed us down even more. At the second crash site traffic was stopped for almost forty-five minutes and I used the stop to stretch my legs and call to let Nicole know I was running late.

"Just take your time, Jazz-beau," she told me. "All we need is for you to get home safely. I went ahead and put the kids to bed. So you can be here when they wake up tomorrow."

When I finally arrived after seven nerve racking hours on the road, Nicole rubbed my neck until the tension was gone. Then she simply held me and when I tried to speak, she shushed me. "You're here safe and in my arms and that's what matters. I took the day off tomorrow so we have lots of time to talk."

"Let's go to the beach," I said. One of the things the two of us liked to do most was to walk together on the beach, even when it was raining.

"Let's see how you feel first," she suggested. "You may decide you've done enough driving." She wrapped her arms around me and held me close. It reminded me of the night she rescued me on the bank of the Arkansas River and I tried to tell her so. She nodded. "I remember. That was the night we made Jack. Now get some rest. I'm so glad you're home...."

I was fast asleep before she finished the last sentence. At some point during the night I got up for a pit stop and when I came back to bed Nicole took me into her arms again. This time I responded the way I did the first time we met and we made wonderful, poignant love. Then I fell asleep again and I didn't wake until Jack, our eldest brought me a cup of coffee. I got up then to see the kids off to school. Like making love to their mother, it's one of those things I never tire of doing.

Strange Connection

8   That weekend at home was wonderful. Nicole and I walked and talked and did the things we like to do all day Friday. Then there was something at the McKee's that evening and on Saturday we joined the other soccer parents cheering the home team on. The other team managed to win with a goal in the last ten seconds, but when we got to the pizza place the loss was quickly forgotten.

It was only when the kids were at the neighbor's watching old episodes of A-Team that Nicole and I finally got around to talking about Trudy. "Are you sure you want to talk about this?" I asked my bride and she nodded.

"I'm surprised it took so long to happen," she told me once we were settled in the den. We were holding hands and I could feel the tension she was going through. "What was it, six or eight months after we first talked?"

"Longer than that, I think," I responded. "It was at least six months after I last talked with Sofya. To tell you the truth, the whole thing took me by surprise and it felt weird. May I ask why you ever brought it up?"

"I wanted to make it a non-issue, Jazz-beau. These things happen and I didn't want it to ruin what we have when it did. I didn't realize how...alien...it would feel. Sofya tried to warn me but I didn't understand what she was telling me. I thought I had it all figured out but I was wrong."

I was very glad to hear her speaking in the present tense referring to our marriage. When she looked at me our eyes met. I could hardly bear the anguish in her eyes. "I am so sorry, Jazz. I put you up to this and I pushed pretty hard. I probably need to apologize to Trudy, too."

"How did you know her name is Trudy?" I responded. "I was

very careful not to mention her name when I called. Did I let it slip?" I asked all this without thinking. It was the kind of query investigators use to catch crooks off base. I worked hard keeping that side of myself out of our home, particularly in dealing with Nicole and the kids.

Thankfully Nicole ignored my slip into cop-mode. "No, dear man. You are much too gallant for that. I did a little research online and put it together. I narrowed it down to Trudy and two other people. One was someone named Louise but she is on the West Coast. The other was named Daniella but I remembered the way you talked about her after you met with the lawyer. So I did a little checking, too." When Nicole said this she looked quite embarrassed.

Suddenly I understood where she was going with this. "So you took a peek at my phone when I got home Thursday night," I said. "You know, I sometimes forget how good you are at the spook stuff, sweetheart."

"I sometimes forget what a good detective you are, too," she replied. Her eyes were fixed on the cushion of the sofa.

"Well, as far as Trudy goes, you don't owe her an apology. Not in her mind. She actually asked if it would be appropriate to tell you how grateful she is. I told her I thought it might be a little over the top." Nicole nodded but didn't look up.

I reached out and touched her face gently and Nicole covered my hand with her own. I lifted her chin until she looked into my eyes again. I put every ounce of love and gratitude I felt for her presence in my life into my gaze. A moment later there were tears running down her cheeks and she hugged my neck so hard I thought it might snap. Then her fingers started tearing at the buttons on my shirt and we left a trail of clothes into our bedroom.

"So you don't mind if I call?" Nicole asked. We were lying in one another's arms, completely spent from our loving. At least, I was. I could barely keep my eyes open and I had no idea what the woman was talking about.

I grunted some inarticulate reply that sounded roughly like

"Call who?" and struggled to stay awake long enough to hear what she was saying.

"Why, Trudy, of course. Who else? Trudy Howard from Jolly Good Times."

I was vaguely alarmed by this but not enough to come fully awake. "Come you're asking me?" I grunted barely able to get my mouth working. *The damned women do exactly what they please, anyway,* I remember thinking. Apparently I gave voice to the thought because Nicole laughed. She sounded light hearted, almost manic, but this didn't register until much later. So I went back to sleep.

This time my slumber was not so deep and I awoke to the sound of Nicole laughing. Her laughter sounded normal, like it did when she was talking to other women. I registered that fact and tucked it away, then went back to sleep.

I was suddenly wide awake. I knew exactly who Nicole was talking to and I felt alarmed. I quickly slipped on a robe and made my way into the den. There I found Nicole sitting on a large rocker in a robe identical to mine and talking on the phone. She was quite animated and waved at me happily as I walked in. I wondered if I was dreaming and stood there for a moment, feeling stupid and trying to figure this out. Then I saw she had gathered all our clothing into a pile and I picked it up and took it into the laundry room.

When I came back into the den, Nicole had hung up. "I take it that went well?" I asked. I still wasn't sure whether I was awake or not.

"She's a wonderful person. What an awful burden she has to carry by herself. Her kids are scattered and they aren't much help. The nursing home does all the basic care and she told me it's very good. But it doesn't cover companionship."

"I understand completely," I told her. "It wasn't as long and drawn out when Nellie died, but it was still awful. Then Jeanne was murdered and I was completely lost. I don't know what I would have done without you. Zilpha took care of the basics of keeping the house going but she has a family she needed to take care of, too. I wasn't very good company, either. You brought me back to life, love. Literally. That's the bottom line as far as I'm concerned."

What was most strange about this conversation is that we had never talked about these things with one another in all the years we had been together. So I was a little concerned. I had talked with Forster when things came up, and Nicole had spent a lot of time with Sofya. Yet we had never talked to one another face to face about some very important things.

A large part of the reason for this was because I am a policeman to the core. Hopefully, I'm not as rigid about this as I once was. Nicole, on the other hand, had been a rather deadly angel of vengeance to serial killers the law did not know about and could not touch. She had given this up not long after Jack was born. Her last hunt had been for the psychopath who had killed my beloved Jeanne and who was trying to drive a knife into my heart when she shot him. Right after she did she told me the whole story of how she had become an angel of wrath. Then we had simply closed the door on that chapter in her life and concentrated on raising our children.

"Maybe so, Jazz," Nicole responded. When she calls me that it means it's time to get down to business. "But you gave me a reason to live, too. I was almost at the end of my rope, too, as you know." She smiled. "Then Jack came along and then Marie. You gave me a life I never expected to have. That's what I was trying to protect. It might have been better if we had talked about this earlier."

"Maybe so, but it's good we're talking now. Are we all right about the thing with Trudy?"

"Yes. I talked with Sofya, too. She pointed out that I can't really carry a grudge when I set it up and encouraged you. I agree with her completely."

"Good. We may need to talk to her together if there's any residual fallout. One thing I need to do is let Trudy know it's over. I think I need to do it in person though, the next time I'm in Newark."

"No, don't do that, sweet man. I changed my mind talking to her. What I want you to do for Trudy is to take care of her almost as well as you do for me." She looked at me pointedly. "I did say almost and that includes in bed, too. I also want to meet her and she wants to meet our kids."

I looked at my bride and shook my head, as if clearing it. "Why do I think our life just entered the twilight zone?"

"We didn't just enter the twilight zone, Jazz-bear. That happened a long time ago, when we first got together to catch a killer. Besides, where else do spooks have to live?"

The question startled me. I have thought of myself as a policeman all my working life. I would have argued that even the work I did for McKee was police work. Yet I realized at that moment my attitudes had been shifting for years. The turning point had come when we were after Victor Quentin Shupe, the Oklahoma slasher. I decided to declare a personal amnesty on her extermination of serial killers the law couldn't touch and went to work with the Queen of Spades. This had turned out to be Nicole.

"Are you sure about Trudy?" I asked, still wondering if this was a dream. "I don't want to set her up to be hurt worse later on."

"Of course I'm sure, Jazz!" Nicole responded. "It's the right thing to do. Trust me on this." That was my bride, mistaken at times, maybe, but never in doubt.

Even so, I was still unsure of the wisdom of all this when it came time to leave for the Big Apple on Monday morning. I delayed my departure and stopped by the office so I could talk with Sofya. Her response was interesting. "Of course it's unusual, Jazz. There's nothing ordinary about either of you, and you, my friend, have had a life that's anything but ordinary. So it seems fitting, what your wife told you. Just be completely honest with her about it all and remember what comes first."

"My family comes first," I told her. "It always has, even when I was growing up."

"Exactly. That may be one of the most normal things about you, my friend. The work you do certainly is not. Nor is your choice of a mate. I think she's right about this. So trust us."

It was late enough when I left the Agency that traffic was not too bad leaving the District. I headed northwest from the office and picked up I495 to I95 north. This would take me all the way to the exit near Jolly Good Times. Since I was running late I pulled into a rest area and called Trudy. I asked her to let whomever might need know that it would be mid afternoon by the time I arrived.

"It's so good to hear your voice," she told me. "You have a wonderful wife."

"Yes, I do," I replied. "I have no idea what the woman sees in me, to tell the truth. It must have been a moment of madness when she decided to keep me."

Trudy laughed. "I think the polite term for that is horse hockey." She paused and I knew she was wondering where I planned be staying. "I was just wondering...." she said and then stopped.

"So was I. Is there room at the inn?"

"Always," she assured me. "Nigel is in the office today and tomorrow. He was asking for you when he came in."

"Good. I need to give him an update. How about Daniella? Is she there, too?"

"No, but she's scheduled to be in tomorrow." We chatted for a couple of minutes more before we ended the call. After I put down my cell phone I felt much better about being there for the next couple of days.

It was still too early to call Dee so I headed north again. I stopped at a Cracker Barrel restaurant for a late lunch and treated myself to one of their pot pies. I exercised some self-restraint when I was done and passed up on dessert. I was drinking a final cup of coffee when my cell phone rang with the unique tone for Dee. This drew some dirty looks from older patrons at the next table. "Police business," I assured them and moved to an empty table in a deserted area. I looked back and saw them straining their ears to overhear my side of the conversation.

Dee told me he was calling from Yuma, Arizona. "Why don't you go to scrambler?" he said and I got out the small flat disk Jack

McKee gave us for phone security.

"I got done in LA and Las Vegas on Friday and Saturday," Dee told me after we were both scrambled. So I came on down here. The bottom line is that the deaths in both places were legitimate. The guy in LA apparently developed a melanoma. I couldn't remember exactly what that was and the doctor told me it was a fast acting skin cancer. None of the paperwork kicked up a red flag and the widow was very grateful he had won the million bucks a few years back."

Dee paused to see if I had any questions but I did not. "So I took off for Las Vegas on Saturday morning and caught the right guy at the PD. The late departed was a guy named Thor Knutsen – honest to God, the Norwegian hammer man – and he was killed in a gang shooting. It's still an open case but the lead detective on the case is a friend of Bill Wilson, too. So we traded drunk stories for a while and he was a lot more forthcoming than he might have been. I told him we were looking for a possible serial and promised to let him know the outcome."

"The thing is, Jazz, he thinks it's most likely a gang related kill or maybe a random death or case of mistaken identity. I tend to think he's right. Yet there are enough loose ends to point toward a serial, too. For one thing, no one has put word out on the street claiming responsibility. The lead guy also tells me the rival gang leader denies knowing the guy who was shot or having anything against him. He claims he doesn't know anyone around him. Second, none of the closed circuit cameras in the area show any known gang member within a hundred feet of the guy killed. It didn't show him arguing with anyone or even bumping into someone.

"The theory the lead guy likes best is that it was a gang initiation kill. You know, pick a random victim and kill them while the other gang-bangers watch. What video footage they have shows the dead guy starting across the street in a big crowd of people and two seconds later lying there in a pool of blood. When they tracked down the people closest around the guy, of course, didn't nobody know nothing. Nor did other people in the crowd. There was street repair going on – jack hammers – so they didn't even hear the shot."

Again Dee paused. I asked. "Where was the victim hit?"

"That's just it. It was a heart shot and the killer used a .22 long rifle hollow point. He knew exactly where to aim, too."

"That would rule out a drive-by. Was he shot in the back?"

"Yeah. There were powder burns on the victim's shirt. My guess is that it was a bump and fire and a short perp, too. All the video shows is the victim falling forward. The heads around him moved aside and kept going. A couple of them looked down but they didn't stop. Nobody did until the light changed. With a crowd scene like that there was no chance of forensic evidence and the bullet they recovered was not in good enough shape for matching."

"It sounds like you did everything you reasonably could," I told him. "Let's set this one aside to look at later if we don't find anything else. What's up in Yuma?"

"I haven't had much luck connecting with the right people here yet," Dee told me. "There was some big festivity going on over the weekend and the police were all covering that. I did get a look at our man's medical records by flashing my home boy's insecurity card and claiming a national security need to know. And before you chew my ear, that's what McKee told me to do if necessary."

"I wonder why he didn't mention that to me, too?" I asked. I didn't doubt for a moment that Dee was telling me the truth.

"Are you kidding? He knows better than most what a by-the-book straight-arrow you are."

That rankled but there was nothing I could do about it. "All right, moving on. What killed the man?"

Dee laughed. "That was a complement, by the way, Jazz. Your integrity is one of the things Sam respects most about you. Me, too. No need to get hinky."

"I know. It just rubbed me wrong. So what killed him?"

"Would you believe cirrhosis of the liver? It may well be that the poor bastard drank himself to death. According to his wife, he managed to blow most of his contest winnings while he was at it. Mostly gambling."

"So why are you still hanging around Yuma?" There was something in Dee's voice that told me there was more.

"Well, I'm no doctor, but I do know a lot about cirrhosis. I don't think the guy was all that sick, Jazz. Not by true drunk standards. I need to talk to his doctor. I don't think there was an autopsy, either. The doctor signed off on death from liver failure due to cirrhosis."

"That means you probably won't get much from him. He's made up his mind and I doubt he'll back down. We need to give him a try, of course, but it's probably a dead end."

"I don't know. Let me talk to the wife again. She wonders how her husband came down with cirrhosis. She claims he didn't drink. On the other hand, us drunks are pretty good at hiding it and our wives at denying it."

"Then you *do* need to talk with the doctor. Find out why he diagnosed cirrhosis. It could be NAFLD."

"There you go speaking in tongues again. What in the hell is norfald?"

"NAFLD. That's non-alcoholic fatty liver disease. I came across an article on it recently. It's very common and can cause cirrhosis."

"What's the fun in having cirrhosis if you don't drink? I'll ask the doc about that if he doesn't mention it. What else?"

"Ask if the guy was on any medication that might cause it, too. There are several, including tetracycline."

"That's an antibiotic, isn't it?"

"A very powerful one. It was used for everything when it first came out. It's linked to hearing loss, too."

"So it's fix your hangnail and trash your ears and liver."

"Something like that." I paused, thinking, and Dee waited patiently. "Why are we even looking at this Dee? Is there any reason to suspect foul play?"

"I get the feeling we're being lied to big time, Jazz. What if cirrhosis wasn't the real cause of death? What if the guy was in the hospital for cirrhosis and died of something else? What if somebody took advantage of the situation and helped him along?"

"You may be right but there are way too many 'ifs' to justify a court order for him to be exhumed. I don't even know if we could get a subpoena for the medical records."

"The wife probably would if she might make some money out of it. On the other hand, you're probably right. The big question I have is how he blew a million bucks."

"Well, talk to the doctor if you can. Tell him the wife says he didn't drink and ask him why he diagnosed cirrhosis. Then talk to the wife again and call me back if something still smells fishy. We'll go from there."

"All right," Dee replied. "Anything else?"

"Where are you off to next?"

"Salt Lake City."

"I don't remember a victim there."

"That's because it wasn't in the list they gave us in New Jersey. Daniella sent it to me. She said it was one they overlooked."

That bothered me. "I wonder why they didn't tell me."

"It wasn't they, Jazz. It was Danny girl and she was most likely just being pissy."

"Yeah, but that could put her on our suspect list. What was the cause of death for the one she forgot?"

"She didn't say. So I'm going in cold. I'll run it down with the death certificate."

I didn't like it. Something was wrong. "Do you think it's for real or is she just wasting our time?"

"I think she did it to jerk your chain and I think she scored. It may be a waste of time but it's on Nigel's dollar. On the other hand, it may lead directly to our guy."

"All right, keep in touch. Go ahead and stay in Yuma if you think we need to go after a court order for autopsy. We'll need to work through the local PD if we do."

"I think it might be better to subpoena his medical chart first. He was in the hospital when he died and that might give us something suspicious enough to get the locals involved."

After I hung up I looked at the reminder list I keep in my shirt pocket whenever I'm on a case. Sure enough, it told me there was something I needed to do, and fairly soon. I looked up the phone numbers I had entered for Willard Nordwald when I took the case. I selected his office number and was lucky to catch him.

"Good afternoon, Jazz," he greeted me when he answered. "I hate to rush but I have a meeting in fifteen minutes."

"I won't keep you then. I'm just checking in. We've made a little progress in the investigation but nothing major. We do have some interesting leads but I think the details need to be passed along in person."

"I agree completely," he answered.

"I know I was supposed to be reporting to you but as things have worked out, I am keeping Nigel up to date, too. It's hard not to working in the home office. Is there a problem with that?"

"Not so long as you keep me informed, too. It needs to be that way to establish you are working for the firm. You need to bill us for your time and expenses. Any written reports need to go through us, as well. We'll pass them along to Nigel."

"Very good. It looks like I'll be back in Washington toward the end of the week. I'll call and see if you are available. We may need help with a medical chart subpoena in Arizona. I'll know more when I see you."

The rest of my trip to New Jersey was uneventful. Daniella was covering the reception desk and greeted me as I walked through the doors. She was almost courteous and took me directly to Nigel's office.

Nigel was his normal effusive self. We chatted for a bit until Daniella arrived with a carafe of coffee and pastries from the bakery at street level. Then she took a chair, which surprised me.

"I've asked Daniella to sit in with us," Nigel said. I saw the shadow of worry flitter across his eyes when he said this.

"Great," I responded and took the initiative. "By the way, thanks for sending Dee the heads-up on Salt Lake city, Daniella," I said. "It will save him some backtracking."

"Salt Lake City, what's this?" Nigel wanted to know.

"Computer glitch. The name didn't get on the first list." She smiled sweetly but when she turned to me it was gone. The look in her eyes dared me to make it an issue. *Busted*, I thought and smiled sweetly. She didn't respond.

I opened my laptop and fired it up. "What I need to discuss with you is James Mills, or whomever he might be this week." I smiled when I said this and I saw Daniella relax a bit. "Just to be clear, I believe that's one name of the fellow you decided not to hire some time ago."

Daniella and Nigel both nodded. "That wasn't the name he used when he applied," Nigel told me. "As best as we can figure that was his original name growing up." Like most of his countrymen, he pronounced it "figger."

"Was that the name on the police record you found?" I asked Daniella.

"Yes," she said. "May only be only on early record. Nothing under that name later."

"Did you get a middle name and date of birth?"

"Arden," Daniella told me. "No date of birth. Can't legally ask DOB on work application."

"Would you care to make a guess how old he was?"

Daniella shook her head but Nigel spoke up. "He would have been in his twenties then, late twenties. That was what, thirteen years ago?" Daniella nodded.

"That would put him in his early forties," I said opening the login page of the National Criminal Information Center database run by the FBI. "Let me see what I can get."

"Dom told me about that computer," Nigel said after I logged on. He smiled. "He wants one."

"I'm afraid these are very restricted," I said. "The people who make them tell me they are totally secure, even if they're stolen. I take their word for it. The only thing wrong with it is that it doesn't make coffee." Nigel chuckled but Daniella just stared at me.

It took me a few moments to log into the NCIC. Then I typed in "James Arden Mills" and the system cogitated for a bit before seven files popped up. Two of these seemed to be what we were looking for. "Tell me which of these is him," I asked, swinging the computer around so Daniella and Nigel could see two faces on the screen.

"They both look like him," Nigel said. "Not spot on but a strong resemblance." Daniella nodded.

"How about these?" I asked, showing them mug shots from the files I had set aside. Both shook their heads.

"Interesting," I replied as I read through the files. "It looks like one of them is dead." I started comparing the files of the two men and found they had a great deal in common. The dates of birth and social security numbers were different, as were the rap sheets, but the physical description was virtually the same. The fingerprints were similar, too, except for some rather severe scars to both hands of the older James Mills that would make print comparisons extremely difficult. The age difference between the younger and the one reported dead was almost twenty-two years.

Compared to the differences, the similarities on the rap sheets were quite striking. Both of the James Mills had multiple aliases, many of which they shared. What was odd was that James A Mills was one alias of the younger of the two men. His legal name, however, was listed as Jaques Auden Michon. Jack Auden was also an alias for James Arden Mills.

"I'd have to have a fingerprint expert verify it but I think the unscarred hands probably belong to the one that's still alive, even though the records show they belong to the dead man. One of the things the record notes for the older guy is three arrests for arson and scarred hands and lower arms from severe burns."

"That would certainly explain the scars on the prints, wouldn't it?" Nigel observed. "How could the lower arms be burned and the palms and finger pads not?" He was talking almost to himself.

"Yes, that's a good point but it raises a difficult question. I think the unscarred prints belong to the younger man. How in the world was he able to manage switching print records in the FBI database? Those files are supposed to be very secure."

"I think you're right, Jazz," Nigel interjected. "Had the man's hands been scarred, we should have noticed during his interview.

As far as I can remember, they were not. Nor was he wearing gloves. I would have noticed that."

I made myself a reminder to check this out and continued. "Another thing I noticed is that the criminal careers of the two men do not overlap at all. There was a twenty year gap between them, beginning when the younger guy was two. A lot of the crimes were different, as well."

Nigel nodded. "You don't suppose we're looking at a father and a son, do you?"

"It certainly looks like it," I agreed and Daniella nodded.

"Well, I'm damned glad we didn't hire him." Nigel looked at Daniella. "Thanks to you, Danny. He would have caused us a world of grief."

"He may be doing exactly that now," I replied. "Taking revenge for not hiring him. So we need to track this fellow down. The problem is that there are just the two of us and the trail is very cold. Jaques Michon has not been active for several years. At least, he has not been caught. So tracking him down may take longer than you care to wait."

"What are you saying, Jazz?" Nigel asked. There was an edge of steel in his voice.

"I am saying that you may need to rethink your strategy for resolving this. Dee and I can continue trying to determine if there actually is a serial killer at work killing off winners. At this point we strongly suspect there is but we don't have any solid evidence of that. Even if we had that evidence in hand at this moment, I would recommend taking the risk and bringing in the FBI. They have the resources to run the killer down and are quite thorough."

"No," said Nigel sternly, shaking his head. "We can't take the risk of letting it be known what is happening. The board would never go along with that."

"All right, then, there is another strategy we can use. I am reasonably sure that killer would have a hard time pulling this off without help from inside the company. Where I would look first would be your West Coast division and their outside subcontractors. I am reasonably sure your operation here is secure.

I have a few more subcontractors to look over before I'm done, but I don't anticipate finding much. No one on the list has any reason to have contact with the players. Not that I can see."

"Let's do that, then," Nigel decided and I ran through what I had done so far. When I was done he smiled. "You seem to be covering a lot of ground very quickly."

"Most of it is in the nose," I said tapping the tip of mine. "Dee and I have been chasing these people a long time. When something isn't quite right, we notice it and start digging. Sort of like a bloodhound." When I said this I thought of Blackwood Unger and his best dog, Beulah.

"What were you just smiling about?" Nigel asked.

"Whenever I think of bloodhounds I think of a friend of mine from Arkansas. He trains search dogs – mostly for dead people – and he helped out on a very important case. More to the point, he looks just like a bloodhound." I made a face and Daniella barked. When she did, what came to mind was the image of an angry Doberman.

Good News

9   Trudy seemed a bit uneasy that evening when I arrived at her front door, suitcase in hand. I had only been able to greet her briefly when I arrived at the office and she told me she had meetings all day. After I gave her a hug I asked her about her disquiet. "It's silly," she said. "I just feel so...wicked. Nicole is such a wonderful person and it feels like we are betraying her."

"Trudy, I can get a hotel room," I replied. "You're not obligated. Not for a moment." I handed her my phone. "Or you can call Nicole, if you wish."

Trudy looked at my phone like I was handing her a viper. I nodded and pushed the speed dial for home. A moment later I was talking to my bride. "How is Trudy?" she asked when I was done saying good night to the kids.

"She's feeling wicked in the wrong kind of way. She feels like we are betraying you."

Nicole's response was an earthy Portuguese epithet she saves for special occasions. "Let me talk to her."

"She who must be obeyed wishes to talk with you," I said and I could hear Nicole laugh in the background. After she took the phone Trudy shooed me out of the room and I went out into the garden. From time to time I heard her laugh and a half hour later she stuck her head out the door.

"It's safe to come back in," she said, giggling. "Poor man. Aren't you freezing out there?"

I allowed it was beginning to get rather brisk and when I came inside Trudy gave me a bear hug and a kiss that shivered my timbers. "I'm sorry to be so silly," she told me.

"You're not being silly. You're just being Trudy, concerned for other people's feelings."

Tears came to her eyes. "That's the sweetest thing anyone has said to me in years. Caring is not exactly valued in this part of the world."

"That's their loss," I replied and more tears came.

"Stop it, Jazz. You're about to set off a cloudburst."

"Trudy, when we're together you can do whatever you feel like doing. You can laugh, you can cry, you can moan, or you can pray, repeatedly."

"Pray?" she asked. "When have you ever seen me pray?"

"I must have misunderstood. I thought I heard you say, 'Oh, God! O God! O God!'"

Trudy blushed and I gave her a kiss I hoped shivered her timbers right back. Things got pretty urgent about then and it was well past nine before I got anything to eat. Yet it was well worth waiting for, Jersey style deep dish pizza cooked just right. That's right up there with Arkansas pork ribs in my book. Between the pizza and the calisthenics before, I barely made it to bed before I fell sound asleep.

Trudy tried to let me sleep in the next morning but my cellular roused me just after seven. "I hope I didn't call too soon," Dee said when I picked up the phone. "I couldn't remember whether the time difference was two hours or three and I've got some good news for you."

"Let me see if someone can bring me a cup of black coffee," I answered. "It was a long day yesterday and I'm still waking up." Trudy smiled and nodded and less than a minute later I was stirring a cup of designer caffeine.

"All right," I said. "Sock it to me."

Dee laughed. "Man, I haven't heard that in years. To cut to the chase, I talked to the widow and to the doctor at the hospital. The doc was a lot more forthcoming than I expected. He knew that the dead guy didn't drink and had spotted signs of NAFLD when he checked out the liver. Yet that didn't seem bad enough to make the guy as sick as he was so the doc ran several other tests.

"One of those was a blood chemistry analysis and things were all out of whack with that. For one thing, the potassium level in the guy's blood was out of sight. So he started to treat that and called the widow to see what over-the-counter meds the guy was taking.

"Sure enough, the late departed was a hypochondriac and very much into self-treatment. He was very secretive too. So he hadn't told anyone anything about all the over-the-counter crap he was taking. Not even on his intake interview. Turns out his GP didn't know about any of it, either. Then the guy died and the liver doc decided it was simpler to put down cirrhosis as the cause of death. He said the guy might have been gone within a few weeks, anyway. Despite medical treatment."

"Wow," I said. "That's incredibly candid for a physician."

"The way I figure, the doc was relieved of a heavy burden when he talked to me. You know how people are after they confess to a crime years later. Well, it was like that for the doc. It had crossed his mind that someone might have poisoned his patient by injecting potassium chloride into his saline drip and causing a heart attack. Yet he didn't have anything but a vague suspicion and then it was too late. The body was cremated right away and the poor doc's been living with it all this time."

"I hope you told him not to fall on his sword with the review board," I said.

"Yeah, I did. No way I could see he was at fault and I told him so. He tried to argue but I told him the one about God playing doctor and pushing to the head of the cafeteria line. He got the point."

"How about the widow?"

"I almost passed her by," Dee told me. "The thing is, I wanted to know how he blew all his money. She wanted to know, too, and gave me his social security number. It didn't hurt that the dumb shit wrote his password on the bottom of his laptop. So I did a little research on the internet and guess what folks? Turns out he had been dumping all the money he told her he lost on the ponies into another savings account, a tax sheltered one that paid good interest. When I told her this and recommended she get a sharp tax attorney to help her recover it, I made her day. She even tried to give me a hundred bucks for the tip."

"Do you think she poisoned her husband?"

"Not really. She strikes me as one of those people who get their news from *The National Inquirer* and celebrity rags. She operates a beauty parlor out of her home and barely scrapes by. She may be angry enough to kill but I don't think she has the imagination to set up something like this. Say she wanted to kill him, her style would be more like stabbing him with her scissors or maybe shooting him with his own pistol. She's way too angry for something slow like poison."

"So we mark this one up as a strong possibility of murder and move on to the next," I said. "Very good work, partner. Good hunting in Zion."

After we hung up I spent a while thinking about what we had accomplished so far. It didn't seem that much for a week's effort, but that's sometimes the way it is. Things can fall into place quickly and there's not much predicting when or how this will happen. So we plug along following procedure and running down leads until something does fall into place.

I still felt lazy so I lay back on the bed and thought about what I needed to do that day. Trudy walked in a minute later to ask what I wanted for breakfast. Seeing me there *au naturale* she shed the robe she was wearing and chuckled at my involuntary response. "My, my," she said, crossing the room and pushing my knees aside. Then she knelt down and smiled. After that things fell into place rather quickly.

An hour later we were washing up from a breakfast of Belgian waffles and poached eggs. She was washing dishes and I was drying them and putting them away. The sight of her beautiful bare derriere inspired me, so I laid aside my dish towel and stood close behind her. Running my hands under her apron and around her waist I cupped her lovely breasts and pulled her close. Laying her head back across my shoulder, she moaned softly and when I moved my hands, lower, she gasped. Then she turned around and we ended up on the bare kitchen floor.

The sound of the doorbell and a key in the lock sent us scrambling for the bedroom. "Cleaning service, Ms Howard," a deep woman's voice announced.

"Come on in," Trudy answered. "We'll be right out." She snickered at the sight of me hopping around on one foot trying to get my pants on. A few moments later she was dressed and back to the kitchen, and I heard her telling someone she had a house guest.

I showered and shaved and put on a fresh shirt and tie. Then I slipped on my loafers and jacket and headed for the living room. I heard the sound of a vacuum coming from the guest area and gave Trudy a peck. "I'll meet you at the bakery," I whispered, picking up my computer and slipping out the front door unseen. Too late I remembered that the bakery was at the office, not in the apartment building, so I visited with the doorman for a couple of minutes until Trudy appeared.

When we got to Jolly Good Times I was surprised to see it was only half past ten. To be discrete, Trudy went up first and I lingered over an incredible cinnamon roll and a cup of designer coffee. They had insulated stainless steel mugs for sale so I bought one before I headed upstairs.

It was exactly ten-thirty when I walked through the doors and Daniella said Nigel wanted to see me. So I followed her into his office. "I've been thinking about what you said yesterday," he told me once we were seated. "You can work here in the office, of course, but I wondered if you might rather work in Los Angeles."

The way Daniella was studying the pencil and pen set on top of Nigel's desk told me she had engineered this meeting. I wondered what she was after in doing so.

"Actually, working here is much better for my family," I told him. "I can get back and forth faster on weekends and there are some projects at the Agency I need to supervise. It works better in person."

"Yes, that's been my experience, too," he said, nodding. "How are things working out with Dom and Trudy?"

"I couldn't ask for better," I assured him. I decided to push back gently. "When we have something sensitive to talk about, I try to do that away from the office. That's strictly for security and I like to stretch my legs, too. Walking seems to stimulate the little gray cells."

Nigel smiled broadly. "Hercule Poirot! One of my favorite characters. David Suchet is absolutely marvelous." He looked at Daniella. "Well, that about covers it, I think. Anything else?"

Daniella shook her head, looking down. I decided to rattle her cage a bit. "Well, I do have one thing. Dee turned up an odd inconsistency with one of your dead winners. At the moment I can't remember the fellow's name but he lived in Yuma, Arizona. There were some odd things about his death that suggest he may have been murdered. Dee's running these down as we speak."

"So what was that all about?" Trudy asked softly a few hours later when we were enjoying a late lunch. There was no one else in the dining area at the time. "I saw Daniella fetch you to Nigel's office, but she didn't come out until after you did."

"I'm not sure. I think she's protecting her turf and sees me as a threat. I really do wonder what she's hiding. Now laugh like I've uttered a terrible pun."

Trudy grinned widely and shook her head. "I sowed a few seeds of misdirection, too," I added softly, patting my lips with a napkin. "I told them we get away from the office to discuss sensitive things."

Trudy nodded. "I've noticed that," she said with a straight face. "Your thing is very sensitive."

I laughed. "And you think I'm bad."

I went back to my work area and started wrapping up the last four subcontractor files. These were all simple single proprietor businesses that provided specific services and the owners had no contact with the players that I could find. The hardest part of the job was running these guys down so I could talk to them.

An NCIC query revealed some criminal records among the owners but nothing recent and no felonies. Having been a policeman I knew, as surely as night follows day, that some of the more serious misdemeanors were probably pled down from minor felonies. I suspect this was to avoid the expense of a trial but it didn't matter. The guys I was looking at had all been clean for years. They were also family men and non-violent offenders. That makes a big difference in my book.

After I had set up appointments with the subcontractors for the next day I tracked down Daniella. I asked her to meet me in my work area and made sure the door to the main room was closed. "I haven't seen any security people around here," I told her. "Am I right assuming you have someone besides yourself on duty?" She nodded.

"I thought so. I'd guess Cleary, Rowan, and Boyle." After gazing at me for a long moment she nodded.

"Are any of them licensed to carry in New York and New Jersey?" Again she nodded, frowning.

"I need one of them who is licensed to carry to go with me tomorrow."

"Why?"

"I'm going to interview four of your subcontractors who may have something to do with what we're looking for. Dee is off running down manner of death in Arizona and Utah. So I need a partner who can keep his or her mouth shut."

"Can't do it alone?"

"Police Science 101," I replied. "The first rule is always be armed going after potential homicide suspects. The second is never go alone. Which of the three would you suggest?"

"Do it myself," she told me. "Keep it quiet."

"With all due respect, Daniella, it needs to be someone I can be at ease with and we rub each other the wrong way. People of interest pick up on conflict between investigators and exploit it. I understand if you'd rather not use anyone from within the office. I can hire someone from an outside agency. There are several I've used from New York."

"Take Cleary. Former FBI."

I knew Bill Cleary worked as an auditor in Human Services. So after I thanked Daniella I looked him up. It turned out we had several friends in common. We arranged to meet the next day at nine and he nodded and asked no questions when I told him I needed him to be armed. "I don't anticipate any problem," I explained. "But all of the guys I'll be interviewing have records and my partner's out of town."

"DiRado," he said, smiling at my surprise. Then he showed me a brass AA medallion. "We have friends in common."

This done, I took a walk around the block to clear my circuits before I tackled the West Coast files. After looking through a half dozen folders I took out my cell phone and called Trudy. "I need to know something," I told her. "Can you come to my work area for a minute?"

"Of course, I can," she said. Then she chuckled. "Just promise not to look down."

"On the other hand, it's sensitive so maybe we better take it outside," I replied and she laughed. "I'll meet you at the bakery in ten," I said.

I was seated at a table and polishing off a second cinnamon roll when Trudy got there. The table was off by itself and offered a little privacy. As a matter of fact, it seemed a bit too well placed for privacy and I took out a security scanner the size of a flip screen cellular. Sure enough the scanner showed a bug and I pushed another button. This was an addition Jack McKee and Toolie Mann came up with recently. Even though it was inaudible to the human ear and was confined to a radius of six feet, the scanner emitted a jamming signal that scrambled whatever was fed into the bug. It also jammed cell phones.

When Trudy sat down I told her about the bug and about the jammer. "Good Lord," she said. "A lot of people at the office come here for a break. We need to warn Nigel and the rest of our office."

"That's right unless it's Nigel who has this place bugged."

"Why would he do that?"

"I don't know. Maybe because he worries about loose lips. Why don't we try some misdirection and see?" I thought for a moment and reached over and switched off the jammer in the middle of a sentence. "....really bad, the worst I've seen. So what I've decided to do is bring in the feds. I just wanted to give you a heads-up so you...." I pushed the jammer button again and smiled. "Now let's see who braces me on this."

"You're wicked," Trudy said, looking at me oddly. She was seeing a whole different side of me, one she was not sure she liked. "What if they ask me?"

"Trudy, if anyone asks, what we were talking about is a different case, one I'm turning over to the feds because I'm busy with this one. The reason I'm giving you a heads up is that I may be hard to reach for a day or two."

Trudy looked doubtful so I added, "Just so you know, everything I just said is actually the truth. There is a rather nasty case someone else is going to have to handle while I'm on this one. I'm thinking it needs to be the feds."

She nodded. "I see. You're putting me in a very awkward position, Jazz. Nigel has been very good to me."

I sighed. "I know, Trudy, but it's not Nigel I suspect. He's the one I'm trying to protect."

"You mean...." Trudy began but stopped.

"Yes, that's exactly who I mean. To put it in the best light, if it is her, she's probably done this to protect Nigel and the company. I'd guess she is also is acting without his knowledge. Look at it another way and she's keeping tabs on your employees. Maybe she's ratting them out or maybe not. Maybe she has another agenda. Or maybe the bug belongs to somebody else who's up to something different."

"I almost wish you hadn't told me," Trudy said, looking so sad I wanted to take her in my arms. "Is this the kind of world you have to live in, Jazz?"

I nodded. "Yes, it is, unfortunately. That's why my family and my friends are so important to me."

"I just hope I'm one of your friends," she said. I could see tears forming in her eyes.

"I wouldn't have told you any of this if you weren't, Trudy. The only reason I do what I do is because of the gifts I've been given.

Sometimes I want to shit-can it all and spend all my time with my family and my camera. I don't have to work."

"Why don't you?"

"Because no one else can do what I do. If I lay down my sword and shield, who's going to take them up? Who has the training or the experience? There are very few of us, Trudy. The people I work for would have a hard time replacing me."

Trudy reached over and took my hand in hers. "I'm sorry I doubted you, Jazz. What can I do to help?"

I started to speak but stopped and shook my head and sighed. "Senility strikes again. There was something else I wanted to talk to you about, something important. At the moment I can't for the life of me recall what it was."

"Well, what were you doing when you called?"

"Oh, right. Thank you. I was looking at the West Coast files and I wondered if the screening process was less rigorous than it is for the office here."

"Yes, it is. That bothered me for quite a while but now I know why it's that way. By the time our projects get to the Jolly Times West – that's what we call it, or simply West – there is very little intellectual property that can be effectively stolen. What we are about is style and innovation, and by the time it gets to West we are so far ahead of the competition in concept that stealing our ideas wouldn't help. By the time a competitor could develop them we'd be six months into weekly events."

I nodded. "So it's simply not cost-effective to do such rigorous background checks as you do the ones here."

"Exactly. Although it might have been cheaper to be more rigorous with our screening in the beginning. Your investigation must be terribly expensive."

"Maybe or maybe not Trudy. Psychopaths are like virus. They seem to come out of nowhere and it's very difficult to come up with a vaccine against them. It's also hard to screen against them. Sometimes they come across as angelic. They can even fool psychologists."

"Angelic? How can such monsters do that?"

"It's very simple. These guys are very good at telling people what they want to hear. Ted Bundy is the classic example of this, but so are Dennis Rader, Ed Kemper, and Gary Ridgeway. You may not recognize the names but Rader was the BTK killer. Kemper was known as the Co-ed Killer, and Ridgeway was the Green River Killer. Rader and Kemper came across as friendly guys who wouldn't hurt a fly. Ridgeway was a strange man his neighbors described as odd but friendly. His camouflage was being so ordinary he went unnoticed. And these are just four among hundreds of others."

"You're scaring me, Jazz," she replied, shuddering. "Let's talk about something else."

I felt restless when we got back to the office so I caught up on my paperwork. I spent an hour typing up a narrative account of the investigation and giving a detailed summary of my time and expenses. I noted that this did not include Dee's time and travel expenses and that those would soon follow. I printed this up and slipped it into an envelope addressed to Willard Nordwald, making myself a note that it was to be updated and mailed at the end of the week.

It was then the nickel finally dropped and I picked up the file for one of the subcontractors I looked at earlier. I don't know how this happens or why these sudden intuitive flashes occur when they do. The best explanation I've heard comes from Dee. "Jazz, your mind works like a pinball machine. You feed a ball in and pull back the launcher. Then you let it go and it bounces around for a while. When it's bounced off all the posts it can it finally goes down the chute and up pops the score."

When I dug out the list of dead contestants and compared the events the dead contestants attended with which East Coast contractors worked these, I got an almost perfect match. One of the last four guys I looked at was Leon Spitz, an electrician who had done a lot of work on Last One Left events over a number of years. He was a family man and had a few misdemeanors in his record. Yet all of these were long before he worked for Jolly Good

Times and Leon had flown straight for over twenty-three years.

Or maybe he never got caught, I reminded myself. Then I chided myself for being such a suspicious soul, knowing I would never change. Given the nature of my work I can't and still be effective. Rule eighteen in my handbook for police investigations was verify everything. The only exception was my hunches. Even then I was only batting ninety-three per cent.

Looking at Leon Spitz's record, all the arrests were for disorderly conduct or public intoxication. It was quite possible Leon had heard what AA long timers call The Pop. As Dee explained it to me, that's when an alcoholic's head finally pops out of his butt and he attains a moment of utter clarity.

I took the list of the dead and Leon's work record for the company and headed for Daniella's office. The assistant there was named Alice and she told me Dan and Nigel had left earlier for a meeting. She said she doubted Daniella would be back in the office until the following morning. "They're wining and dining some new clients and you know how that goes," she said. There was a wistful note in her voice. "Some girls have all the luck."

I told Alice what I wanted wasn't that urgent and headed for the Human Services office. I caught Trudy just as she was about to leave. "I was just thinking about you," she said. "Wicked thoughts," she added.

"You'll have to tell me about them," I replied. "Let me ask you something before I forget it forever. You'd be in a position to know."

"Now that sounds delightful, being in a position to know and be known," she quipped. "You must have been reading my mind." Then she clapped a hand over her mouth and blushed. "I'm sorry, Jazz" she whispered. "That's totally inappropriate for the workplace."

"That's all right," I assured her. "It's almost after hours and I won't tell. Let me show you something."

"You can show me whatever you want, big guy," she told me and then blushed. "See what you do to me, Jazz? I'm so bad."

"Then maybe my question needs to wait," I replied. "Let me

grab my jacket and we'll go play cops and robbers."

"So what was your question?" Trudy asked. We were lying spooned together on her rug, watching the gas logs burn in the fireplace.

"I don't even want to think about it now," I answered. "I'm not on the clock. At least, not on Nigel's. It can wait."

"You're spoiling me, you know," she murmured.

"I certainly hope so," I murmured back. "You deserve it."

"So what am I going to do when the case is over?" she asked. "I've gotten so used to having you around."

"*Carpe diem!*" I declared, grasping her firmly in a tender spot.

"Oh!" she gasped sensuously. "Is that what that's called? But you're right. The day is all we have, you and I."

"It's all any of us have," I replied. I looked at my watch. "I need to say 'good night' to my kids."

Just then her land line rang and she reached out to answer. A moment later she covered the receiver and said, "I better take this. It's my daughter." I nodded and headed for the bedroom.

"No, sweetie," I heard her say. "Now is fine....Yes, someone came over for supper....No, it's someone from the office....Yes, we're working on a project. So what's up with you?"

I slipped into a long sleeved tee-shirt and a pair of soft jeans and made myself comfortable on the bed before I called home. "Your timing is impeccable," my bride told me when she picked up. "Your brats are being little hellions." Then I heard her tell them it was Daddy on the phone and an argument broke out over who got to talk to me first.

"That's me!" I heard their mother say. "Whoever gets ready for bed first gets to talk to him first when I'm done." The noise level dropped immediately as I listened to the kids running down the hallway. "It must be the weather," Nicole told me. "They've been like this since I took them to school this morning. The teacher said all the kids were wound up today."

The little hellions were back in four minutes flat and Nicole and I talked for almost an hour once they were settled in for the night. "How do families with four or five children ever do it?" she asked and I confessed I had no idea. Yet when I offered to come home and work from there, Nicole was adamant. "No, Jazz. You need to be exactly where you are. This is important and not just to you. It is important to me, as you know. Someone has to hunt these sick assholes down."

I knew exactly what Nicole was saying. Even though she had retired from the business of tracking down serial killers, the skills she used were still there. I know there were times that she wondered if she had done the right thing in standing down, even though she was sick and tired of it. While it might be true that she had young children and had no intention of ever taking up the hunt again, I knew that she kept her skills well honed. She insisted this was to make herself fit to train other agents, but we both knew this was only partly true. She wanted to be prepared in case she ever was forced to go back to it.

This was the closest we had ever come to talking about this and I said as much. There was silence from the other end of the line and I knew my bride was trying not to weep. So I decided to take a risk. "Woman, I said we need to talk about this!" I declared sternly. A moment later I heard her snort and I knew we were all right.

"You're so funny when you try to be stern," she told me.

"I know, my love, but all joking aside, we do need to talk about it." I knew I was being unfair because I was speaking Portuguese, the language we used for love.

"You are so lucky you are not here," she answered in the same patois. "You might not survive me jumping your frame."

"Oh, but what a wonderful way to go," I replied, completing our ritual. Switching to English I said, "You know, I can be there in four hours, my love."

"No," she told me firmly. "I'll see you this weekend. We'll talk about it then."

After I hung up I heard a soft knock at the door. I opened it and Trudy came into my arms, tears in her eyes. "The reason my daughter called," she told me. "I'm going to be a grandmother.

Paydirt

10 Trudy took off for Seattle the very next morning. Before she left she arranged for me to move into the small apartment Jolly Good Times kept for visiting firemen. "I'm really going to miss you, Jazz," she told me over breakfast. "It's good having you in my life. You can stay here at the apartment if you wish. You could be my house sitter."

"That's very tempting," I told her. "This is a very comfortable place but I think it would be lonely without you."

"You could have Nicole and your kids visit if you wanted."

I laughed. "You don't know my little hellions. They'd be into everything in the first ten minutes."

"You could take them to the zoo or the dinosaur exhibit at the Museum of Natural History. Kids always like that. One advantage of living here is that the city has lots of wonderful things for kids."

Bill Cleary met me at the office as we arranged and he agreed to drive when I asked. "This is your personal car?" he asked and I told him it was a rental. "Couldn't you make it look more like a cop car?" he replied with a smile.

"Well, I thought about a black Suburban," I shot back and he chuckled. "Nicole and I tried to get along with a couple of small cars But with the kids we needed something bigger. We're considering a minivan."

"Yeah, but Crown Vic rentals come in other colors, Jazz."

"That's true but the best deal was on a white one with plain wheels, tan leather upholstery, and a spotlight. I think it was a special order for some city official that fell through."

"Well white is the safest color after yellow or that God-awful green they use on fire trucks," he replied. "And you can't beat the Crown Vic for comfort."

"It's fun watching other drivers slow down, too," I told him.

"I bet it is," he said, grinning. "Where we going?"

I read him the first address and entered it into the Garmin. Ten minutes later we were at the coffee shop where my first interview agreed to meet. I knew within two minutes that the guy we talked to had nothing to offer. His primary service had something to do with computer software and he had almost no contact with anyone but Dom and Daniella. Nor did he recognize anyone in the photo array I had put together from random mug shots, including one of James Mills. So I thanked him for his time and paid his tab.

The second interview was much the same. This owner specialized in event logistics – things like food and general supplies – but most of his work was done by phone and his computer system. He did work directly with some of the office staff in both the East Coast and West Coast locations, but this involved very few face to face encounters. He was also curious about our inquiry but I assured him it was just part of a general company assessment.

"Well, I hope you guys are satisfied with my work," he said. "I like doing business with you. If something's wrong I hope you'll give me the chance to make it right. I've worked for you guys a long time."

"I don't suppose you recognize any of these fellows do you?" I asked, showing him the mug shot array.

The owner shook his head and we left soon after that. When we got to the car Cleary asked if he could see the array. As he looked at them, he chuckled. "I know this asshole, Jazz," he said, handing me a photo. "I helped put him away." It wasn't anyone I recognized. Then he showed me another photo. "I know this guy, too, but I can't figure where. Maybe around the office. I think it's been a while."

I looked at the photo. "His legal name is Jaques Auden Michon," I told him.

"That doesn't ring a bell," Cleary replied.

I tried a shot in the dark. "How about James Mills?"

Cleary shook his head. "I don't know. That feels warmer somehow but I can't say for sure."

The third interview was with Leon Spitz, the electrician who had worked almost every show tied to a fatality. He was a wiry, cheerful little man in a Spitz Electric shirt with his first name embroidered over a pocket filled with pens and tools. He was as outgoing as Nigel and the way he moved told me he was probably strong as a mule. He also had a lively sense of humor and I liked him immediately, so much so I had to remind myself to be objective.

When I asked Leon about what he did for Jolly Good Times I was surprised to learn that he had actually been on site for every season he had worked. "There were only three events I couldn't make. One was right after I remarried and I thought my wife's children and I needed the time to get to know each other. The second time I was as sick as a dog with flu and the third time I was out with a ruptured appendix. Other than that I was there for them all. They seemed to like my work. There was always a bonus."

"What did you actually do?" I asked.

"It would be easier to tell you what I didn't do. My main job was making sure the electrical systems kept working and that kept me hopping in some of the places we went. You know, bad weather and moisture in the electronics. Other than that, I did just about everything from driving a jeep to helping the contestants with their luggage to filling in for a drunk cook. That one was a mistake. They liked my cooking so much I thought I'd never get out of the kitchen."

"So you were in direct contact with the contestants?" I asked.

"Oh, yeah. They were a great bunch of people, too. You know, there were the usual butt-holes but ninety-five percent of them were good folks. They appreciated what you did for them."

"So you got to know them pretty well?"

"Yeah, I really did. Mostly by watching. Competition like that brings out the best and the worst in people. I used to wrestle quite a bit and I've seen it before. Some of the guys were real pieces of work." He shook his head, remembering.

"What about the other staff for the event, Leon? What did you think about them?"

"They were good people, too. For the most part they knew what they were doing and pulled their own weight."

"For the most part?"

"Yeah, there were a couple of guys who didn't fit in. Three of them, as a matter of fact. Lots of attitude. A couple of them washed out pretty quick but the third guy seemed to do his job real good and they kept him on. Thing is, around everybody else but me he was Mister Nice Kiss-ass but when he thought no one was looking he was surly as hell. I couldn't argue with the quality of his work when he worked, but I hated to work with him. Couldn't trust him. He took credit for other people's work and blamed other people for his mistakes. I never understood why they put up with it. I couldn't see how nobody else could see him for what he was. It tickled him knowing I did and couldn't do a damn thing about it."

Leon stopped abruptly. "Sorry. I don't usually go on like that. I don't like people who do and I hope you don't think I'm like that. I like to give people the benefit of the doubt but I guess that sumbitch got under my skin more than I thought."

"Ain't nobody here but us chickens," I assured him and saw Cleary smile. He knew the joke. "Even if you're biased you know about it, at least. Seeing him through your eyes will help us understand the man. What else can you tell us?"

Leon thought for a moment, then nodded. "All right, then. He was always pissing and moaning when none of the big shots were around. Seemed to think the world owed him something. You know what I mean. That kind of attitude."

I nodded. "Unfortunately, I do. I've fired a few. How did he get on with the contestants?"

"Oh, he was Mister Sweetness and Light around them. Kissing ass so much I wanted to kick him." Realizing what he had said, Leon looked at me and quickly added, "Not that I ever would, of course. It's just that a man ought not to grovel like that. Didn't fool all the players, either. I heard a couple of them laughing about it. He didn't have them fooled at all."

"Do you remember this fellow's name?" I asked.

"Yeah, I do. It was Jimmy Bob Miles."

When I heard this, my antennae went up. "Are you sure it wasn't Mills, Leon?"

"Miles is what I remember. I'm not that good at names except the ones who piss me off and he sure did that. I guess it could have been Mills. I am pretty sure his first name was Jimmy Bob. That's what we all called him."

"That's been a few years ago," I pointed out. "How about faces? Are you able to remember those?"

"Faces are something I never forget." Leon tapped his forehead and chuckled. "A few of them I wish I could. Like my first wife and her mother." He shuddered. "Wicked witches of the West."

Cleary and I laughed politely and I pulled out the photo array. "How about these guys? Recognize any of them?"

Leon looked at the first picture and laughed. "By golly, he looks just like Victor Mature! Everybody knows him."

"I'm surprised you recognize him," I responded. "He was an old guy when I was growing up."

"I'm an old movie buff," Spitz told us. "He did a lot of religious...." He stopped and pulled out a picture. "That's him. Jimmy Bob Miles. Or Bitchy Boy, as I call him. The man could wake up with a million bucks in his hand and a hottie in his bed and still find something to gripe about." He frowned.

"What else can you tell us about him?" I asked.

"He was the laziest bum you ever wanted to see when the boss wasn't looking." Leon stopped. He looked troubled.

"What are you thinking?" I asked.

Leon looked down and shook his head. "I don't like to smear people for what they can't help," he told us.

"All right. We'll take it with a grain of salt. What is it?"

"Well, I think Jimmy Bob's a little light on his feet. I think he had the hots for a couple of the players, the men. They were pretty open about being that way they are, you know, and they're the ones I heard talking about him."

"Do you remember their names?"

"Wouldn't do you much good if I could. They were killed in

a car wreck a couple of years later. I wouldn't have remembered their names but their pictures were in the paper."

"Can you remember when this was?"

"No but I can look in my scrapbook. I got pictures of the whole cast for all the events I worked."

"That would be great," I said, giving him one of my cards. "Why don't you give me a call when you spot them?"

I looked at my note pad. "Do you know how many episodes he was on, Jimmy Bob?"

"Four or five that I can remember. But he may have been on the ones I was out sick. I came back the year after I had my appendix out and he was gone." He shook his head. "That was a tough year, financially. I really had to hustle to make ends meet. What saved my ass was the extra bonus Nigel sent. Right at Christmas, too. He signed the note 'Santa' but I knew who it was."

We talked a while longer but little came of it. I did make myself a note to ask Trudy to run down the year Leon was out for surgery and also how many seasons Jimmy Bob Mills worked on the support crew. I added a reminder to get in touch with Leon about which event the gay men were players.

It occurred to me that one of them might have been the winner that season and I needed to check that, too. Even if they had not, it was possible that they had offended Jimmy Bob in some way. Were he the killer we were after, that could have been deadly. Car wrecks can be faked quite easily to appear accidental and police officers are like the rest of us. They often see what they want to see and they carry a big case load in most major cities. There is always the temptation to go with the obvious and to clear a case quickly.

Our final interview wasn't until after lunch and I asked Cleary if there was a smaller place around where we could get lunch. He knew of a place not far from where we needed to be later. It was well known for its Texas-size turkey burgers and baked fries, and the food was up to its billing. While we ate we traded war stories about the Bureau. As it turned out, we knew many of the same people and the time went very quickly. He offered to split the ticket but I assured him it was covered by my per diem.

The final subcontractor interview turned up little that we did not already know. Like most of the other subcontractors, this lady had no significant contact with the contestants. Her service was to provide two EMTs and a helicopter for emergencies and the people she worked with were the event staff. She was a chopper pilot and was trained as an EMT. The other EMT she used had worked with her for years. "We started in a bus," she told us, smiling, "but I qualified as a chopper pilot thanks to Uncle Sam. So we pinched our pennies and switched to air service and the rest is history. We have two other teams in the New York area now but Liddy and I keep the fun stuff for ourselves."

When we showed the lady our photo array she picked out James Mills right away. "I've seen this guy around but I don't know where." I asked her if it might have been on one of the Last One Left episodes she nodded. "Yeah, that sounds right but I don't remember. We must not have had much to do with the guy. I remember Leon Spitz very well. He's a super guy. Great cook, too."

When we got back to the office I thanked Cleary for coming along. "Hey, it was my pleasure, Jazz. I don't get out of the office much. Thanks for lunch."

I decided it was time to touch base with Dee. I started to dial his cell number but stopped. I wanted to keep what he had to tell me to myself for the moment and I didn't know if the office mikes were on just then. So I headed for the apartment reserved for company visitors. It was within easy walking distance of the office but I took the car. Even though I was well armed, there was no way a mugger could know that until he braced me. Even in broad daylight I thought walking the street carrying a laptop and a suitcase presented too easy a target.

The apartment was quite comfortable. It was smaller than Trudy's place but the décor was light and bright and it was high enough above the street to give a nice view of the city. Since it was also on the east side of the building it overlooked the Hudson

River bay, and like Trudy's building, it had a twenty-four hour doorman.

Trudy had alerted the building manager and the lady gave me a key and a visitor's packet after checking my credentials. I was glad to see the building provided secure internet service and I checked that right away. Then I swept the place with my pocket bug detector and was pleased to find it clean. Later I did find a bug in the living room and another in the bedroom but neither was active.

I was unpacking my clothes when my phone rang. It was Alice, Daniella's assistant. She was calling to let me know that Leon Spitz had called and given her two names. He told her it was urgent so she called me right away. The names were Rick Hobart and Loren Springer. Hobart had been the winner that season and Springer may have helped him do it.

I sensed that Daniella's assistant had more she wanted to tell me so I asked, "What else, Alice?"

"Well, I don't want to talk out of turn but there was a big fuss with those guys. One of the other players accused the two of them of cheating. She claimed they were...you know, partners, and that Loren helped Rick win. She thought they had split the prize and threatened to sue the company. Daniella and our company lawyer had to go talk her out of it."

"Any idea how they did that?" I asked.

"No, and please don't let on that I told you about anything. I like my job."

"Who else knows about this?" I asked.

"I know Dom does and I think Trudy does, too."

"Was the lawyer Willard Nordwald?"

"Yes, how did you know?"

"I just do, Alice, but don't worry about it. You did right telling me about it and nobody will hear a word from me. I promise. What was the name of the lady who threatened to sue?"

"It was Roselle Hoffstadt. She lives in Dallas."

"Do you know how they got her to keep quiet?"

"No, and I don't want to know. I've said too much already."

The line went dead. I wrote out the basics in my case notes without identifying the source. Then I finished unpacking and made myself a cup of tea from the supplies I found in the kitchen.

Kicking off my shoes I tried a leather covered recliner that was so comfortable I found it hard to stay awake. Flipping it over I copied down the name of the manufacturer and the model number and filed it in my shirt pocket. Then I sat back and covered my legs with a lap blanket, intending to call Dee and immediately drifted off to sleep.

I might have stayed there all night if my phone hadn't rung an hour later. It was Dee and he sounded excited. "I hit the jackpot in Salt Lake City, Jazz. There were two guys killed in a car crash and both of them were on the same season. One of them was the winner."

"That sounds like Rick Hobart," I said. "Was the other one Loren Springer?"

"Now how in the hell did you do that?" Dee said. He sounded completely exasperated.

"Pure luck," I told him. "I just got off the phone with a reliable source that filled me in on Hobart and Springer." I passed along all Alice had told me.

"Well that confirms what I found out in Salt Lake," he replied. "The two of them were killed in a car crash but they didn't live here. They were tourists from upstate New York and they were legally a domestic couple. The thing is, they didn't get legally connected until after the Last One Left event they attended. I haven't confirmed it yet, but I think that may be where they first met, on the show."

"I think you're right. I think Leon mentioned one of them was from Arizona and the other was from Seattle."

"Who the hell is Leon?" Dee demanded. I wondered why he was so testy but didn't ask. Dee would tell me when he was ready.

"Sorry, I just talked to him this afternoon. His last name is Spitz and he worked for the Last One events as an electrician. He worked on site on almost every season with a dead winner."

"Do you like him for it?" Dee asked.

"Actually I don't," I said. "My sense of him is that he is exactly who he seems to be. I could be wrong, of course, but that's my cop's nose report."

Dee chuckled. "So what you smell is what you get. How deep do you want to me to dig here?"

Something about the way he said this told me something was bothering him. I decided to ask. "What's going on, Dee?"

"Oh, I had a dust-up with Salt Lake City's finest," he told me. "A real jerk. He pulled me over for allegedly speeding – one mile an hour over the posted speed limit of 45, if you can believe it. The thing is, I wasn't driving over forty just then. I was looking for a place to get a bite and I signaled my turn, too. Then he gave me a hard time over the insurance card."

This surprised me. Dee is normally very good with local officers. "So how does it stand?" I asked. "You need me to bail you out?"

"No, when he started pulling that crap I asked to see his sergeant. He tried to ignore that but I insisted. Finally, he backed off and let me go with a warning – after wasting thirty minutes of my time." He laughed. "Then I ran into Officer Shit-heel again when I was at the motor vehicle office asking for a copy of the crash report. I was talking to the DVM sergeant who happened to catch the crash. I think Little Boy Shit-heel thought I was making a complaint."

"So what about the car crash?"

"Other than when it happened, it looks pretty cut and dried. It wasn't clear who was driving. The two guys were both over the legal blood-alcohol limit and neither was wearing a seat belt. They were driving way too fast and lost control of the car. The car bumped into a truck, bounced into the curb, flipped, and tossed them both out. Unfortunately it was steep embankment next to a deep concrete storm drain and they bounced all the way to the bottom. The post mortem didn't include a full autopsy. Both bodies had multiple fractures, including severe skull fractures the ME put down as cause of death. The sergeant told me their heads looked like deflated soccer balls."

"What was odd about when it happened?"

"It was ten-thirty in the morning and they were drunk as skunks. That's not easy to do around here."

"What about the driver of the truck?"

"Asshole never stopped. Could be he never knew it happened but I doubt it. No one got the plate number, either."

"Did you look at the crash site?"

"Yeah, I did. Even after all this time there are wheel marks on the curb and down the side of the storm drain, but no sign the truck ever braked. The drain is solid concrete from the curb to the bottom and it could have been an accident. I think it was a homicide but I can't prove it. The official ruling is death by misadventure."

"You need to stay in town and dig some more?" I asked.

"Yeah, I really do, but I'm heading home for a long weekend. I've been gone too long. Nothing's wrong and Karin hasn't said anything but I need to spend some time in Mountain Home."

I sat and thought about what Dee had told me for a long while. I had a sense of *déjà vu* hearing the details of the Salt Lake City wreck. It took me back twenty-something years to our first serial homicide. A reporter had been investigating what looked like official corruption at the highest levels of state government. She had been murdered, her car run off a steep concrete embankment by a large truck. The details were so similar I would have wondered if it was not the same killer had I not seen half his head blown off as he was about to kill me and one of my investigators.

I made myself a note to talk to Dee about this the next time we spoke. Over the years we had come across several cases where an auto crash had been used to cover up a homicide. Then I thought about what I needed to do next. The most urgent item was tracking down James Mills or Jaques Auden or Jimmy Bob Michon or who the hell ever he was being by now.

The problem was that I was working for an attorney in the private sphere. I was not connected to the case through any official agency and did not have the resources of an agency behind me. While I was sure Sam McKee would help me out, I was hesitant to ask. He had helped me on criminal cases before but was very clear that neither he nor the Agency was concerned with law enforcement. Sam, in fact, operated mostly in the gray areas beyond the boundaries of the law. When our work turned up simple criminal activity, as it often did, he quickly turned it over to the FBI or the proper agency. We dealt with high level corporate crime, conspiracy in the board room.

Even so, it was crucial to get this killer stopped before anyone else was murdered. Aside from the issues of public safety and the repute of Jolly Good Times, I wanted to nab him before he realized that anyone was on his trail. The last thing I wanted him to do was for him to take our presence as a challenge and accelerate his pace. Up to then he had not killed that frequently. At least he had not killed prize winners that often. He may have been killing others, too. Were he provoked, he might expand his pool of targets and there was no telling who this might be.

Even so, it didn't seem like I had much choice. So I picked up the phone, turned on the scrambler, and started to call Sam. Then the clock caught my eye and I stopped dialing. It was getting late and Sam needed family time as much as I did. My call could wait.

At that point my stomach reminded how little I had fed it that day and I checked the refrigerator. The top third was a freezer and I found a frozen pizza there with a note from Trudy. "I thought this might come in handy," the note said and I turned on the oven. While I was waiting for it to warm I explored the fridge. It was well stocked with the essentials and there was another note inside a heart. It said, "Check the freezer. I miss you! T."

I took a quick shower to wash away the grime of the day and popped the pizza into the oven. I set my phone to ring in eighteen minutes and called Trudy. We talked for over an hour, stopping only for me to take out the pizza. When I thought about this after we rang off it started to bother me, talking so long with Trudy. Nicole was the only one I did this with, though I had done the same with Jeanne and Nellie. I realized what I was doing and imagined Forster telling me to cut it out. What surprised me was that it worked and I slept like a baby. No, more like a log.

Moving On

11 Thursday morning I was up early and working on my laptop at the apartment. On an impulse I picked up my phone and called Sam McKee. I was lucky to catch him at the Agency on what he said was shaping up as a slow, lazy day for him. "It's hard to believe," he said. "There was a time in my life when I actually craved action. These days I can't quite remember why I was so driven. Or how I kept up the schedule I did."

This was a conversation we had before, many times. We have been friends long enough that I knew he was aware of this. I was also aware he knew I knew. All it meant was that he was bored with running the Agency and not ready to face the paperwork *du jour*. When he's like this all we can do is be patient, so I grunted my general assent and waited for him to finish.

Nor did Sam disappoint me. "Of course, that was before Doctor Bob taught me a better way to deal with my demons than run from them. Now I find myself perfectly content to sit on the bank and watch the river flow." Then he sighed and laughed at himself. "Who the hell am I kidding, Jazz? I'm lucky if that lasts fifteen minutes."

"Yeah, but it's nice to stop and catch your breath once in a while," I pointed out. His response was a protracted hum and we visited for a while, swapping snide observations about the state of the world and the antics of current candidates for reelection. We do this from time to time. It's the closest Sam ever gets to complaining and Willie Dill tells me Sam doesn't do it with anyone but me. I think this is because I'm the only one he knows who has managed an agency. I know how it is to live in the hot seat.

After a few moments, Sam turned serious. "You know, Jazz, I've been expecting a call from you. How's the case going?"

"You have?" I asked, surprised.

"Yes, from what you told me about it I thought it might be a bit of a challenge. You don't have official status so you can't use some of the resources you normally do. Like me, I suspect you're reluctant to ask any favors."

Sam didn't suspect this. He damned well knew it. When I allowed that might be the case I could almost hear McKee grin. "What you are far too self effacing to realize, my friend," he added, "is just how much we owe you for what you do around here. It's a lot more than busting bad guys. You help keep us honest."

I didn't know quite how to respond to this so I just shrugged and made a noncommittal response. When I did, Sam chuckled. He's as familiar with my quirks as I am with his. "So what do you need from us, Jazz? We're a little short on F-14s or Abrams battle tanks but we're good for everything else."

"I need to find a man who dropped off the face of the earth ten or twelve years ago, more or less. He has a record and I've got a fairly clear mug shot, but he seems to have been clean ever since he vanished. Or maybe I should say he's not ever been caught. Hold on a second and I'll email you his ugly mug." I attached the rap sheet and a police photo of James Auden Michon. "I thought your facial recognition software might be able to pick him up off a driver's license photo or something like that."

McKee opened my email and studied the photo. "He's got strange eyes, doesn't he? Or is that just odd resolution?"

I looked at the photo on my desktop. It was high resolution and quite clear and I spotted what Sam meant. "Yeah, he does, doesn't he?" I responded. "How in the world did I miss that?"

McKee laughed. "Just goes to show you're human, Jazz. That's a big relief to the rest of us. Why don't you make a copy of the best print of his mug shot and bring it by when you're in town. I'll alert Michael to give it priority. You'll be in this weekend, won't you?"

"Of course, I will," I told him. "The kids have soccer." This struck him as funny and he was still chuckling when we ended the call. Nor did I even bother reminding him that the image I sent was the best I had and that there was little sense converting it to printed paper and then back to digital. Instead, I sent an email to Michael Angelino, his executive right arm, explaining what I needed and attaching the high resolution photo I'd already sent Sam.

I was hard at work on the West Coast files late that morning when Dee called. He was still in Utah. "I just now talked to the Motor Vehicle sergeant again," he told me. "I'm looking at the file right now. There were some critical details he didn't think to mention before. For one, he wasn't completely convinced it was an accident at the time and I think you'll see why. There were two separate witnesses who did the right thing and stopped to see if they could help. They were trailing behind the victim and were close enough to hear a loud noise just before the crash. They reported it sounded as loud as a gunshot and they saw the victims' car bounce over the curb immediately. They pulled over and climbed down the wall of the drain but both guys were dead by the time the good Sams got to them. They called it in right away and then waited around for the officers to get there."

"What about the tire?" I wanted to know. "It sounds like a blow-out to me."

"That's just it. It was the right front tire that blew but both of the witnesses said it looked like a big truck bumped them twice just before the car flipped. Hitting the curb could have blown the tire. The sergeant couldn't tell it for sure by looking at the car – it was pretty beat up from rolling down the drain – but the lab turned up some common white truck paint on the victim's car. It was on the driver's side."

"Any idea why the Salt Lake police didn't follow up on this?" I asked.

"Oh, yeah," Dee growled. "This is Mormon country, Jazz. The two guys were what they call gentiles around here. Our two guys were from New York, Sodom and Gomorra to a lot of people hereabouts. When the sergeant found out that they were a gay couple – he honest to God called it an abomination, Jazz – it was easy for him not to push. He didn't say as much but I think he believes they pissed off Jehovah who kicked their sorry asses into the ditch."

"Sounds like a true believer," I replied. "You know, not all Mormons think that way, Dee."

"I know. Self-righteous, stiff-necked assholes just piss me off. It doesn't matter if they're Mormon or Baptist or Big Book Nazis. Or paint their butts blue and dance in the moonlight. Where do they get off taking inventory on the rest of us?"

"Sounds like someone might need a meeting," I told him.

"Ain't that for sure? Good luck finding one around here."

"Come on. Wouldn't hurt to try, would it?"

"You know, Jazz, you can be a real pain in the ass," he told me.

"I know. That's what you love about me," I replied.

"Actually, that ain't so far from wrong," he chuckled. "I'll give it a shot. I promise."

After we rang off I sat there thinking about the case. I felt sure there was a killer at work and I couldn't shake the feeling that the killer had inside help from Jolly Good Times. Everything I had learned so far seemed to point to that. Yet, aside from Daniella, there wasn't anyone who seemed to fit the profile that was coming together in my mind. This didn't feel like a murder for profit. The only place I saw for that was with the fellow from Arizona. It was possible that someone was after the money he had squirreled away. Yet his death was one of the latest ones.

So what was our killer after? It always comes back to that and these things are driven by a fairly basic list of motives. I couldn't see the basis for any kind of sexual gratification, which is the most common motive for serial killers. Nor did the killer seem to crave attention and notoriety like some. Quite the contrary, he had kept himself well hidden. Crossing off financial gain left thrill seeking, gaining a sense of power, unresolved rage, punishing wrong doers, and revenge for being wronged. Every killer's motivation is unique to his or her life history but investigators don't normally piece that together until the killer is identified or caught. Even then it doesn't make sense except within the twisted logic of the killer. Yet it all comes back to an incident, or a series of incidents that pushes these people over the line and leads to the first kill. So we look for those triggers.

I made a few notes to go through later and set motive aside for the time being. There were files to read and it is basic police work that normally catches these guys. The Green River killer is a case in point. It took twenty-something years to bring Gary Ridgeway to justice even though he was a person of interest early on. The investigators never gave up and kept digging until they found the right lead. This is tedious and time consuming process but it eventually pays off. A case file comes together that limits the suspect pool until we have our harbingers of death. Sometimes it's a team of killers. Most often it is not. Either way we have to stay on the ball.

I was plowing through my third file of the afternoon when my cell phone rang. I saw it was Trudy and was glad of the break. "Hello, there sweet thing!" I said. "You saved me from a fate worse than death. I'm drowning in personnel files."

There was silence from the other end of the line. Then I heard an unknown voice. "Dr. Phillips?" it asked formally.

"Yes, this is Dr. John Phillips," I replied. "To whom do I speak?"

"This is Billie, Trudy Howard's daughter. Are you the one they call Jazz?"

"Yes, that's what I go by. How can I help you?"

"My mother's in intensive care. She was in a coma until early this afternoon. When she came out of it she asked me to give you a call."

"Yes, I'm doing some personnel work for her company. Why is she in intensive care?"

"They think she had a stroke last night. We're lucky it wasn't as bad as it might have been."

"How can I help? Your mother's a dear friend."

"How do you know her? You're a policeman, aren't you?"

"I retired from that a while back. These days I work mostly as a consultant and trainer. I'm consulting for her company. That's how we met. How can I help?"

"It doesn't sound like a very professional relationship," she said.

"It is at work, Billie. She and my wife and I really hit it off right away. Your mother has a wonderful sense of humor." It was on the tip of my tongue to ask what business it was of hers but I exercised some self restraint. She was newly pregnant and her mother was in intensive care. "Why did your mother tell you to call me?"

"I don't know. She wasn't that lucid but she kept saying, 'Call Jazz. He needs to know."

"So she never talked about what I needed to know?"

"No. She tried to say something else but I couldn't understand her very well."

"Well, she was helping me with a project I'm doing for Nigel, her boss. Have you talked to him yet?"

"No, but I talked to Helen, one of mother's assistants. She told me Nigel was not in town at the moment but she would let him know."

"Maybe that's all your mother wanted you to tell me, that she's had a stroke and is in the hospital. When did the stroke happen?"

"It was just after we went out to dinner. Fortunately, we were on the way home and not far from the hospital. So I took her directly to the emergency room." Billie suddenly started sobbing. "It almost killed her, Jazz. One minute I was talking to her and the next she looked so awful. I was so afraid she was going to die."

"Are you taking care of yourself, Billie? It's none of my business but I have a daughter and that's what I'd want her to do."

"Is she married?"

"No, that's a few years off, thank God. I didn't have children until late in life and I dread the thought of her leaving home."

That seemed to break the ice. We visited for a while longer and Billie promised to keep me posted on Trudy's progress. I told her to call me anytime she needed and to let me know if there was anything I could do. I mentioned the fact I would most likely be in the District that weekend. "I'm a soccer pop," I said. "Most of the other parents think our children are my grandkids. They think my wife is my daughter." Billie thought that was funny.

The news about Trudy was unsettling and I didn't feel like rummaging through any more files. I had reached a point of diminishing returns and needed to do something else for a while. So I looked through my notes for follow-up. I spotted the one about James Spradley being an amateur illusionist and wondered how I could check this out quietly. Then I thought of Leon Spitz and I looked at the list of dead winners again. Sure enough, Leon had been with the show the season that Spradley won.

I dialed the number I had for Leon and was passed directly to his voice mail. I left the message that I needed to run something by him and then looked at my to do list. There was nothing there that got my attention so I decided it was time for coffee.

I had picked up my cup and was almost out the door when my cell phone rang. It was Leon, returning my call, and I went back to my desk. "I'm just running some details down," I told him. "I believe you worked The Last One Left event the season that James Spradley won, didn't you?"

"Oh, yeah," Leon said. "You couldn't meet a nicer guy. It's a damn shame he bought it so young. He was one of those guys you enjoy being around. Always had a smile, even when he was dead beat, and he wasn't afraid to pick the others up when they felt down."

"How did he do that?"

"Oh, he always had a funny story nobody else had heard, and he was a wizard at card tricks. Not just the ordinary ones, either. He was a magician, or an illusionist he called it. When he did his tricks he always said that what he did was pull off illusions. He always said if you want to see real magic, look at a rainbow."

"Sounds like a good man," I said. "Did you ever figure out how he did some of his tricks?"

"No, and he pulled some really good ones, too. Once I saw him make a whole tray of food disappear. Then he pointed behind us and there it was on the other side of the clearing."

I had a pretty good idea of how Spradley made that happen but I kept quiet. What illusionists will tell you is that what they control is how people perceive things and I wondered. How in the world could James Spradley set up and successfully pull off a fake auto crash? And if he had, then who was incinerated inside his car?

Leon was surprised when I thanked him for his time. "What was it you wanted to know?" he asked.

"What I wanted was a better sense of who James Spradley was," I told him. "As a man. So far as I know, nobody around here ever met him in person."

"What about Daniella?"

"Did she know him?"

"Are you kidding? The two of them were thick as thieves. No, that's not right. Maybe I should say thick as Romeo and Juliet."

"Daniella? Nigel's assistant?" I found this hard to believe.

"You bet your sweet bippy. She may come across as the Ice Queen but James – nobody called him Jim – pushed her hot button. And she pushed his. They tried to hide it but I saw them sneaking around. The funny thing is, I think I was the only one who noticed it. Still, it wasn't any business of mine and I kept my mouth shut. I like doing business with Nigel and she's way up there on the company food chain. You know how it is."

"Yeah, I know how it is."

"I hope you don't mention me talking out of turn to Nigel."

"Talking about what?" I asked and Leon chuckled. "Don't worry," I assured him. "I appreciate your candor."

After we ended the call I sat there and thought about this. Try as I might, I couldn't picture Daniella as sweet and tender. Maybe Dee could. I made myself a note to ask him. Then I had another thought. Had Daniella helped Spradley win? I didn't see how that could be managed. I added a note to talk to Dee about this, too. It could be that a lot of the anger Daniella carried might stem from the loss of her lover. Even more important, did her anger over his death push her over the edge into serial murder? I knew it could, combined with a troubled history, and I decided we needed to know a lot more about Daniella Cooper. The trick would be doing it quietly.

I started to call up Daniella's personnel file but stopped before I hit enter. Assuming Daniella was somehow involved in the murders, it was a good bet that she probably had electronic trip wires set up to warn her. I had accessed her personnel file once, which was to be expected. To access it again would suggest I considered her a person of interest.

Even if she were not our killer, she might have done so just to protect her privacy. I knew Nicole had done this when she was hunting down serial killers but I was reluctant to ask her how she did it. While she volunteers things now and then, we treat that period of her life as don't-ask-don't-tell. At least we did up to then. Asking her help might be a good thing for us as a couple.

On the other hand, Sam had offered to help however he could and he had the resources and technology I needed. So I made myself yet another note to ask him that weekend. As I did, I suddenly felt incredibly homesick for my bride, our kids, and our friends in the District. I glanced at my watch and decided I needed to sleep in my own bed that night. So I called Nicole to let her know I was on the way. I also left a note for Nigel telling him that I was running down some leads in the District and would not be back in the office until Tuesday afternoon at the earliest. Then I thought of Willard Nordwald and set up an appointment for Monday afternoon. As his agent I could talk freely about the information I had and my suspicion of Daniella.

I got home in record time that evening. Even though it was still the rush hour when I left, the weather was beautiful and traffic was not bad at all. "Goodness," Nicole said when I walked in the door. "I didn't expect you for at least another hour. Let me call the kids. They are next door watching the Three Stooges."

"I have a better idea," I said and gave her a kiss that left no doubt of what I had in mind.

Sam McKee was surprised to see me already in the office the next morning when he showed up and we swapped friendly insults. "There's something I'd like you to look at if you've got time," he told me as we sipped our coffee. "I know you're in the middle of a case but I don't think it will take more than a couple of hours. If it does, you can set it aside. There's no rush."

"To tell you the truth, I'd really like a break from the case," I answered. "What do you have?"

Sam handed me a couple of thick files. "These appear to be kosher but they didn't feel quite right to me. I don't know why."

"It's probably the aroma of four-day fish," I said and he smiled.

Fifteen minutes later I went back to Sam's office to ask him to clarify something I didn't quite understand. It was a small ambiguity but when I asked, he looked thunderstruck. "How in the world do you do that?" he declared for the umpteenth time. "It seems so damned obvious to me now. You just saved us hours of work."

"Well, fresh eyes help. Nicole does that with me all the time."

"Aye, but the woman's possessed of the second sight," Sam answered with a Scottish burr.

"Not really," I chuckled. "Mostly it has to do with where I put something to keep it safe. She knows me better than I know myself."

"Ain't that the truth," Sam replied. "It's the same with me and Megan. I think it's gender linked. So tell me about your case. Thanks to you my morning just got clear."

I quickly summarized where we were and some of the issues that troubled me. "What I need right now is a lot more information on Daniella Cooper. I can't seem to rule her out as a suspect and I need to know her history. I can't figure out how to do that without risking tipping her off."

"Nicole could probably help you with that," Sam pointed out. Seeing the look on my face, he added, "On the other hand, that might not be a good idea. I don't mean to intrude."

I sighed. "That's just it, Sam. I don't feel I can ask her to go back to what she did for so long."

"You do realize it's pretty much what she does for us, don't you?" he asked gently. "She hunts people down for me, evil folk. And she does it without letting them know who wants to know. I've never seen anyone better at it."

I smiled at what Sam left unsaid and he nodded. Were I to ask him to get the information, he would do so and Nicole is the agent he would ask to do it. "You're right," I chuckled. "Why not cut out the middle man?"

Sam smiled and nodded. "Exactly. All you'd be asking is for her to get the information. It's not like you're asking her to act on it. Run it by Sofya if you need to but I think she'll tell you the same."

My bride smiled and reached out to caress my face when I told her about my conversation with Sam that evening. The kids were already in bed and fast asleep and we were talking in our bedroom. "You are such a good man, Jazz," she said, "so good to me and our children. Thank you for being so careful but Sam's right. I am the one he would ask to do this. So leave it to me. It may take a couple of weeks before I find anything."

I reached out and opened my briefcase, taking out the manilla file for Jaques Auden Michon. "This is the guy we think might be the killer taking out million dollar prize winners. There's a very old mug shot and his rap sheet is attached. When you look at it you'll see he goes by a number of aliases. A fellow he worked with one season told us he thought Jimmy Bob Miles, as James Mills was known on the event, is gay. This may or may not be related to one of the murders."

Nicole nodded and set the file aside without looking at it. "We? Was Dee with you?"

"No, I borrowed an auditor from Jolly Good Times, a former agent who retired from the FBI. Dee is back in Arkansas for a long weekend. He's headed out west next week to look at more...."

I suddenly stopped cold. Nicole tells me it is startling, and even a bit intimidating when I do this. But it's completely involuntary. Nor do I have any idea what sets these sudden flashes in motion. I had not mentioned James Spradley and he was not in my conscious thoughts. Yet I suddenly realized exactly where he might have gotten the torso that was incinerated in his car crash and exactly how he might have set up his accidental death.

"Sorry," I apologized to my bride. "Something just came

together. I need to get this down before I forget." I started to
scribble myself a note on an index card to look at this again. It
took three cards.

Torso in Spradley crash
  • a cadaver that had been stolen?
  • lower arms, legs, and head removed?
  • disposal of these
  • thrown into sea earlier? later?
  • alternative – bones from biology class skeleton?
  • natural bone skeleton – no other tissue?
  • stolen? theft written off as prank?
  • theft from morgue?
  • skeleton bought on dark net?
Staging wreck
  • use cruise control to get car up to high speed?
  • runs along side car to steer it until cruise kicks in?
  • lots of gasoline in plastic jugs for accelerant?
  • alternate – alcohol? acetone? ether?
Run all this by Dee...

When I finished Nicole was looking at me intently. "Are you
done now?" she asked politely. That should have been a warning
but I didn't see it coming. When I nodded she grabbed me and
threw me down on the bed, attacking the buttons on my shirt. I
responded by grabbing the hem of her tee and pulling it over her
head. As I thought, she was wearing nothing under it and any
further thoughts I might have had about the case flew out of my
mind like bats from a burning steeple.

"You seemed to be rather inspired, my love," I observed a bit
later. I was speaking Portuguese, the language we use for love.
    Nicole smiled and kissed me gently. "You have no idea how
hot you are when you play detective," she murmured softly in the
same patois. Then she touched me gently in a tender place, and
things got rather urgent once more.

Touching Base

12 We had a wonderful time as a family that weekend. Nicole didn't have anything pressing on her schedule so she took Friday off. I left the office at half past ten and we spent the rest of the day bumming around the District doing things we loved to do. Mostly we simply enjoyed one another's company and ended the morning with a long, leisurely lunch. With children there are not many days we can do that. Then on Saturday morning there was soccer for both Jack and Marie, followed by subs at our favorite shop and a trip to the Smithsonian to see an American heritage display we all enjoyed. Then we went home and polished off a couple of home baked pizzas for supper, followed by frozen yogurt. While the yogurt did not quite measure up to Arkansas' finest, it was plenty good enough for seconds.

On Sunday, after two days of glorious sunshine, the clouds rolled in and we spent the day lazing around the house. It was wonderful to light the gas fireplace and fill the hours with board games but by the end of the day my thoughts returned to the case. Then the neighbor kids called and Jack and Marie were off to watch some old black and white Tarzan movies. When they door closed behind them I looked at Nicole and she looked at me. It was clear we shared the same thought. It was time for a long autumn nap and we took off down the hallway to our bedroom.

Monday morning I got to the Agency much earlier than I normally do. Sam was not in yet but Michael Angelino already was hard at work. Even so, he waved me into his office. "Good morning, Jazz," he greeted me. "I got your email on Thursday evening but you didn't indicate you needed priority. Would tomorrow morning be good enough? We did a major update to our system over the weekend and everything is running behind."

I assured him that would be fine and headed for my desk. Space is always at a premium in the Agency and I share an office with a couple of other people. When we are all there at the same time it gets a little crowded but it's not often that happens. I am rarely gone these days and the other two guys are rarely there. When they are, I normally work from the house unless the Agency project I'm on is highly sensitive.

I was just getting settled in when Willie Dill stopped by to ask how my case was going. I was surprised to learn he was a fan of the show. "I don't get to watch it often but I like the challenges," he told me. "It seems better grounded in normal reality than other shows and I like the people they get as contestants. I've watched what passes for reality on some of the other series and they seem to generate a lot of unnecessary drama. Most of it seems pretty silly to me."

"On the other hand, it's gotten pretty real on Last One Left," I told him. "I wanted to talk with you about some of it. Not the drama but the investigation."

I sketched out what we thought was happening and Willie listened intently. "I don't get it," he said. "I know these guys you go after are crazy but I don't understand why they are doing it. What's their motive? Money?"

"That's the sixty-four dollar question," I told him. "This is not your run-of-the-mill slasher. He, or possibly she, is incredibly organized and very patient, very much like a chess master. He seems to enjoy the challenge of the hunt more than the kill. That ends the game."

"Now that I can relate to," Willie told me, nodding sadly. "One of the things that surprised me back when I was a sniper was the let-down after a successful mission. We were taking out ranking officers in the North Vietnamese army and I came to hate it. Yes, the missions were righteous. The guys we took out were the enemy and nasty people to boot. So why was I left with the taste of ashes when the adrenaline wore off? Why did I feel so unclean?"

There was no answer to this and we sat there reflecting for a long moment. Then something came to me. "Maybe it's because tasting ashes after taking human life is how we're supposed to feel, Willie. Maybe it means you were a good man forced to do something that is evil in almost every other situation."

Willie sighed and cleared his throat and I hoped I had not gone too far. "You think he might be doing it out of spite, Jazz?" he asked. "Simply because he can?"

I nodded. "I'm sure that's a big part of it, rubbing our noses in it, too, but I think there's more. If I had to make a guess, I'd say another big part is probably revenge."

"You think he might be taking out what was done to him as a kid on his victims? That would make some warped kind of sense. Or because he was born the way he was? Like Richard the Third?"

"'Now is the winter of our discontent...?'That fits, too. Richard the Turd, as Dee calls him, was a real piece of work. He couldn't be the best so he became the worst of the worst. The irony is that he was so successful...for a while."

Willie nodded. "Well, I better get going. I'm sure Michael's left me a huge pile on my desk. Let me know if I can help."

"What do you mean?" I asked. "You already have. You helped sort out my thinking."

Willie gave me an odd look. "I don't see it but I'll take your word for it. I don't see how I helped."

"You helped me stir the pot. It's like one of those big bingo cages. Turn it around and around and every once in a while a number pops out. Do it long enough and a pattern comes together. Bingo!"

Willie nodded vaguely and left. Looking around I saw Michael had left a stack of items on my desk, too. I was working my way through it an hour later when Dee called. He was on his way to Little Rock to catch a flight to the Twin Cities where Jared Michaels, another of our dead contestants, had lived. This one was a straight-forward homicide and the St. Paul police thought it looked like a mugging or possibly a serial killing. The victim was on his way home from a show at the old Fitzgerald Theater downtown and had parked on the street several blocks away. He had been killed with a single stab to the heart with a long, thin, pointed blade, much like an Italian stiletto or German Army dagger.

Michaels was unusual for a victim. He was tall and lean and the medical examiner noted that he was in very good condition. Slight contusions around his neck indicated that he had been taken from the back with a choke hold and the knife had been driven up to the hilt directly through his heart. The entry wound was just below the sternum and the angle of the wound indicated he had been pulled backward and stabbed by a right handed attacker. The medical examiner went on to state that in his opinion the killer had known exactly what he was doing. "Very precise," was how he put it.

"So you're thinking commando training?" I asked.

"Could be," Dee answered. "Or it could be a gifted amateur who studies old war movies."

"Or an actor who has been taught how to do it in a convincing manner," I replied.

"You know something I don't?" Dee asked.

"Besides what I had for breakfast?" I responded and he laughed.

"Are you kidding, Jazz? There's an eighty-seven percent chance you had scrambled eggs or egg-beaters, turkey bacon, and multigrain pancakes served with honey."

Dee was dead right. "What is it?" He asked. "You have a hunch that our killer is an actor?"

"No, except this whole case is about show business. Even player selection is more like an audition than a job interview. Jealous actors have been known to kill over not getting chosen for a part. This many of them seems a little over the top, but with actors, who knows?"

"Drama freaks!" Dee added. I could almost see him shake his head. "I ever told you how many actors it takes to change a light bulb, didn't I?"

"Yeah, that was one of Nellie's favorites, but remind me."

"There's one to hold the ladder, one to change the bulb, and four others to stand on the sideline and say 'That should be me up there.'"

We swapped light bulb jokes for a couple of minutes before I asked, "Seriously, Dee, what do you think?"

"Well, you may be right about an actor connection, Jazz, but I can't see how that's going to help us catch the killer." It was his way of gently reminding me we had not been on the case that long and of our need to stay open to other possibilities.

"It was just an idea. God only knows what's in our killer's mind. And She ain't talking."

"No kidding. There were a couple of things about this mugging that says it may be a serial. The victim's body was completely stripped and left behind the driver's seat of his car. There's no sign of his clothes or shoes, either."

"How was the body displayed?"

"I'm not sure. I'll have to read the case book first and look at the crime scene photos. I'll give you a call once I've read it and talked to the guys on the case."

I had just hung up and picked up the folder I was reviewing when my cell rang again. The caller ID said Trudy Howard and I thought it was her daughter. So I was careful how I answered. "This is Jazz Phillips," I said. "How may I help you?" Even to me my voice sounded a little stuffy. All I needed was to plug in an extended harrumph.

"Jazz, is that you?" Trudy asked. "You sound funny. Is everything all right?"

I explained that I was being careful and why, and Trudy laughed. "No wonder Billie gave me the third degree. When I tried to pin her down why she was asking all that she got rather evasive, too."

"So how are you? The last I heard it didn't sound good."

"Oh, I'm fine now but Billie and her husband won't let me do anything."

"Trudy, you had a stroke. They're trying to take care of you and you need to let them."

"No, Jazz. It wasn't a stroke. Didn't Billie tell you? It was some kind of reaction to a strong chemical substance. The police here have dragged me over the coals about it. I didn't understand why they were being so nasty. I still don't."

"What was the chemical, Trudy?" I had a bad feeling about this.

"That's just it. They hemmed and hawed around and finally told me it was methamphetamine. They demanded to know how long I had been an addict and who sold it to me. They wouldn't back off until I got a lawyer." She giggled. "Then it was kind of fun after he got there, seeing him turn the tables on them. Who Billie got is a guy who's known as a legal Rambo. He kicked butt and took names."

"Are they sure it was meth? Did you have it on you?"

"No, Jazz. They picked it up on my blood work when they brought me into the emergency room. Apparently meth can have the same symptoms as having a stroke but I didn't learn that until I talked with my doctor. It was awful. I don't see how anybody could enjoy taking that stuff."

"How did the police get involved?"

"There was an off duty officer doing volunteer work at the hospital. He overheard a couple of the lab technicians talking about it and called the detectives."

"You were very wise to get a lawyer," I told her. "The volunteer was way off base passing along your medical information without your consent. Did they search your luggage?"

"They were going to but Billie refused to identify my luggage. So they seized it all, along with her car, and they wound up with egg all over their faces. The lawyer filed a civil suit against them this morning and he says he's going to push for criminal action, too."

"Sounds like you're in good hands," I told her. As much empathy as I might have for fellow officers, it sounded like they were either poorly trained or simply ignored standard guidelines. Either way, they had gone off the reservation and deserved any legal consequences they might experience. There is simply no excuse for shoddy police work.

"Oh, I wish I was. I wish I was in your hands."

"I hope Billie's not listening in."

"Give me a little credit, Jazz. I may have been rather muddled this weekend but I'm all right now."

"I'm sorry. This caught me by surprise. Have you been able to figure out how you ingested the meth?"

"No, but I'm convinced it wasn't accidental."

"What do you mean?"

Trudy's voice changed. It was clear she was very angry. "I think someone deliberately poisoned me, Jazz. Are you all right?"

"Of course, I am. Why do you ask?"

"The only place I could think of where someone might do it was at work or at home. That would be very hard to do at work. If it was at home, it would have been in the food we both ate. I was afraid the same thing would happen to you. I asked Billie to call you and warn you. I told her your number was in my phone. Didn't she do it?"

"She told me you kept asking her to call me, but she couldn't make out what you wanted her to tell me. Apparently the meth really messed you up, so bad you couldn't get across what you wanted to say. Why were you worried about me?"

"I was afraid you might eat or drink whatever I did. We had the same thing, didn't we."

"Yes, but I didn't have any sweetener in my coffee and you did. I drank it black. Let me have it checked. Why do you think someone may be trying to poison you?"

"I think it's tied to this whole business of winner murders." I had never heard anyone at Jolly Good Times put it so frankly. Nor had I heard her ever be so blunt about the company. "I think Nigel should have called in the FBI right away and let the chips fall where they may. On the other hand, it's not my company. I own a few token shares, but he holds the majority stock. We all love the man but he's wrong about this."

"I need to check this out, Trudy. Could you call and ask the super at your building to let me in? All I need to get is the bowl on the table with the sweetener you used."

"I'll call and let the doorman know to expect you," she told me.

"There is an envelope addressed to you in my center desk drawer. It has a key and I told my secretary you might need it. Please call me and let me know what you find."

"It may be a few days before we hear," I said. "I'm going to use an independent lab. Assuming I do find something the biggest questions are how the poisoner got into your apartment and why he attacked you."

"I have no idea why anyone would want to poison me. And if they did, why use meth? Why not use rat poison?"

"We may never know for sure. It could be that he knew that a lot of symptoms are similar to people having strokes. Meth is harder to spot if you're not looking for it. Since they took you to the emergency room, they probably routinely tested for it along with a number of other things. Meth is also easier to come by than other things."

"What really bothers me is the who," she replied. "It's has to be someone who knows enough about me to know my habits. Do you think it's someone who's been stalking me?"

"No, I don't. To tell you the truth, I'm pretty sure it's someone inside the company or our killer's accomplice. Or maybe someone else with easy access to the offices."

"You mean like a custodian? Ours have been with the company for years. I had them thoroughly vetted." Then Trudy realized the full implications of what I'd just said. "You think it's somebody we know, someone in the office. That's scary even if it's only the killer's accomplice."

"No, I *suspect* that may be true. I'm not completely sure even though it would explain a lot of things. The point is that we need to keep this quiet, just between you and me. The last thing I want is for the killer to know what we're thinking."

"What about Nigel? Are you going to tell him?"

"Not at the moment. Once I'm sure, I'll inform him. Until then the fewer people who know about this, the better. Dee needs to know but no one else. We are dealing with a very clever perpetrator and it's all too easy for someone to inadvertently let something slip."

It was at that moment I had a deluge of cascading thoughts. We had not run a background check on Nigel, himself. Did he have a criminal record, and, if so, could he be the one who set this whole thing up? Was he acquainted with James Mills and was Mills Nigel's hatchet man, literally?

The thoughts rendered me speechless and I was silent too long. "Jazz?" Trudy asked. "What is it? Is something wrong?"

"I just had mental train wreck," I told her. "Four or five different trains of thought intersected all at once. It's going to take me a while to sort it all out. The main thing I'm concerned about right now is your safety. How long do you plan on being gone?"

"Originally a week but I can extend it for at least another week for convalescence. Nigel expects a lot but he is very liberal with executive benefits. He called and told me to take my time."

"Well, you need to stay put. I don't think you're in any danger of the poisoner coming after you there. Just take reasonable precautions. I actually think it's more likely that the killer was coming after me rather than you."

The moment I said this, I regretted it. "What?" Trudy demanded. It was the first I had ever heard her being angry. "That's it. I'm going to Nigel! He needs to bring in the FBI. Enough is enough."

"Trudy!" I said sternly. "That could wreck the whole investigation."

"I don't care. It's not worth your getting hurt."

"It's part of my work, Trudy. It's a consequence of going after the bad guys. They fight back and some of them have come after me. Yet I seem to be rather hard to kill."

"How does Nicole live with this?"

"She used to be a uniformed police officer. She knows the risks and she accepts them. She also knows somebody has to step up to the plate. Call and ask her. The point is that if you go to Nigel and insist on bringing in the FBI, that will not help. These killers are like dogs with a bone when they get an idea about something. Most of them simply can't stop once they start. This guy is trying to scare us. Doing so gives him pleasure and he's going to continue coming after me. That's what is going to get him caught."

We talked a good while longer and Trudy reluctantly agreed not to go to Nigel. I promised to let her know the results of the sweetener analysis as soon as I had it and when I hung up I felt like I'd been in a marathon. Not that I could speak from experience. I can walk a good many miles and feel great when I'm done, but I'm not built for running or even speed walking. Besides, walking that way looks funny.

I decided I needed a shower before my meeting with Willard Nordwald. There was supposed to be a new spa attached to the gym at the Agency and I decided it was time to check it out. Sure enough, it was equipped with treadmills and exercise bikes, each with its own small television set. After fumbling with the controls I was able to get the close captions up and running. For some reason my electronic jinx didn't seem to apply to the treadmill but I was totally overwhelmed by the choice of a hundred channels. By the time I found one I liked I had walked over two miles according to the meter. So I soaked in the hot tub, relaxing my tired legs and wishing my bride was there with me.

No sooner had the thought entered my mind than Nicole walked through the door. Two minutes later she appeared from the ladies' locker room dressed in a minimal Brazilian bikini and slid into the water beside me. Seeing the look on my face, she grinned. "Do I dare give you a hug?" she asked sweetly.

"Woman, you just about ruptured my bathing suit," I assured her. "You're going to get us thrown out of here." I opened my arms and she slipped into them.

Nicole chuckled. "Now that sounds like fun," she said, returning my hug with interest.

"I thought you were going to work at home today," I told her, kissing her lightly on the lips.

"So did I but Sam called. He needed someone to fix his computer. Michael is out for the day and Jack is not in town. So he called me." She shook her head. "You know what the problem was?" I confessed I had no idea. "The main power cord wasn't completely pugged into the surge arrester," she told me, shaking her head sadly.

"Well, that's not all bad," I replied. I didn't have a clue what she was talking about. "It means we get to spend some time together, doesn't it?"

"Yes, but we need to do something nice for Louella." This was the neighbor whose kids loved old movies. "She's been so good about taking the kids at the last minute."

Then something changed. The way she looked at me meant it was time to get down to the nitty gritty. "So how is your case going? I just got a call from Trudy. She is very upset."

"That was fast," I said. "She must have called you the minute I hung up." Nicole nodded and I continued. "The truth is that it's driving me crazy. I can't seem pull much together. All I have is bits and pieces that don't fit into a coherent picture. It's like a jigsaw puzzle that doesn't have a straight edge or a picture to go by and where both sides of the pieces look the same. Our killer seems to like complicating things and I think he may be taunting us."

"Tell me about it," Nicole said. I was so surprised I had trouble talking. I looked at her and started to ask if she was sure, but I knew she was. Her eyes were grave and held an almost frightening resolve. "I mean it, Jazz," she murmured. "We're a long way from New Orleans."

Nicole was reminding me of the first serial killer she took down. It was righteous and it was done in self-defense. What was most remarkable was that the killer struck the first blow, knocking her down, paralyzing her left arm and almost taking her out. She had only touched him twice. Falling to the street, she first swept him off his feet with her legs, leveling the field. When he fell his head bounced off the pavement, which the ME said most likely would have killed him. Even so, she didn't know this and she struck him once more to make sure he could not attack her again.

Nor had she reported this, mostly because the killer was a prominent surgeon and a close friend of the Chief of Police. After that she had become an angel of wrath, tracking down other monsters the law could not touch. The only time we had worked together was going after the slasher who had murdered my bride and two dozen others, and who was coming after me. That was her last victim and she shot him to protect me.

"All right," I said. "Let's go somewhere more private." Then my eyes fell on the clock. "No, I've got a meeting with the Jolly Good Times lawyer. I need to type up my report. Let's do it after I meet with him tomorrow afternoon."

"Why not tonight after the kids go to bed?"

I shook my head and smiled. "No, my love, first things first. Murder can wait. I've got plans for you and that bikini."

The meeting with Willard Nordwald took over an hour. I gave him my written report and summarized our findings. Then I brought him up to date with details I had not included in the report. He was quite distressed to learn of the attack on Trudy and asked if I was sure I wanted to continue. I told him I did and that I could speak for Dee on that matter. "Someone has to do this," I said. "Dee and I are trained for it and we probably have more experience than anyone else. For better or worse, this has been a big part of our life's work and we are very cautious. That's why we're armed and work either as a team or with another experienced officer when we deal with suspects. That's why I took Bill Cleary with me when I interviewed the subcontractors. I didn't expect to run into trouble, but I didn't take the chance."

"Steve DiRado is on his own right now, isn't he?" Willard asked.

"Yes, but he is dealing primarily with law enforcement officers and public officials. The only exception was the widow in Yuma and he would not have gone in alone if he thought there was any danger at all. As it turned out, she offered him a hundred dollars for tipping her off to the scam her husband was working on her." Seeing him frown, I quickly assured Willard. "He didn't accept it, of course."

Nordwald nodded though his frown did not go away. "The danger really does concern me, Jazz. Please be careful. Now what are you not telling me?"

"Well, for one thing, I have a strong hunch we are dealing with someone connected to Jolly Good Times. I think James Mills may be our killer, but I believe he may have had help from inside the company. I am not quite sure how this insider has helped the killer, but I think it is someone who has access to company information. I am reasonably sure that neither Dom nor Trudy is involved and I cannot see how Nigel could benefit." Willard blinked when I told him this but said nothing.

"What I can tell you is that going through the personnel files has not turned up anything the least bit suspicious. So far. Nor can I see how any member of the board could benefit. On the other hand, I am convinced that we are probably dealing with a serial killer and they operate by a whole different logic and motivation."

Nordwald nodded. "I noticed you have not mentioned Daniella Cooper. Has she been cooperative?"

"She does what Nigel tells her to do. Aside from that...." I shrugged.

"I also noticed that you did not include her with Dom and Trudy as not being involved."

"Her behavior has not been reassuring," I answered. "We have also been told by a reliable witness that she was emotionally involved with one of the victims. I am not sure quite what to make of that. Naturally, I have not mentioned any of this to Nigel. That's up to you but I'd suggest waiting a bit. We're turning up bits and pieces and those are beginning to coalesce."

Willard nodded. "So what's next?"

"I've been thinking about that. At the top of the list is taking a close look at Daniella Cooper, and we need to be very careful doing so. After that, I don't know. I have gone through some of the personnel files of the West Coast operation. I need to go over the rest of these with Dee. Unless something develops in New Jersey, I think the two of us may need to visit the West operation and interview event staff in person."

"Really? Why is that?"

"For one thing, more than ninety percent of what human beings tell one another is nonverbal and we need to observe that in person. We do it together because separately we have a greater chance of missing something critical. We also kick things around quite a bit as we go and every once in a while another piece of the puzzle falls into place."

"Well, I'm very concerned about your interviewing the West Coast staff," Willard told me. "These are some pretty sharp people and they'll want to know what you're doing. What do you plan to tell them?"

"I don't know," I replied. "The truth would be best. The closer you stay to the truth the more you create trust. One possibility is that there have been some issues raised about the quality of the experience for the contestants and we have been brought in to assess these issues. The Roselle Hoffstadt complaint comes to mind. Normally we would take a close look at her but the timing isn't right."

"Very well, but please be careful. I am very concerned for your safety. We have eight people dead, seven of whom were winners and in top condition. At least, they were when they were contestants. I'd feel better if you worked with a partner in New Jersey. Is there someone else you can call on?"

I thought for a moment. "I am sure I can find someone. Bill Cleary would will do for now, but I will need to use someone outside the company to work with Dee. Do I need to clear it with you if I find someone?"

"No, not within reason. Just report it to me so I can do the paper trail."

As I drove back from my meeting with Willard Nordwald there was something tickling the back of my mind. I couldn't quite grasp what it was and I have learned I cannot force these things. So I surrendered whatever it might be to the tender mercies of the universe and turned on the car radio. It was tuned to a station I like that plays mostly mellow jazz and I settled back into the seat and let myself be carried away by the music. The first song was a favorite of mine by Kenny G and found it very soothing.

Sure enough, at the very next traffic light I spotted the sign of a donut shop and I remembered what had been tickling my memory. It had been weeks ago and that morning it was my turn to take the kids to school. On the way to the office after I dropped them off I spotted a bakery I'd never seen before. So I stopped to sample their wares. Nor was I sorry I did. The coffee was on a par with the place I normally visit and at a better price. Unfortunately, the pastry was not. It wasn't bad but it wasn't worth bringing a bagful home, either.

Just as I was getting up to leave two plainclothes policemen walked in. Nor was there any mistaking they were cops. One of them was Hispanic and looked familiar. The other was an older male and did not. Nor could I place the officer I recognized. "Jazz Phillips!" he said with a smile, offering his hand. I took it and he introduced me to his partner, a large African-American named Otis who ignored my offered hand. "I bet you don't recognize me," the Hispanic said shaking his head at his partner's discourtesy.

"I know the face and the voice but I can't recall your name," I told him. "I think you were at a seminar I gave in Denver. That was maybe six years ago?"

"Eight, actually," he told me. "It was a seminar on financial crime and what I learned there led to some great busts."

"Delgado," I said, nodding. "Detective Robert Delgado from Fort Collins. You were in your late twenties but you looked sixteen at most. You also asked some very good questions."

"This is the guy I was telling you about," Delgado told his partner. Otis nodded brusquely but didn't smile. "Oats is FBI," Delgado explained. "They're trying to recruit me." The man in black man frowned at the slurring of his name but said nothing.

"They are known to do that," I said. "You can't beat the training and they certainly pay well."

"Phillips," Otis murmured. "You the one they call the beast buster?" His face looked like he'd bitten into a sour pickle.

"I'm never going to live that down," I confessed, shaking my head. Delgado grinned but Otis was not amused. "Actually, my hot button has always been corporate financial crime."

"I heard you led the team that took down Kwan Tea," Delgado said, nodding.

"No, I was part of the team," I corrected him. "Another guy led it." That was not exactly true but no one likes braggarts. I did lead the team but McKee was the boss.

"Man, I would have liked to have been in on that," Delgado told me. "Listen, I know you need to go. You got a card? I'd like to bounce a couple of ideas with you."

I realized Delgado was telling me he didn't want to talk in front of Otis and I handed him one of my Agency cards by mistake. Delgado looked at it and Otis read it over his shoulder. When he did, his face grew grim. "I do a lot of consulting for these people," I told them. "I also do some work for the Bureau from time to time." Otis looked even more sour hearing this. I'd had enough attitude from Otis and decided to rub it in. "They still use a couple of my books as training texts."

Otis glared at me but said nothing. I told Delgado it was good to see him and left the bakery. As I drove to the office I took myself to task. Why had I let Otis get to me so much? I had a choice to take the higher road and it felt like I had failed miserably. Then I remembered something I had heard Dee say on a number of occasions. When you spot it you got it. I didn't like the thought much, but I had apparently seen something I didn't like about myself reflected in Special Agent Otis. Or as Pogo might say it, I had seen the enemy and he was me.

At that point, I decided I had given Otis too much of my life. I turned my thoughts to what Nicole had said. Then an inconsistency in the case struck me. Assuming Daniella had been involved with the younger James Mills, why had she deep sixed his attempt to work at Jolly Good times? I pulled over and wrote a note to myself to look at this later and stuck it in my pocket.

I was at my desk at the Agency two hours later when my phone rang. It was Robert Delgado and he got right to the point. "I need some career advice, Jazz. Can you spare me some time?"

I told him I could. When he asked where we could meet I asked, "Have you seen the National Cathedral?"

Robert told me he had not. "It's easy to find and a good place to meet," I told him. "You'll see why." We set up a time late that afternoon and I gave him directions where to find me in the nave near the western visitor's entrance.

I arrived at the cathedral a half hour early and used the time to sit quietly in the nave. I described Delgado to my angels before we left and on my way out I told McKee I might have a live one for him. He is always scouting for new talent and our operations had grown considerably over the last three years.

Robert Delgado found me sitting exactly where I told him I would be. He greeted me warmly again and followed me to a place we could talk privately. "Man, this is some place," he said reverently, looking around as we sat down. Then he leaned forward and spoke softly. "I don't know if you made them, Jazz, but there are a couple of people following us. Not together, either. They were at the bakery this morning, too."

I nodded and explained they were part of my security detail. "Man, you must have totally made somebody mad," he replied. "Kwan Tea?"

"That and other things," I replied. "I don't want to rush you but I've got a dinner date with my family. You said you needed career advice."

Robert nodded. "To put it in a nutshell, I'm tired of gory crime scenes and it feels like that's all that's coming my way lately. That's my reward for clearing a lot of homicides. So I'm looking to make a career move to financial crime. I'm looking at the Bureau and the IRS. It looks like all they have to offer is paper-pushing and morale doesn't seem very high either place." He paused and I knew there was more he wanted to say. "The job with the Fort Collins PD was good but, like I say, I burnt out on homicide and asked to be moved to the fraud and theft squad. Unfortunately, that was after the job lost me a marriage. Thank God we didn't have any children."

Delgado sighed. "About four or five years ago I started looking to change. Then we caught a really big real estate scam tied to a homicide and I really liked working it. Who broke the case was an accountant the department hired as a consultant and I learned a lot from him. So I decided to take a few accounting classes and those turned into a CPA. What's so funny, Jazz?"

"What's so funny is that you just described the early part of my career. I never went for the CPA, but I do know what you're saying. You ever work any other financial scams?"

"I should be so lucky," he told me. "After I switched over it was simple fraud and embezzlement. Most of what I did was gather evidence but that gave me time to study. I just finished up my CPA hours and got certified. I guess I could hang out a shingle but I don't want to be shut up in an office all the time doing tax returns. I'm an investigator and I thought you might have some ideas. Or need some help."

I nodded. "You have your CV with you?"

Delgado smiled. "You bet!" He reached into his jacket and I made a quick hand signal telling my angels it was all right.

"What was that?" Robert asked, looking in the direction of one my angels sitting forty feet away. The angel still had his hand inside his jacket. "Oh," Delgado said. "You were dead serious."

I nodded. "Unfortunately. There is a price on my head, Robert. I seriously torqued some bad guys over Kwan Tea. Over some other things, too." I took the CV out of the envelope. It was three sheets and looked very professional. "No padding, I hope."

Delgado smiled. "No bullshit, Jazz. I actually left some good stuff out."

"Good," I nodded. "That will give you something to add at the interview. I'll look this over and if I think there's a match, I'll pass it on. Don't hold your breath. It may take a while. If the fellow I have in mind doesn't want to follow up, I have some other ideas. There's always a demand for competent investigators."

"I really appreciate it, Jazz," he told me.

There was something I'd forgotten at the Agency that day and I stopped by Sam's office on my way home to drop off Delgado's resume. Sam was still there and he nodded. "I take it this is not the FBI guy. Your angels mentioned that you'd been accosted at the bakery."

"That's the man. I don't know him well, but Robert is a quick study. He asked some damned good questions at the seminar I gave. Were I still at the CID, I'd hire him if he cleared the background check."

"Any idea how long he's going to be in town?"

"No, but I can check my cell record and give him a ring. His call was the last one I got this afternoon." Somehow I managed to call up the number and read it off to McKee. Not knowing quite why, I had also entered the number into my list of contacts.

Remembering all this, I dug out my cell phone. Sure enough, Delgado's number was there and I gave him a call. "Hey, Jazz," he greeted me cheerfully. "I was just about to give you a call. What can I do for you?"

"Dee and I need a third partner if you're available," I told him. "Are you still licensed to carry?"

There was a long silence, so long I thought the call had been dropped. "Yes, I'm still on the rolls as a sworn officer in Fort Collins but I'm on terminal leave. Your friend, McKee, has been recruiting me pretty hard and I was just about to take his offer."

"So why haven't you?" I asked. I knew the answer but I needed to hear Delgado say it.

"I think you know why," Robert answered. "I'm a police officer, not a spook. I already turned down an offer from the NSA. Besides, my hot button is white collar crime. What do you have?"

"I've got a case that's driving me crazy," I said. "It looks like there is a serial at work but we don't know who it is yet. We're also working for a law firm investigating it. I can't tell you much more until you are on board. What we're working under is lawyer-client confidentiality. The law firm is our client."

"Damn!" Delgado said. "You catch some strange ones, don't you. What else can you tell me?"

"There may be a lot of travel involved and what I have been doing so far is trying to find a paper trail. It looks like our best suspect dropped off the radar some time back and we need to find him. Whoever is doing it seems to have a lot of inside help from the client company involved. There's also been an attempt to take me out. That's what's behind the need to carry."

"Sounds like fun but I hate to let the opportunity with McKee pass. He's got some good people working for him."

"Let me talk to Sam," I replied. "I can probably work something out."

Dee called late that afternoon, updating what he had found in St. Paul. "There's not much to add. The local police classified this as a potential serial and searched their files to see if there are similar cases. There weren't. They also posted the crime on NCIC, but got no response to date. There was some genetic material but no match on CODIS."

"Sounds like you're done there. What's next? Atlanta?"

"Yeah, that should wind it up unless we get a fresh one."

There was something in Dee's voice that concerned me. "What's bothering you, Dee?"

"Well this is a pretty slick asshole, Jazz, at least so far. I'm beginning to feel a little nervous working alone."

This tripped a red flag in my mind. Dee's sense of danger is much more acute than mine and has saved our lives more than once. "Then stand down," I told him. "Right now. Head for DC and we'll go to Atlanta together. I need to clear some things off my desk. No, come to think of it. Take a few days off at home. You've been working pretty hard without a break. I'll call you by next Monday. Query Atlanta by phone if you get bored."

Dee laughed. "We been working together too long, Jazz. I was just about to suggest that myself."

"It won't be just us, either. I think we have a new man coming on the payroll." I told him about Delgado and he laughed.

"Sounds like you were looking in a mirror for recruits," Dee said.

"No, he's a lot better looking than either of us," I told him. "Who he reminds me of is the Trini Lopez way back when. What Nellie would have called a real heart throb."

"Careful, partner, you're dating yourself."

"You spot it, you got it!" I laughed.

Surprises

13 After I hung up I debated what I needed to do for a while. It was close to quitting time and I checked to see if Sam was back in his office. I needed to talk with him about Robert Delgado, but Sam was not in and his secretary told me she didn't think he'd be back. "I think he had some family thing," she told me. "I think he'll probably go straight there from his meeting."

"Please leave him a note I need to see him," I said. "I'll try again tomorrow. It's nothing that urgent but I do need to talk with him."

Normal business hours were past but it a little early to head home. So I woke my laptop and ran D. Cooper through the NCIC database. The machine hemmed and hawed a bit and informed me that it had over ten thousand responses. This was way too many to sort visually so I tried Dan Cooper. This brought up over two thousand hits but these were almost all men. Nor were the files sorted by gender. Running Daniella Cooper narrowed it down quite a bit but it would still take me too much time to review them all.

The problem was that I had no idea what her middle name or initial might be or if I was even using the right spelling. That information might be in the Jolly Good Times database but I couldn't figure out how to get it without tipping her off I was snooping. Then I had to laugh at myself for not seeing the answer right in front of me. I picked up my phone and found Trudy's number in my contacts folder.

Then I realized I was at my Agency desk and cancelled the call. I wasn't particularly worried about the security of the Agency but Trudy was my personal business. It was past normal office hours but I didn't want anyone wandering in or overhearing me. Like any other group of human beings, spooks thrive on gossip. Since they cannot talk about work, it is open season on one another so long at it doesn't compromise what they do. Nor is it allowed to be vicious. Sam sees to that, as does Sofya. Even so, I didn't want to give the grapevine more ammunition.

Ten minutes later I was polishing off a large serving of frozen yogurt in the Agency canteen. The place wasn't busy since most everyone else was gone for the day. I took a table in a secluded corner and dialed Trudy again. She answered on the third ring.

"I was just thinking about you," she told me. There was no mistaking the warmth in her voice or the hint of longing. "Then you called. That's nice."

I wasn't too sure about that, at least not for me, but I didn't disagree. The truth of the matter is that it was uncomfortably pleasant to hear her voice. I seemed to be developing feelings I didn't want and couldn't honor, pleasant though they might be. So it was unsettling to hear myself agree so readily. Nor was I lying and that was even more unsettling than if I had been.

We visited for a while before I explained what I needed. She laughed when I told her. "That's because her first name is Edynella and her last name is Keupir." She spelled them out for me.

"No wonder I didn't get a hit. You don't happen to know her middle name, do you? Please tell me it's something simple like Mary or Janice."

Trudy chuckled. "Believe it or not, it's Leighanne." Again she spelled it out. "I think her parents didn't like simple names."

"Apparently not. Hold on a moment." I fired up my laptop and typed the correct spelling into it. The result was a single response. The mug shot with the file was definitely a younger Daniella, but neither Daniella, Beth, nor Cooper appeared in the file. "That's rather odd," I told Trudy. "The name she uses now doesn't show up even as an alias." I scanned the file and quickly learned why. Aside from a couple of tickets for speeding, Edynella *Leigh* Keupir had been arrested only once. This was as a material witness in New York pending extradition to Great Britain. To me that suggested she might currently be in Her Majesty's witness protection.

"Thanks, that worked," I told Trudy. "How did you learn her real name?"

"Believe it or not, from her birth certificate. She gave me her real one by accident. What I mean is she gave me two birth certificates. They were in a file folder she gave me. The one with the name she uses now was on top and the one in her old name was stuck to the back. She was very upset when I told her what had happened and I promised not to put her former name in her file."

Trudy paused and I was sure there was something else she wanted to tell me. Then it occurred to me what it was. "You kept a copy of her original certificate, didn't you?" I asked.

"Yes, I did. As upset as she was, something didn't seem right. So I made a copy to protect the company. I put it in my personal holding file."

Daniella's response made it sound even more like she was in witness protection to me. "So what's her middle name now?" I asked.

"Beth," Trudy replied. "And not Elizabeth, either. She was very emphatic about that."

"Daniella Beth Cooper," I said. "It has a certain ring to it. Do you know if she had it legally changed?"

Trudy was quiet a moment. "You know, it never occurred to me to ask. I do know she has a Social Security card in her new name, as well as a passport. We keep Social Security numbers in a separate file for security."

"Do you know if Nigel knows about this?"

"I imagine so but I never thought about it. He would have to, wouldn't he?"

"Not necessarily," I replied. "He may have assumed that you had collected all the necessary information when you first started. Do you know anything at all about her background? Is she still an American citizen?"

"She must be. She travels on an American passport and her new birth certificate says she was born here. I know because we have a tickle file for those of us who travel out of the country. So we keep our passports up to date."

"What about your contestants? Do you check passport information for them?"

"As a matter of fact, we do. We have to. Some jurisdictions require the company to surrender passports while an event is going on. Of course, most of the contestants already have passports. We just make sure they're up to date."

I thought about this a moment and she asked, "Are you onto something, Jazz?" There was a lot of concern in her voice.

I laughed. "I have no idea, Trudy. Part of it is force of habit. When I was at CID I taught our investigators to just follow their intuition. Beyond getting some basic information and following some basic procedure, there is no way you can really plan an investigation. All you can do is follow the leads. I told my people to follow their hunches and fish here and there. Sooner or later they'd catch something."

"So you're fishing now?"

"No, I'm talking to Trudy. I apologize for slipping into cop mode."

"Actually, it's kind of a turn-on. I wish you were here so I could show you."

"And shock Billie?" I replied and we both laughed.

After talking to Trudy I called home to let Nicole I was running late. I started to run a deep background check on Edynella Leigh Keupir. Then I decided I'd done enough for the day and made a cryptic note to myself to run it the first thing the next morning. I started to stick it on my computer screen the way I used to do in my home office but remembered being warned about not doing this at the Agency. This was part of the office security policy. So I folded it and stuck it in my pocket. I left an electronic reminder on my laptop calendar, hoping I'd remember what I meant by "Leigh 1st." Sometimes I get so cryptic I totally baffle myself. I am lucky my bride knows me well enough to puzzle it out. Most of the time.

I got home that evening early enough to have a couple of hours with the kids. This included a cut-throat game of pachisi, pronounced parchesi in rural Arkansas and called Aggravation in our family. We played it on an antique oak board made by my grandfather when he was a young man. Marbles and dice have been lost and replaced and the finish was restored several times over the years, but the board was a strong anchor in family history. Quite often a lively discussion or debate slowed down the play, often intense but never with rancor. This was considered a legitimate strategy for distracting one's opponents.

That night the play was intense and I was worn out by the time Jack won the game. I confessed as much to Nicole as we sat cuddled in front of our gas fireplace. She nodded. "I know you wanted to tell me about the case this evening," she told me. "So if you need to do it now we can but I hate to break the mood. I kept tomorrow morning open in case something came up."

I nodded, relieved. "That would be much better. Then we won't have to worry about little ears overhearing."

"Good," she said, reaching out to snag a trade blanket and spreading it over us. Snuggling even closer she said, "Let's pretend it's deep winter and that we're in the McKee's line shack." She gave me a kiss that brought back many sweet memories of the shack, then gave me a look that was pure mischief. "There's something else I'd like to bring up.... Oh! I think I already have."

I slept in Tuesday morning, getting up only to say goodbye to the kids. I was showered and dressed by the time Nicole was back from taking them to school and had a fresh pot of coffee brewed. It was time to get down to serious business and with silent consensus we took our customary seats at the kitchen table. Taking a sip of my coffee I began telling her about the case, starting with the first meeting with Willard Nordwald and ending with my last conversation with Trudy. During the telling I included most of my thoughts on the case and my throat was parched by the time I was done. When I glanced at the clock I noticed I had been talking for almost two hours.

By the time I was done, my bride was out of her chair and pacing like a caged tiger, totally focused on what I was telling her. "I think you're right," she told me as I poured myself a therapeutic cup of mocha. "I think there is a serial at work and he or she must have help from inside the company. There's no doubt in my mind that the auto crash in Utah was murder. The stabbing in Saint Paul sounds like the work of a serial killer and I don't think the shooting in Atlanta was a random act of violence, either. It would take a lot of convincing for me to believe it was a random attack. I think the evidence you have so far points to Daniella as an accomplice though I don't understand her motivation. It sounds like she is quite close to Nigel, and she comes across as quite loyal to the company."

"She is from all I've seen," I agreed. "Assuming Leon Spitz is right about Daniella and James Spradley, it's quite possible that his death was the event that set her off. Either that or he is the killer and she's his partner, but I think that's a reach."

I paused and Nicole waited patiently for me to continue. "So assuming Spradley is dead, the question is what aimed her or them toward other winners of The Last One Left. That's the part that doesn't make much sense to me. The only thing that comes to mind is her resenting other winners for being alive and having the opportunity to enjoy what they've won. I think that alternative assumes Spradley's death was an accident or suicide and that he was not murdered. That's a rather elaborate way to murder someone. There's too much likelihood of things going wrong and getting caught. The same goes for faking it."

"I wish we knew more about her," Nicole said. "I have the feeling that there is some critical factor in her background that would help us understand."

"Well, let's see what I can find," I answered. Getting up and setting my laptop up on the table, I turned it on and got us another cup of mocha. Then I started to log into the NCIC database but Nicole stopped me before I finished. "Wait a minute, Jazz. Don't log in as yourself. It is possible to alert her if you're not careful."

Seeing my surprise, she smiled. "How do you think I kept

ahead of the game so long? It's easy to set up an alert if you know what you're doing. How sophisticated is Daniella with computer systems?"

"I have no idea. I imagine Dom or Trudy could tell us," I answered.

"Just a minute." Nicole left and came back a minute later with a small leather address book. "This is my little black book," she told me. "It holds real user names and passwords I used to remain anonymous in Cyber World. Sam knows about it and part of my job at the Agency is keeping it up to date. How comfortable are you taking a leap into Spook Land?"

I sighed. "You know how hard it was for me to convince myself we needed to work together in the first place, sweetheart. On the other hand, my comfort zone has stretched quite a bit since I changed my mind. The bottom line is that I would prefer to do this my old fashioned way unless there is a real and present danger."

"I think Oliver Wendell Holmes was talking about the First Amendment, Jazzbeau, but I do appreciate how it is with you. It's one of the things I love most about you, Chief Straight Arrow." Nicole smiled sweetly to take any sting from the words. "Go ahead and do it your way. I was just feeling very protective. Like I am with the kids. Sorry."

I chuckled. "No, you're not. You're not a bit sorry." She grinned and I smiled back. Then I logged into NCIC my normal way. "Since I'm working for a lawyer, *I* need to keep it kosher. You, on the other hand are working for Sam, not for Nordwald, the lawyer who hired me for this case."

"Nordwald? He doesn't sound Jewish," she quipped. Then she became serious as I sent a query for Edynella Leigh Keupir.

The results of the query came back to us very quickly this time. There was not a lot information to be had and it came from several different sources. Yet what I found surprised me. Daniella, as I continued to call her, had been born in a small town near Cleveland, Ohio, in 1962 and graduated at the top of her high school class in 1979. She won a full ride scholarship from the

University of Cleveland and pursued a degree in criminology, finishing in three years. During her senior year she had been chosen for a post-graduate student exchange and spent the summer and following year studying in Canterbury. Her field of study was applied criminology and she finished with honors in June 1984.

Edynella had returned to England after graduation and returned to the United States in late 1984. Just before she came home something happened in England. This, however, did not prevent her return to Ohio for Christmas. She returned to Canterbury and finish her fellowship in 1986. She then moved to New York City where the British legal system finally caught up with her. I am not sure why, but a warrant for her arrest as a material witness had been issued some time before and she was extradited. After that she fell off the grid and I could not see why. Try as I might, there was nothing more I could find out about her.

I sat and thought about this for a while and Nicole respected my silence. There was a lot left unsaid in the NCIC report but there was nothing more I could do without going beyond the constraints of my agreement with Willard. There were no legal grounds for me taking the investigation of Daniella farther except for my own suspicion and I was not a policeman. I told Nicole as much as she was leaving for work and typed up a summary of everything I had, to date, including my dilemma. I printed three copies and gave one to Nicole when I got to the office. Another was for Sam and the third was set aside for Willard Nordwald if, and when, I decided to give it to him.

"This is crazy since you will be working for Sam," I told her. "But this way I can tell Willard that I have done everything by the book. Sort of." She smiled and gave me a tender kiss. "Don't ever quit being Jazz," she murmured. "We all love you for being who you are."

Sam was not in his office when I dropped by so I left the envelope in his secure mailbox. I sealed it first, addressing it to Sam. On second thought I marked it "For Your Eyes Only."

Sam thought this was funny, "Shades of Graham Greene," he

said when I saw him in his office late that afternoon. "It reminds me of those cover sheets we used back in the early days of fax. You know, the ones stamped CONFIDENTIAL that had dire warnings against unauthorized reading. As if that would stop any self-respecting snoop from peeking."

Sam opened a drawer and took out a thin file he handed to me. "Michael brought this by earlier. It's the result of the facial recognition search we ran with the mug shot you sent us. I'm not quite sure what to make of it. It looks like Jaques Michon, AKA James Mill *et al*, fell off the grid for a few years and then turned up as an anonymous murder victim in Bethlehem, Pennsylvania, about eighteen months ago. Nor were there dental records that could be found to confirm this. At least, so it appears. The only fingerprint hit belonged to a dead man, James Auden Mills, who departed this life some thirty years ago."

McKee smiled. "Of course, there was no DNA match from CODIS to verify this. Since it was such a brutal murder the local police ran the anonymous victim's picture in the paper. It was pretty battered but our facial recognition software affirmed who it was. The mug shot they published also turned up a long lost sister who showed up out of nowhere to make identification and claim the body. Three guesses who that was. That's right, sports fans, one Daniella Beth Cooper. What I can't figure out is why she didn't show up in an NCIC query, assuming the local police ran one. Surely they would have checked her out."

"One would think so," I replied. I opened the file and scanned it quickly. "I imagine there was no hit because NCIC was never queried. Nor would there be anything for Daniella Cooper to find. She is neither a victim nor a perpetrator, so she wouldn't have been listed with NCIC. I see she had a valid driver's license showing her to be a resident of Linden, New Jersey, and I imagine that's all the identification the Bethlehem PD required." I looked at McKee. "How did you come by all this information, Sam?"

He chuckled. "Oh, I called and talked to the chief. I may have left the impression she was the subject of a background check for security clearance in the District. I said her brother had come up as a potential security risk. The chief was also Special Forces and he told me a lot more than I wanted or needed to know. Among other things he told me that the long lost brother was cremated."

"That figures," I said. No possible autopsy down the road. I wonder if Nigel was aware of Daniella's ties to Mills the younger."

"That's a good question. It gives you some leverage with her if you need it."

"I don't think so. She is pretty...obdurate. It depends whether I can clear Nigel. I don't suppose the chief sent along any pictures of his victim, did he?"

Sam smiled broadly. "He emailed me one and you'll find it tucked into the back of the file. It's not pretty."

I riffled through the file but there was no photo. Sam was startled when he heard this but looked at his printer and laughed. "I must be ready for the old people's home," he said, handing me a full page gloss. It was printed in color which highlighted the victim's injuries. Yet it matched both the mug shots of both James Mills and Jaques Auden Michon quite well. The question was which one of them it was. Or if both were dead.

I said as much and McKee nodded. "So what does your gut tell you?" he asked, looking at me intently.

"My gut tells me Daniella is in the UK equivalent of witness protection. I don't know why I think so but I had that impression early in the investigation. It would certainly explain the trouble we're having getting much background information. I really lucked out with Trudy discovering her original birth certificate. I may be barking up the wrong tree and I'd really like to clear her, guilty or not. Background could be very helpful help doing so."

Sam nodded. "Let me see what I can do about that. I have some friends in low places." He smiled and I knew our conversation was over.

I glanced at my watch. "You know what my gut is really telling me, Sam? It's time for lunch and frozen yogurt. Care to join me?"

"I truly wish I could, Jazz," McKee said shaking his head sadly. "I've got what is shaping up to be an excruciatingly boring interagency meeting. I swear, the time we waste fighting turf wars.

You know what I mean."

"Unfortunately, I do. Would you give me a call later? I need to talk to you about Robert Delgado."

Sam stopped and looked at me sharply. "We're in the process of hiring him," he told me. "Is there some reason we should not?"

"Not for a moment. I need to borrow him for a week or two before he starts here," I said. "The law firm I'm contracting with will pick up his salary while he's working for me."

"Sure," Sam said with a wave of his hand. "Just send me a reminder. And let me know how he works out."

I could tell my bride was very pleased with herself when I got home that evening. Not limited by the constraints that even Sam McKee had to abide, she had dug up a wealth of information. While no one else might have noticed, except the kids, I knew that she was dying to tell me. The kids, of course, sensing something was up, were bouncing off the walls. Even so, she remained patient until they finally wore themselves out and fell asleep.

Glancing toward the hallway to our bedrooms, she said, "I think we need to take this to the garage."

Grabbing a couple of warm throws, I followed her and joined her in the front seat of the Forester. "They don't make these things for sparking, do they?" I observed.

Nicole laughed. "I bet if we set our minds to it we could figure out a way."

We were quiet a while before Nicole started talking. "Don't ask me how I got this information, Jazzbeau," she said. "You need to be able to honestly deny knowing the source."

I nodded. We had never discussed just how Nicole had been able to get the information on serial killers the police could not. I was not completely comfortable with this but I accepted it. What she could tell me without poisoning the evidence tree was where to look and what to look for. Nor was she a sworn peace officer.

"Do you remember the 1983 Brinks-Matt robbery at the Heathrow Trading Estate?" she asked.

"Yes. They called it the crime of the century and I think they even made a movie about it."

"That's right. The movie was called *Fool's Gold*. Sean Bean starred in it. To refresh your memory, a gang of six robbers broke in with the help of a security guard. They were after three million English pounds in cash but ended up with a haul of twenty-nine million in bullion, diamonds, and cash. After the robbery some of them were caught, others were murdered, and some went to prison for a long, long time. There were at least five homicides tied to the robbery and there was talk of a curse attached to the robbery. The bullion was never recovered. Any questions so far?"

I shook my head and Nicole continued. "Not long after the robbery two of the gang members were caught. One of them was Anthony Black, the security guard who let the gang into the warehouse where the stolen goods were stored. The other was his brother-in-law, one of the original five-man team."

"Where Daniella comes into the picture is that she witnessed something related to the robbery. At least, the police believed she did. They were under a lot of pressure to solve the case and recover the loot. So they were desperate and pulled in everyone with even the least connection to any of the robbers. It was her bad luck that she had been photographed dancing with one of the robbers at a Brixton night club several months before the robbery. She had dated him off and on for several months before they broke up on Halloween 1983. That was about a month before the robbery and the guy she was actually meeting apparently stood her up."

"Wait a minute. That was over a year before she was extradited. No, a lot more than that."

"Yes, there were a number of things the police failed to follow up in a timely way. There was also a lot of incompetence. A couple of days after the robbery a sharp eyed busybody spotted a white hot metal crucible in a neighbor's back yard. She called the police right away but the officers who responded said it was out of their assigned area. They did promise to notify the police for that area but it fell through the cracks. No one ever took a statement and the witness was never called to testify."

"So it took all that time for them to get around to Daniella?

I wonder why the Brits even bothered with witness protection."

"I wondered that, too. So I dug a little and apparently she demanded it in return for testifying. I'd guess that she liked the idea of becoming someone else and I can relate to that. What little I could learn about her family back ground tells me it was toxic. Like mine. It looked good on the outside but was rotten all the way through." Nicole's eyes were so sad when she said I took her in my arms. She began to sob softly.

"Why is mommy crying?"

I looked up to see our son, Jack, standing in the open door into the house.

"She was remembering something sad that happened a long time ago," I explained.

Nicole slipped out of my arms and opened the car door. "Come here, Jack. Mommy's all right. I was just very sad. I didn't have you or your sister to cheer me up back then."

Jack climbed into his mother's lap and Marie's head popped out from behind the door. She ran and climbed into my lap. The front of our sporty little SUV was getting rather crowded. "You know what we need?" I asked and my bride rolled her eyes, knowing what was coming.

"Who votes for ice cream?" I asked and there were cries of delight.

"You're shameless," Nicole said as we carried our children into the kitchen.

"I hope so," I told her and started to chant. "I scream, you scream!"

"We all scream for ice cream!" the children chanted back. Nicole just shook her head, but I noticed she ate her share, too.

New Partner

14 Wednesday morning there was a message in my voice mail to call the lab I'd used to analyze the sweetener in Trudy's apartment. The message said that they had sent a hard copy of the report to my address in Washington. It also gave me an extension number to call if I wanted a verbal summary of their report.

When I called the number given and the call was picked up by someone with an unfamiliar voice. After going through the security protocol we agreed to use when I had delivered the items I wanted screened, the technician who had done the analysis told me it was only the artificial sweetener that had been spiked. "All the other stuff was clean," the technician told me. "There was nothing in the salt or the pepper or in the salad dressing or other condiments. Nor in the lemons, croûtons or orange peel, either. It's lucky that no one was killed. If anyone had used more than two of the packets, they might have died. The particular form of meth that was used was highly concentrated and could have easily been lethal."

I asked the technician how the sweetener had been poisoned. I had taken a close look at the packets but had seen nothing. "It was very carefully done," she answered. There was a tiny hole in a crease in the bottom where the packets were crimped. I'd guess whoever it was used a very small hypodermic needle and sealed the hole with a tiny dab of transparent paper glue."

"So they went to a great deal of trouble to keep the meth from being detected," I replied, mostly talking to myself.

"Yes, that's what I think but that's your department. Personally, I think someone who would do something like that deserves to be fed their own poison."

"You may be right," I agreed. "On the other hand, that would make us just like them, wouldn't it? Thanks for being so quick. I may need to get back to you once I've read the full report."

I was thinking about this when my cell phone rang. It was Robert Delgado checking to see if I'd had a chance to talk to Sam McKee. I told him I had and explained the arrangement I had worked out with him. "Sam doesn't skimp on the important things but he's a real Scot when it comes to saving a few dollars. So this is a trial run to see how well we all work together. He's also a lawyer who doesn't like lawyers, so it tickles him having a law firm pay the piper."

"That part feels a little weird, you know, working for a law firm," Delgado told me.

"I know what you mean. Just remember, Dee and I are policemen, first and foremost. We follow proper procedure and our job is to investigate. When we're done we turn what we have over to the lawyers. Their job is to decide what needs to be done with what we give them, just like with the DA's office. The biggest difference is that we don't normally arrest people. When we do, it's a federal bust."

"I can live with that," Robert replied. "When do you want me to get started?"

"Let's shoot for the first of the week. That will give you a few days to do whatever you need to do. In the meantime, why don't you come to dinner tonight? I'd like you to meet my family."

I had no sooner hung up than my phone rang again. This time it was Nicole. "I ran your client through NCIC and checked him out in a couple of other places," she told me. "I found some interesting things. We need to talk."

I glanced at my wrist watch. It was just past eleven. "Well, how about an early lunch?" I suggested.

"All right, but let's talk first. Let's meet in the gym."

This surprised me but I agreed. I was surprised again to see Sam McKee sitting at a side table with Nicole when I arrived. "I asked Sam to sit in," Nicole told me. "I have a bad feeling about some of this and want his opinion."

"Of course," I said, wondering what in the world she had found.
"The first part is pretty straight forward," Nicole told us. "Nigel
was born in 1960 and grew up in the Bow-Bell district of the East
End of London. He went to neighborhood schools, made high
grades, and earned a scholarship to the Central School of Art and
Design. It's very prestigious. There he studied theater design and
photography and graduated *summa cum laude*."

Nicole paused and consulted her notes. "That was in the early
'eighties. Not long after graduation Nigel did his national service
in the RAF and ended up serving as a photographer and an aerial
photographer. He was promoted to intelligence officer during the
Falklands War and continued in the service afterward. Then he
was badly injured in a helicopter crash in 1985 and took medical
retirement in 1986."

Nicole looked at us to see if we had any questions, then went
on. "After he recovered, Nigel went to work with a public relations
firm and married for the first and only time in 1988. About that
time the company he was working for fell apart and Nigel went to
work for one of his clients as a cameraman and later as a producer.
He moved up the corporate ladder fairly quickly but in 1994 he
left his job to form Jolly Good Times. At first they subcontracted
with other production companies, including the one he had just
left, and then did a number of projects for BBC. Their first reality
show event was produced in 1998 but only scraped by until it was
renamed The Last One Left and became popular in the UK in
late 2001. The ratings went viral when Last One hit the American
market in the fall of 2002, and they began to produce two contest
events per year in 2004."

Nicole looked up and said, "This is where it gets strange. Nigel
and his wife moved to New York in 2002. They had been here
almost two years when his wife was brutally murdered in their
home. As the husband, Nigel immediately became the leading
suspect. He was cleared fairly soon by a strong alibi. He and his
Human Relations Director were cultivating a client at the time
of the murder, though the police tried to find a connection to a
hit-man. They were not successful and Nigel lived under a cloud

for almost a year before the perpetrator confessed after being arrested for two similar crimes. To date Nigel has rarely dated and has never had a significant other, male or female, since. He has, however, been known to employ high price call girls from time to time. To date he has never been arrested or convicted, not even for a parking violation."

I was stunned. "Why hasn't Trudy mentioned this?"

"Exactly," my bride agreed, her eyes as cold as glacial ice. "What other secrets has she kept from you and Dee?"

"Who is Trudy?" Sam asked.

Nicole looked and me and I nodded. "Trudy Howard is Nigel's HR director," Nicole told him. "She was Nigel Pleyer's alibi in the murder of his wife."

"It's none of my business but it sounds like you and Dee need to talk to her," Sam said, looking at me.

"No," said Nicole, her eyes even colder. "Jazz and I both do. She set herself up as Jazz's ally and then she weaseled her way into being my friend, too."

"I'll talk to Willard," I said. "Team Jazz is pulling off the case."

Sam held up a hand. Later he told me he had never seen me so angry. "This is none of my business," he said. "But you two are my friends. I'm here if you need to talk this through. I would suggest not making any hasty decisions."

I looked at Nicole and she nodded. "Thanks, Sam," I said. "We really appreciate it. You've got too much on your plate already. I think it would be better for us to talk to Sofya." Had I not been so angry I would have laughed at the look of relief on McKee's face. Then I had one of my intuitive insights. I knew Sam was aware of exactly why Nicole and I were so angry with Trudy and felt embarrassed. When we talked about this later Nicole told me she had the same sense of it.

I was in a much calmer frame of mind when I talked to Willard Nordwald late that afternoon. Nicole and I had gone directly to Sofya's office and, seeing the look on our faces, she had cleared her schedule for the rest of the morning and that afternoon. What ensued were two of the most intense hours of my life and when we were done, Sofya looked as wrung out as we were. "I know you both feel betrayed," she said as we were leaving. "That's natural to us who work in a world where betrayal is the norm. My sense is that it is probably a benign omission. It is likely Trudy never thought to mention this to you. It is equally likely that Nigel would assume you were aware of this since it is a matter of public record. I, of course, may be fooled. Naturally, I don't think so," she added with a tentative smile. Had the situation been less tense, that statement would have been funny. A detached side of me did note, however, that the more tense the situation was, the less accent Sofya had.

Fortunately, Willard was able to see me late that afternoon. Nor did I waste any time with polite preliminaries. "I don't walk away from cases, Willard," I told him, "but I am about an inch from doing exactly that right now. Your clients have been lying to me." I tried to keep my voice and my face calm as I said this but I felt myself trembling.

Willard sighed and shook his head sadly. "They always do, Jazz. They always do. How bad is it?"

"I don't know. It could be very bad. I'm convinced this is a case of serial murder and Dee and I are putting our lives on the line investigating it. Now it looks like the head of security was romantically involved with one of the contestants and may well be the killer's accessory. That, in and of itself, does not bother me. Daniella has been a suspect from day one, at least to me. What gets me is that no one bothered to mention that Nigel was involved in a murder investigation several years ago. Yes, he was cleared but Dee and I are both policemen. To us, hiding that fact puts him way up there on the suspect list."

Willard sighed again and shook his head. "I'm sorry, Jazz. This is my fault entirely. It simply didn't occur to me that you needed to know. It's public knowledge. I knew about it when Nigel became our client but it's a painful subject for him. What you probably don't know is that his wife was carrying their first child when she was murdered. Dom and Trudy told me he was completely devastated. Please believe me when I say there was no attempt to hide this. Not by me nor by anyone in our firm. Nigel probably assumes I told you."

I thought about that for a moment. Then I realized Sofya was probably right and Willard was probably telling me the truth. When I did I also realized that the only reason I felt so badly betrayed was my involvement with Trudy. I was sure this was also why Nicole was so angry, too.

I sighed. "Then it looks like I owe you an apology," I told him.

"Not at all," Willard assured me. "You're simply doing your job the way a policeman does. As a matter of fact, you strike me as far less cynical than most in your line of work. So let's move on. I'm very concerned over the situation with Daniella."

So I laid it out for Willard, chapter and verse. When I was done I summed it up. "Any one of these things can be explained away, even if they are combined with any one or two of the other items. Taken as a whole, they're pretty suspicious. Not conclusive, but quite suspicious. There could be an innocent explanation."

Willard gave me a wry smile. "But not beyond the reasonable shadow of doubt. From what you've told me, I think you may well be right. Assuming you are, please be very careful. This could be utterly devastating to Nigel."

"Oh, it gets worse," I told him. "A lot of my secondary information has come to me from Trudy Howard. She may be involved, as well. I tend to think she is not but you do need to know."

There was no mistaking Willard's surprise when I told him this. "Dear God, Jazz. She is the last person I would have suspected. I've known her and her husband for years."

"Like I said, I don't think there is anything there but I do need to look. I can't afford not to."

"Are you sure you want to stay with this investigation, Jazz? Given your suspicions, I wouldn't blame you for dropping it."

"No, I'd rather see it through if we can. Let me talk to Dee and see what he says. I imagine he'll want to stay on the case, too." I started to mention Robert Delgado but something kept me quiet. Nordwald had already given approval of hiring a third investigator and I had heaped enough on his plate for one day. So I took my leave and headed for home.

I was less than a block from Willard's office when I had a thought that chilled me to the bone. Robert Delgado had appeared in my life again out of the blue and was now almost part of our investigation team. Was this truly coincidence or had he subtly inserted himself into the investigation? This was something which serial killers were notorious for doing and I had just invited the man into the life of my family.

Pulling over I called Nicole and explained the situation. "Am I being unreasonably suspicious?" I asked my bride.

"Not really," she answered quite calmly. "At the moment I think you're still reacting to the situation with Trudy. I am, too, but Robert stopped by the office just after you left to talk with the lawyer. We visited for a while and nothing popped up on my slay-dar. After he left I checked him out again. I'm ninety-nine point nine percent sure he's exactly who he presents himself to be." Then Nicole's tone changed. "And if he's not, he just outsmarted himself and stepped straight into the lions' den." I knew better than ask what she meant.

The District of Columbia lies between Virginia and Maryland and was originally made up of parts of both states. Even though the city grew into a cosmopolitan cultural center, the original residents continued the traditional customs of the South. Among other things, this means that Wednesday evening is considered church night and teachers are encouraged to give minimal homework. The original intent may have been to give families time to attend midweek prayer services together, but the reality is that it quickly became a midweek family night.

Since that evening was a Wednesday, it meant it was pizza and take-out night at the Phillips' place. While Nicole and I like to mix things up ordering in, the kids always wanted pizza. This didn't mean they didn't poach a couple of bites from our plates, of course, but it didn't work the other way. To tell the truth, Nicole and I didn't care for the combinations they chose. Anchovies are fine once every year or two, but every week is way too much.

What was unusual that Wednesday evening was that we had a special guest and the kids loved it. We normally don't do this on family night but I had wanted to look at Robert Delgado in a different setting. Our kids took to him immediately, initially because he insisted they call him Bobby and shared their love of anchovies. Yet they also got to stay up later which is always a treat and he told them funny stories about his eccentric family. "I hope you don't mind the familiarity with the kids, Jazz," he told me as he was leaving. "I'm the youngest child of my family and I have nieces and nephews older than me. Your kids remind me of a couple of their kids."

I assured him it wasn't a problem. When he had left I fired up the gas fireplace and poured us each a glass of wine while Nicole put the kids to bed. "So what do you think?" I asked my bride as we sat in front of the fireplace sipping our wine.

"I think he's a lot like you," she answered. "I think he'll work well with you and Dee both. What I wonder is why he's still single."

"Two things," I said. "He told me the job had cost him a marriage when we first talked. He also said he was glad they didn't have any kids but I think he regrets it, too."

Nicole nodded. "That makes sense, especially with him being Roman Catholic and from a big family."

"Did I miss something? I don't think he mentioned being Roman Catholic."

"That's right, he didn't, did he?" Nicole said, staring into the fire. "He wasn't wearing any religious jewelry, either."

I started to ask how she knew he was Catholic but then I realized what my love was not telling me. She turned to me and smiled. "I like to know who's coming to dinner," she explained. "Particularly when he may be a suspect."

"Is there anything else I need to know?" I asked.

Nicole shook her head. "No, his resume is factual," she said. "Modest, too, as a matter of fact. Just like someone else I know."

She looked at me pointedly, then smiled. "Poor Dee. One of you is more than enough."

I realized then she had not just run a background check, but had gone much deeper, too. Then I realized the full implications. She had done this long before I asked Delgado to dinner and she had used sources unavailable to me. As usual, Nicole was way ahead of her doddering husband.

Seeing my comprehension, Nicole nodded. "I protect my family, Jazzbeau. That includes my man. If I'd had any questions, I would have cancelled out. I wouldn't let him anywhere near the kids." Seeing my next question in my eyes, she added, "No, I never looked at you or Dee. I knew I didn't need to."

"Nor I, you," I told her. "There was no way I could without...."

"I know," she said. Then she gave me a look I knew well. "Even so, maybe there is something you need to look into a little more deeply."

"Yes," I murmured. "Maybe there is."

Thursday morning I called Dee to find out how he was doing. As I thought he might be, he was feeling restless after a few days at home. "I love this place, Jazz. But there's only so much fishing I can do and so much golf before I start feeling stale. Thank God for the Internet but even that's not enough."

"That's why I'm still in the game, partner. As you know. And I have a new partner for you to break in if you like him." I told him about Robert Delgado and added that a copy of his resume was headed Dee's way. I also shared my reservations about the timing of his appearance. "Nicole checked him out, our sources and hers, both, and she is ninety-nine point nine percent sure he's legit. Like always, you've got veto if you want it. You're the one he'll be working with mostly, starting with Atlanta. And Nicole sends her condolences."

"Oh?" Dee asked. It was amazing how much meaning he packed into that single syllable.

"Yeah, she said he's very much like me."

"Two of you? I must have really pissed God off," he laughed.

"When do you want us to get started?"

"Monday morning if you can stand a couple more days in paradise." Dee and Karin's place is near Mountain Home, Arkansas, one of the most beautiful places on earth. "Or I could fly him up on Saturday if you want Sunday to get him up to speed." I gave him Delgado's phone number. "I'll check with Sam and see if we can get him a Homeland Security ID."

It turned out that Sam was a step ahead of me. When I called him about the official ID he told me one was already in the works. "I should have it for him by late tomorrow afternoon when I swear him in," Sam told me. "It will only be a provisional Agency ID for now. Once Robert is past his probationary period we'll think about whether he needs the full Homeland credential. For right now he should be all right flying with Dee. Just so you know, he will be required to carry, 24/7."

After Sam rang off, I sat there thinking where the investigation needed to go next. Looking through my notes to myself, I wrote out a list of questions I had not yet answered:

- What Last One events had Daniella attended personally?
- Who was responsible for the bug in the bakery table in the Jolly Good Times building?
- What was Daniella hiding – aside from what we had turned up so far?
- Do we need to take a closer look at Daniella's family background?
- What about the stalker fan theory? Who suggested it?
- Why did Daniella identify Mills if they are partners?
- What jurisdiction did she get her information from?
- Did killer set the records fire to protect himself or was the fire accidental?
- Is it true Mills is not in the electronic database? How to check this out without alerting killer?
- Is Mills dead or alive? Is/was he a real person?
- How do we handle situation with Trudy?

I was reaching for my phone to call Nicole about that last question when it rang. It was Trudy's ringtone and I was tempted to pick it up and confront Trudy. Yet this was Nicole's issue, too. So I let it go to voicemail and started to call Nicole once I was sure the line was clear. Just then my phone rang again, Nicole's ringtone this time, and I answered.

"Trudy just called me," my bride said. "I let it go to voicemail."

"The same here," I replied. The timing told me she had called Nicole first which was interesting. "I think we need to talk about how we want to handle this."

"We could pretend nothing had ever happened," Nicole suggested.

"We could if we thought she was a suspect," I replied. "Do we think that?" I could well imagine what a defense lawyer could do with the fact of my involvement with Trudy.

"I don't and I don't think you do, either, lover. So we need to talk. This whole situation points out how risky your involvement is. I'm not pointing the finger, either. I was my idea but it has the potential for a whole lot of grief. Not least of which is wrecking the investigation."

Even though I didn't believe what the three of us had done was wrong, we weren't the only people who would be affected if things went south. I knew Dee would be disappointed, as would Robert Delgado. I didn't anticipate any fallout from Sam or our friends at the Agency but it would be embarrassing for them. Word would get around, too, and my professional reputation would be tarnished.

"I think you and I need to spend the weekend in Seattle," I said.

Nicole chuckled. "Funny, I was just about to suggest that. Let me be the one to call. Or do you want to yourself?"

"I would really appreciate your doing that," I said. "I feel like a damned fool."

"There's a lot of that going around, Jazzbeau. If you really think about it, the whole thing's pretty funny. We'd probably laugh if we saw it on a sitcom."

"I'm afraid I don't see the humor in it just yet. Silly is about the best I can do." Yet when I hung up I realize I was smiling. Jazz the Beast-buster meets Inspector Clouseau.

Looking at my list of questions, I selected the first. What Last One Left events had Daniella attended personally? Digging through my briefcase I came to the master list I had requested, the one that included the original contests in the late 'nineties. Counting them I realized that there had been more than twenty last-man events and I wondered why it took so long for someone to see the pattern. My answer lay in the list of dead winners. Sorting these by cause of death I underlined violent deaths and double underlined suspected murder. What I came up with was nine dead, only three of whom were definitely homicides.

- James Spradley – auto crash Oregon coast
- Rick Hobart (winner) auto crash Utah – probably murder
- Loren Springer (partner) auto crash Utah
- Arnold Ritter – Yuma – cirrhosis or murder?
- Jarod Michaels – St Paul, murder (stabbing serial)
- Ronald Henley – Atlanta – murder (shooting)
- David Herold – Los Angeles – cancer
- Thor Knutsen – Las Vegas – (gang related shooting?)
- Hailey Beck – San Diego –?

Looking at the list of dead contestants, I saw that only four others could be homicides, too. Spread out as they were all over the country, it was no wonder why no one had seen the pattern. Based on that, it really was hard to discern the deaths as more than tragic coincidence. It had been Willard, not Daniella, who had noticed what he thought was a pattern after the death of James Spradley. It was he who pointed it out to Nigel. While this may have been a simple oversight on Daniella's part, it may have been deliberate, too. As Nigel's junkyard dog it would surely be within her job description to be on the lookout for anything out of the ordinary.

Looking at the master event list again, I saw that Daniella had been present at all but one event. Oddly enough, that was the one in which Hailey Beck, our player from San Diego, had competed. Suddenly I realized I didn't have any additional information on Beck or on Dee's trip to LA, and I wondered why. So I picked up my phone and called Dee.

"My mistake, Jazz," Dee told me. "I meant to tell you about Hailey Beck. I was focused on the guy in Yuma right then and it skipped my mind. I tried to call Pendleton and get some basic information but I hit a leather-neck wall. Nobody would talk to me and I had to drive ninety frigging miles each way. Then, when they saw that super dooper Homeland Security ID Sam gave me, they couldn't jump through their asses fast enough to oblige. The long and the short is that nobody seems to know where in the world Master Sergeant Hailey Beck is. He was last seen on a night training exercise off the coast and is now presumed lost at sea. He is/was quartered on base but none of his stuff is gone but the BDU he was wearing. Nothing in his secured workplace is missing, either, except the equipment he was carrying. That, by the way included his sniper gear. His spotter places him in the boat when the exercise started but he lost track of Beck during the assault. Now you see him, now you don't kind of deal. Makes me wonder."

"Yes, it sounds rather familiar, doesn't it?" I asked. Dee and I had worked more than one case where an alleged dead sniper had come back to life as a serial killer.

"Shades of Ed Posey and Wally Keller," Dee affirmed. "Not to mention that guy that killed the federal judge. You know who I mean, the McMullen cousin, the one who crapped his pants."

"Otis Dan Searcy," I replied. "So what else did you get from the Marines?"

"Not a whole lot. They didn't want to talk about what Beck actually did for them but they did allow he was a sniper and hinted around black ops. One of his cohorts did let it slip that he didn't know why Beck was even on the training exercise. He wasn't really a member of the unit. The company captain confirmed that. He was surprised when I told him Beck was a survival show prize winner."

"Beck wasn't a winner," I replied. "He was a contestant and was on the dead list we were given but he didn't win the event. I think the event winner that time was James Spradley."

"My bad," Dee said.

"Don't worry about it. What about his personal life?"

"The captain wasn't aware he had one. He told me Beck was a loner and was not married. Never had been according to his file."

"I'm starting to like Beck as our killer," I told Dee.

Dee blinked. "Now you mention it, I see what you mean. No ties, low profile, very secretive and gets paid to kill people. We should all have it so good. Wasn't sitting on a cool million, either. Be easy for him to resent those who were."

"From what you say about Pendleton, I don't think we'll get very far with the Corps. I think this may be a job for Sam."

"I think you're right and he did tell you to ask," Dee pointed out. "He has the connections."

"You're right about that," I said, making myself a note to call Sam. "You been in touch with Delgado yet?"

"Yeah, he's coming in Sunday morning. I'll meet him in Little Rock and we'll head out on Monday. Seems like a sharp kid." Then he laughed. "Your wife's right. He comes across a lot like you."

I sat at my desk after I hung up. I had the feeling there was something important I had overlooked. It had something to do with James Mills, something I should have asked Sam. Then, when I thought back over our conversation, I realized what it was. I had focused on other details and never asked how James Mills died.

Despite what Sam had told me, I had the feeling that the balance of markers lay in his favor. So rather than bother him I decided to go directly to the source and called the department in Bethlehem, Pennsylvania. I'm glad I did. Talking cop to cop I think I got a lot more information.

I was lucky to catch the Chief of Police still at his desk and it turned out he was someone I had met earlier on another case. "So what are you up to these days, Jazz?" the chief asked. "Still going after serial killers?"

"Actually, not so much these days. The case I'm on looks like one at work but mostly I go after corporate criminals now."

"Well, you keep some interesting company. McKee and I go back to Vietnam." The way he said this told me this was not necessarily favorable.

"Believe it or not, Chief, a lot of the crime I go after goes all the way back to then, too."

"I can believe it. That was a real cesspool. Still is from all I hear. What can I do for you?"

"Sam told me about your John Doe murder victim and I think he's tied to the case I'm on. I'm not sure exactly how, either. He may have been an accomplice to the killer I'm after. Or not."

The chief agreed. "Yeah, that might fit if there was a falling out betwixt them. Our first thought from the beat up condition of the corpse was that it either a random mugging or a drug deal gone bad. That didn't really make a lot of sense considering the bullet was a single military hard ball .223, and that it penetrated the victim's chest exactly in the center of the sternum. It looked like precision shooting. We decided it probably was not a random killing by some citizen playing with his new assault rifle. Current thinking is that we were looking at two, or possibly three, separate crimes, two assaults and a difficult homicide shot from over five hundred meters."

"You found the sniper's nest?"

"No, we found three possibilities, but no tracks, no brass, nothing but random trash. Take your pick, but it was damned accurate shooting from just over five hundred meters out to a little over seven hundred and fifty. Not your everyday hunter."

"What time of day do you think?"

"That's just it. It was damn near a night shot if the ME got the timing right – a half hour after sundown to right about midnight. It wasn't a well lit area, either. I don't see how he did it."

Things came together in my mind then in one of those intuitive leaps Dee talks about. I realized exactly how it could have been done. "Are you an ex-smoker, Chief"

The chief snorted. "No-ex about it, Jazz. Why?"

"How about the victim. Was he a smoker, too?"

"The ME reported he was. Stained fingers, lips, teeth. What do you have?"

"A wild idea, Chief, but bear with me. Imagine you're standing outside at night having a smoke. Go through the motions of taking a puff just a moment before taking a second puff. Where does your hand rest in between?"

"Well, I'll be a coon-ass cajun! That *ventre du biche* shot at the cigarette glow, didn't he!"

"What did your ME say about the age of the victim's bruises?" I pushed on.

"Said most of them were at least a week old. Only a couple on the face looked new. Now, you tell me something, Jazz. Why didn't McKee ask me all this? All he seemed interested in was the woman."

"McKee's not a policeman, Chief, not like you and me. Our mission is to keep the peace. We're trained to be prepared for emergencies and to respond whenever the bad guys pop up on the radar. McKee is military, Special Forces. He was trained for intelligence analysis and tactical assessment. His mission is to find the enemy and to go after him before something happens."

"I see." The chief sounded unconvinced.

"A big difference is that the law does not allow us to be proactive the way McKee can be. A lot of what we do is reconstructing crimes and gathering evidence to go after a conviction. What Sam does is gathering intelligence and going directly after the bad guys before they can act. Rough justice is fine with him. Where you and I have to have probable cause, all he needs is probable intent."

"Yeah? Well, he sounds like a spook to me. So what do you do for him, assuming you can tell me?"

"I sometimes wonder. I'm mostly his policeman, I think. That's especially true when it comes to detecting crime in the corporate boardroom. I seem to be able to find lies in spreadsheets. Sam claims it's voodoo."

I paused, wondering how far to go. The chief sensed this. "So what are you not telling me, Jazz?"

"Well, I may be right or I may be full of crap, but it seems like Sam depends on me to help keep things honest. His agency operates in the gray areas of the law sometimes. That's where the bad guys operate and I help keep things righteous as opposed to strictly kosher legally. I'm like a bellwether Sam uses to keep from being one of the bad guys, too."

The chief chuckled. "That's a term I don't hear very often these days and you're talking to an English major here, Jazz. Are you aware of the origins of bellwether?"

"Yes, I am. That's why I said 'like a bellwether,' Chief. Nobody wants to think of themselves as a neutered billy-goat. I wish you well but you won't hear me wishing you a 'nice' day, either."

The chief laughed. "That really used to tickle me, too. When I heard someone say that I sometimes asked if they meant lewd, lascivious, or just plain bawdy."

The chief cleared his throat and I knew he wasn't quite done yet. "You know, Jazz. what would be useful to me is an outside opinion. I know you don't have much information but what do you think? Is the shooting tied to the bruises, you think, or are we looking at two separate crimes."

"Well, off the top of my head and with my feet firmly planted in midair, I can imagine the victim having something the killer wants. It could be money the dead guy owes or information the killer needs or something the killer wants done. There's not much telling which one but the killer beats the tar out of the victim just to let him know he – the killer – is serious. Say it's money owed. The killer gives the victim so many days to deliver and sets up the date and place for exchange. The killer has already scouted his killing field out and zeroed in his vectors. On the night appointed he tells the victim to show up at a certain time and to stay put for an hour, maybe more. At the appointed hour the killer makes sure the coast is clear and sets up in his nest. When the victim lights up his cigarette the killer waits for just the right moment and fires. One shot dead center of central mass does the trick. Killer waits and watches through the scope to make sure victim is dead."

"Damn, I can see it happening exactly that way. Any way this ties into your case?"

The chief seemed eager to get rid of the case and I couldn't blame him. On the other hand, I needed to be honest. "You don't know how much I wish it did, Chief. Or maybe you do. I just can't see any way it fits. The facts we know just don't line up. Except for who the victim is, I can't see any tie.

The Emerald City

15 Our trip to Seattle turned out to be a wonderful adventure. We left the East Coast on a direct flight Friday morning that seemed to arrive earlier than we departed. Nicole and I also treated ourselves to first class seats round trip. Of all the amenities our extravagance bought us, the ones I appreciated most were ample personal space and the quality of the food. The best result, however, was that when we stepped off the plane I felt rested and so did my bride. She was feeling frisky, too, and the moment the bellhop closed the door, I found myself pinned to the floor.

Since Trudy was tied up until late Sunday evening with a family gathering, we spent what was left of Friday and all the next day doing the tourist things. Even though I thoroughly enjoyed this, I found myself feeling a little blue. Nor could I figure out why when Nicole asked if something was wrong.

"Is it confronting Trudy?" Nicole asked. "Are you worried about what she might tell us?"

"No, I actually feel pretty good about that. I don't expect any real surprises. When did you first notice me sinking?"

"It was yesterday afternoon when we started talking about what we wanted to do while we're here. We were talking about the rain and the clouds. You seemed bothered that we might not be able to see Mount Rainier."

Then it was there, as clear and undeniable as the mid-day sun. "I'm sorry, Nicole, it never occurred to me."

"What never occurred to you, Jazzbeau?" she asked gently.

"The last time I was here was just before I was almost killed by the bomb. I was on a case and Jeanne flew out to keep me company. Her flight almost crashed in Portland and the two of us drove up to see Mount Saint Helen that evening. It was a clear night and a full moon."

"That sounds very romantic," Nicole murmured. I realized my silence didn't fool her for a moment.

When I looked into her eyes I saw nothing but love and I made a decision. So I told her how Jeanne and I had made love in the back sear of the convertible I had rented and Nicole laughed when I told how we had almost been interrupted by the Oregon highway patrol. "The serial bomber we were after had struck again in Seattle," I said, "and Sam put out an APB to find me. We ended up chasing the patrol officer at high speed under a full moon with the top down all the way back to the hotel."

There were tears in Nicole's eyes when I was done. She reached out and touched me gently on the cheek. "No wonder you were sad, Jazzbeau," she told me. "I wish I had known Jeanne. She seemed like such a wonderful person."

"I'm sorry it intruded in our time together," I replied.

"I'm not. It's all part of the story of how the wonderful father of my children came into my life. I'm not jealous of Jeanne or Nellie or any of the women who were part of your life. They are part of what made you who you are." She smiled. "That includes Trudy, too."

"I take it we've forgiven her?" I said, surprised.

"I have," Nicole said. "I hope you have, too. We need to confirm it by talking to her but, yes."

"Does that mean I'm off the hook?" I asked.

Nicole laughed. "Of course, you are, silly man. You make it sound like durance vile. I'm not going to force you back into her bed. I'm not going to be jealous if you choose to do so, either."

"Why would I even want her in my bed when you're there?" I asked. I was dead serious.

Nicole gave me a look that pushed my tachometer from normal to the red line in a split second. "Somebody better watch out talking like that," she murmured. "He just might get jumped."

While I had not been to Seattle for a number of years I was

delighted to find it had not lost its charm. We happened to pick one of those rare weekends the clouds cleared away and it was easy to see why the place was called the Emerald City. Even so, we still wore waterproof rain parkas and had umbrellas folded away in our backpacks, as did most of the people I saw on the street. Wind chill is always a factor, too, particularly when it's wet, and it was getting late in the year. Christmas was not that far away.

Seattle is not only a major seaport and industrial center, it is also a wonderful place for tourists. The problem is not finding something to do but choosing which ones. Since the weather was so good, we decided to put Woodland Park Zoo and the Space Needle at the top of our list for Saturday, with Chihuly Garden and Glass in reserve if the weather changed. I also wanted to visit the Museum of Flight History and the Pacific Science Center, and Nicole wanted to take a tour of Safeco Field.

We did make it to the Space Needle and to the zoo on Saturday, but we spent most of our time walking and talking and being lovers in a user-friendly city. Along the way we visited specialty shops and somehow I ended up with a new camera I had been lusting after for years. On my own I don't think I would have bought it, but Nicole insisted. She clinched the deal by offering to pose *au naturale,* and she made good on her promise the very next morning. Our room was on the east side of the hotel and the light on the balcony could not have been better. Nor could the lovemaking that followed.

Even so, the surprises for Jazz weren't over. Nicole was very mysterious about it when she asked me to get dressed in a coat and tie that afternoon. Nor did she yield a thing when she got a taxi and handed the driver the address. When the driver started to ask her something, she just shushed him. "It's a special surprise for Daddy," she told him in a deep Delta accent. "He's from Arkansas," she added, as if that would explain everything!

Apparently it did. "Ah," he said, a bright grin breaking across his dark face like a sunrise. Looking at me, he nodded and said, "Well, you're in for a wonderful time, sir."

I was so baffled I really didn't have a clue what Nicole was about until our cab stopped in front of a large church building. Yet I still didn't understand why we were there. The sign in front told me we were at the Mount Zion Baptist Church. It wasn't until we walked in the front door and I heard the music that I got it. "This is a little late for Sunday services, isn't it?" I asked Nicole. A man walking by looked at us and laughed.

"It's a special benefit concert," Nicole told me as we joined the line going in. "I was afraid you had seen the poster at the hotel. The desk clerk told me about them. He says it's the best gospel music around."

The woman with the man walking by said, "Amen, brother!" I didn't know if she was talking to me or about the desk clerk.

"All proceeds go to the Soul's Rest homeless shelter," said an usher with a wide grin, handing us a program. "So reach deep, brother! The poor folk down there need it worse than we do."

We found seats and just as we were getting settled the organist kicked things off with a mighty chord. What followed was three hours of incredible gospel music unlike anything I'd ever heard. Some of it was lively and I found myself singing along, clapping my hands like a fool and shuffle dancing in the pew. Two minutes later my bride was right there with me, her long dark hair flying in every direction. Some of the hymns were soul wrenching and brought tears to my eyes as I remembered the many times Jeanne and I attended the little black church in Oak Grove, not far from where she lived in Hope. Some of the more contemporary pieces were satire, poking fun at pastors with "narrow minds and wide lapels." All of it was deeply moving and at the end of the service I was surprised how quickly the time had gone.

At the end of the service one of the junior clergy and his wife both insisted on giving us a ride back to the hotel. They seemed a bit disappointed when they learned we were from the other side of the country. I think the point of the ride was to recruit us and when he learned I was a policeman, the deacon a bit looked rather nervous. I wondered what lay behind it, personal history or simply a guilty conscience over some venial transgression. Yet I assured him I was on vacation and didn't even bring my cuffs. When I did I could see my bride was having a hard time not laughing.

"That was the most incredible experience," Nicole told me as I unlocked the door. She looked both awestruck and frightened. "I don't know what came over me, Jazzbeau. I've never done anything like that."

"The folk at Mount Zion would tell you it was the Holy Ghost."

"Oh, God! I was afraid you'd say that. Did I embarrass you?"

"Of course not!" I told her. "This is the way these folk worship all the time. Did I embarrass you?"

Nicole shook her head. "No. I need to talk about this, but not right now. I think I just hit the wall. I'm totally beat."

"Of course, sweetheart," I replied. I began to undress her and toss aside her clothes. When I was done I slipped an extra big tee over her head and tucked her into bed. Then I undressed and joined her but she was not yet asleep.

"I never heard you sing like that before," Nicole told me. "Could you sing me that hymn again, the one you really liked at the end of the service? The one about grace?"

So I took my bride in my arms and I began to sing softly. As I did tears began to run down her cheeks. Yet it was after I started the second verse that the floodgates burst. Even so, I didn't stop singing.

'Twas grace that taught my heart to fear
And grace my fears relieved.
How precious did that grace appear
The hour I first believed.

It was the next thing Nicole said that stunned me. I knew she carried a great burden of self-imposed guilt, but until that moment I hadn't realized just how great. "Don't you see what that means, Jazz?" she sobbed when I was done. I didn't answer and simply held her close until she was done weeping. "Do you remember telling me about the look in Victor Shupe's eyes just before he died?"

I nodded. Shupe was one of the most vicious serial killers I have ever seen. "I don't think I will ever forget," I told her. "Or what Forster says Victor saw in my eyes, either." The old priest had told me that what Victor saw in me was the joyful face of a celestial Father waiting eagerly to bring his lost son home.

"Well, I always had trouble believing it was true. Then that song really brought it home to me, Jazz. What it means is that if there's hope for serial killers like Victor Shupe, then there's hope for people like me, too."

Nicole was still wiped out the next morning, so much so that she slept late. This was very unusual. So I decided to stay in Seattle another day. Nor was there a problem arranging child care for our kids. Jack and Martha were in town and the kids were having a wonderful time with the McKee clan. Then Nicole got up about noon and insisted on going ahead with the interview with Trudy. "I'll feel better if I am up and around," she declared and by the time Trudy arrived at the hotel, she seemed mostly recovered.

Nor did we spend much time in pleasantries when we began. Since I was the lead investigator, I intended to take the lead with the interview once we were seated. Yet Nicole preempted me smoothly. "There's an issue we need to clear up about the investigation before we visit," she told Trudy bluntly. "What we need to know is why you didn't tell us that your boss has been involved in a murder investigation once before."

Trudy was startled by the hard, almost cold look in Nicole's eye. "I started to tell Jazz a couple of times but it didn't seem relevant," she answered, holding Nicole's intent gaze. "The two cases didn't seem related."

"That may be true, Trudy, but Jazz was the one who needed to make that determination," Nicole replied. "I think any policeman would think it necessary to make sure of that."

"I certainly wasn't trying to hide anything," Trudy told her.

"You do understand how that would seem from our point of view don't you?" I chipped in. "Particularly with us sleeping together."

"Do you honestly believe I seduced Jazz to hide the facts?" Trudy snapped at Nicole, ignoring me. "I thought we were friends."

"I thought so, too," Nicole said calmly. "That made it worse in my eyes." The two women glared at each other for a long minute. I was about to say something when I saw something happen. Their eyes filled with tears and suddenly they were holding one another.

"I'm not your killer," Trudy told Nicole. "It hurts me that you might think so. I have a hard time swatting flies."

"I never really did think so," Nicole assured her gently as I sat there struck dumb by what I had witnessed. "Why don't you tell us about it?"

Trudy pulled back a bit and nodded. "Nigel was courting a new client, a new event sponsor, as a matter of fact. So it was a major pitch and he asked me to help him with the presentation. Since there was an elaborate dinner before the actual presentation we ran late into the evening. And since it was a business meeting, Susan didn't attend. She really wasn't interested in the company or the business end of things, though she did like to come along on competitive events once in a while. She even made some suggestions that we used to make the events more attractive to our viewers."

She paused a moment, gathering her thoughts. "Anyway, Nigel and Susan had moved here from England a couple of years before she was killed and Susan was not happy about it at all. They apparently had quite an active social life back home and that all went away when they moved. Nor was Susan able to see her family very often. She was very close to them."

Trudy shook her head sadly. "Looking back, I can see it was a recipe for disaster. They had no children and Nigel was very busy with the company then. Even more than he is now. He traveled a lot all over the United States and took Susan with him whenever he could. Yet there wasn't much for her to do while he was conducting business and she began to hate road trips. She was not hesitant to tell him about it either. So he left her home more and more often, traveling with me and Daniella, scouting locations and making assessments. This only added fuel to the fire of Susan's resentment. She became jealous of both me and Daniella, and she did not hesitate to make her displeasure known to us."

Trudy stopped speaking and we waited patiently. "Unfortunately,

Susan did not hesitate to express her feelings at the office, too. Nor could we predict when she might storm in out of the blue or fly off the handle. And all this was much worse during the two months before she died. Now we understand what was behind 'this. Susan was pregnant but no one knew it. Nor did we know she was having an affair, too. I am not sure even she knew she was pregnant and Nigel, of course, didn't have a clue. I have never seen him so surly. Staff morale went to pieces and I had to confront him about it more than once."

Trudy smiled. "Yes, Jazz, I can be blunt and implacable when necessary. Nobody likes me much when I do." Nicole smiled when Trudy said that. "This is particularly true with Nigel and every once in a while he gets angry and fires me. Then the next day, he calls and hires me again. This has happened several times and it used it to drive my husband crazy."

"Were Susan and Nigel living in New Jersey or New York when the murder happened," I asked.

"Oh, they were living in New Jersey. Nigel doesn't mind spending for quality but he is a real Scot when it comes to pitching a penny. The truth is, you can get the same quality for a lot less on this side of the Hudson."

"I don't suppose you remember the names of the investigating officers, do you," I asked.

"Actually, I do. One was a tall black man named MacIntosh and his partner, Winston, said, 'Like the Apple.' When we were done, Mac told us – my husband sat in on all the interviews as my attorney – that murder cases were very rare in the part of the city where they lived. I could tell neither of the officers liked Nigel very much. They were very methodic when they put him through the wringer but they were not abusive. Later I told Nigel that the reason the officers were so rough on him was because of his attitude and not theirs. That was one of the times he fired me, and for two days! I told him the only reason he hired me back was to have a friendly character witness. By then, he had calmed down a bit and he actually laughed. Then he absolutely fell apart." The memory brought tears to Trudy's eyes.

I had a sudden flash. "So it was you who held the company

together through that time, wasn't it?"

Trudy nodded. "Yes, me and my husband, Norman. That's how we became partial owners of Jolly Good Times. Cash flow was a problem and we let Nigel pay us in shares."

"How much of the company do you own?" I asked.

"I'm not sure. My accountant could tell you. It's only ten or twelve percent. I let Nigel vote my shares."

"What about Susan's affair?" I asked. "What do you know about that?"

"Very little, actually. I was surprised to hear about it and poor Nigel was devastated. There was apparently a mystery man involved but not even the police could find out who the man was. He was very elusive. They grilled all of us very thoroughly. Nobody had a clue."

"Didn't the police say anything at all about him?"

"They were very reticent about what they knew. That was one of the big issues Nigel had with them. They wouldn't tell him anything."

"How did they find out about the mystery man?" I asked.

"I'm not sure," Trudy answered. "That was one of the things he wanted most to know."

"Well, I would have done the same if I had been the investigator," I said. "I imagine they suggested he might have hired it done. That is something I would check out carefully, too. The mystery man could have been the killer. Since they could not find out anything about him, that itself would suggest that he was a contract killer. At least that's what it suggests to me. Professionals are very good at leaving no trace. That is how they stay out of prison. With some of them it seems like the Devil is taking care of his own. They seem to have incredibly good luck. Of course, for a lot of them that luck runs out at some point. I suppose they grilled you about the mystery man, too."

"They sure did. They even suggested that Nigel and I were lovers. That was a big mistake. They did not realize it at first but the company lawyer – Nigel's lawyer – was also my husband. Norman is a big man and he was in their faces in a New York second. Winston was the one who asked and I thought Norman was going to punch him out. The way Winston asked was way beyond impolite. Mac came as close to apologizing as a policeman ever does."

"I never understood that," I replied. "There is no excuse for poor manners. Nor is being judgmental called for. Our job is to collect evidence and turn it over to the prosecutor. It is not really any of our business after that. Except to testify in court. Even then our job is to present the evidence in a professional manner. That may not be very entertaining to the jurors or the audience, but we are police officers, not actors."

I suddenly realized that Nicole and Trudy were looking at me oddly, and I also realized I was ranting. "He as a thing about celebrity cops and judges," Nicole explained to Trudy. "You should hear Jazz talk to the TV when one of them comes on. Sometimes I have to remind him that little ears are taking in his colorful language."

"Oh, they learn it from their mom, too," I assured Trudy and she smiled. "That's who taught them to cuss in Cajun." Turning to Nicole, I asked, "Is there anything else you need to know, love?"

Nicole shook her head. "We can always call and ask if there is." She got up and stretched. "I'm still sore from all that religious exercise," she told me. To Trudy she explained. "We went to Mount Zion Baptist last night for a gospel benefit. Things were really jumping."

Trudy and I got up, too, but Nicole shook her head. "No, please stay, Trudy. I need to go for a long walk, to be with myself and get the kinks out. I'll be back in a couple of hours and we can visit then. Jazz can bring you up to date." Nicole smiled and then looked pointedly at me and Trudy and the bed. Then, without another word, she slipped on her rain parka and left. A moment later Trudy was in my arms.

Trudy insisted on taking us to the airport on Tuesday morning. She picked us up at the hotel and we had an unhurried breakfast together at the airport before our flight. When we were finished,

Nicole hugged Trudy and waited with our carry on stuff while I walked Trudy back through security. "Thank you, Jazz," she told me, kissing me lightly on the lips. "That was wonderful, meeting Nicole in person and being together with the two of you. You're a wonderful couple and you fit well together. I want to meet your children soon."

"They have their moments," I said. "They can really little hellions, too, when they put their minds to. Fortunately, they don't choose to do that very often."

"What do they call you, if you don't mind my asking?"

"Would you believe Papa Jazz?" I told her and Trudy laughed. "They think it's funny when some of my adopted grandkids call me Grandpa Jazz."

"My goodness, you have a complicated family," she told me. "One of these days, I'd like to see your family pictures."

"Oh, it gets even better," I replied. "The agency I work for is run like an extended family. As a matter of fact, a lot of the people who work there are closely related."

"How in the world they get around the nepotism laws?"

"I have wondered that myself," I confessed. It has something to do with the original charter and a lot of our people were not married to each other when they went to work there. Our acting head is a lawyer, himself, and he has apparently figured out a way to do it. For me, it is mostly don't ask don't tell. Nicole and I are both independent contractors, which allows for a lot of flexibility."

"This was quite a weekend, husband," Nicole said as we snuggled together in our seats. That was easier said than done. First-class seats are not built for snuggling. "I had no idea I was in for such a religious experience. It was wonderful but I'm glad I didn't know about it ahead of time. I don't think I would've suggested going."

"Suggested is not what comes to mind," I declared. "Kidnapping was more like it."

"Well, you seemed to get with the program pretty quickly," she said with a smile. "As a matter of fact, you were the source of my inspiration. So it's all your fault."

I laughed. "Well, my love, maybe it was and maybe it wasn't. I think Someone is messing around in your life and in mine, too."

"That is what makes it so scary. I know you and I trust you. I'm not so sure about a Someone I don't know very well. The Someone I encountered at Mount Zion was about joy. That's not the Someone I was told about growing up. If I had to name that someone, I would call him Killjoy. There's not much room for joy in all that hellfire and brimstone they talked about."

"Well, that gets back to the preachers that lady was singing about. You know, the ones with narrow minds and wide lapels."

Nicole smiled and nodded. "I really liked her. And speaking of joy, how was your...reunion with Trudy?"

I sighed. "It was wonderful, what else would it be? It was almost as wonderful as reunions with my wife."

"So not an A+?"

"More in the high B range, I'd say," I told her. "But I'm feeling a little uneasy about this, sweetheart. I think we're wandering into minefield, giving grades. If there's much more interrogation about it I think I'm going to have to plead the Fifth. Besides, it's like comparing apples and oranges."

"You're probably right, but I'm curious. Which one am I?"

"The apple," I said with conviction. "Of course. You're definitely the apple of my eye."

"Well, as long as it's not the apple of your horse...."

Due to the change in our flight, the return trip home was not direct. We were able to stay with the same airplane, as was our luggage. However, there was a ninety-five minute layover in the Twin Cities for cleaning and maintenance, refueling and taking on supplies. So all the passengers were herded off the plane while the ground crews were at work. We were told to take our carryons with us, which slowed the process down.

Nicole used the layover to stretch her legs walking up and down the concourse while I guarded our things. I hadn't heard back from Dee about the investigation in Atlanta so I decided to give him a call. When I took out my phone I saw that I'd had two calls from him while we were in flight. One was just after we boarded the flight in Seattle, when I had put my phone on airline mode. The other was just before we landed in Minneapolis-Saint Paul.

As always, it was good to hear Dee's voice and even better to listen to his humor. "I've got to tell you, Jazz, working with Bobby Delagdo is like turning the time back thirty years. He's so much like you I keep expecting him to know stuff you would remember better than me. Only he doesn't have a clue what the hell I'm talking about."

"There is a just God!" I declared, laughing. "It's atonement for all your sins against truckers."

Dee thought that was funny. "Seriously, Jazz, the kid is a real go-getter. Just watching him makes me sweat. Once he gets his teeth and something he's worse than you are and he's got damned good instincts. He loves frozen yogurt too. The only thing is, yogurt doesn't like him, not at all. Honest to God, Jazz, when he eats the stuff we have to drive with a window open."

"So there is justice," I said, reminding him of all the years we spent in a patrol car. It was so bad I started calling Dee Gasius Maximus and it caught on with other guys in the Patrol. "What do you have on the case?"

"Turns out our contestant from Atlanta was a retired Marine gunnery sergeant," Dee told me. "That makes two jarheads as victims, but I don't think there's a connection. They were on different events. This one's name was Ronald Henley and according to the detective on the case, he died being in the wrong place at the wrong time. He was a runner and ran a river trail along the Chattahoochee. First time the local dick said that I said, 'Gesundheit!' Ron's course took him by the only convenience store for miles. It's a popular resting point for runners. But it was a very cold morning and the sergeant was out early. No one was around that morning but the store clerk."

Dee cleared his throat and I heard the sound of ruffled pages. I realized he was filling in the blanks from his case notes. "What killed him was a through and through gunshot wound to the throat. The bullet tore out the main carotid artery and part of the spinal cord. So the gunny died very quickly, from bleeding out or hydrostatic shock. From the damage done, the ME thinks the weapon was much bigger than a ten millimeter or a forty-four caliber full metal jacket, but the slug was never found. What surprised the ME was how much damage it did without spalling. Said he had never seen a wound quite like that from a handgun."

"So what are the local police looking for then, a rifle or a shotgun?"

"They're actually leaning toward a twelve gauge sawed-off shotgun using a slug but that doesn't make much sense to me. There's not much cover near where the gunny fell. Closest good cover was thirty-odd yards away. Not many could nail a running target that small at that range with rifle, much less a sawed-off or a pistol. Not even with a scope."

"A shotgun?" I asked. "Maybe the shooter was aiming for the torso and hit high," I said. "A twelve-gauge or a twenty-gauge rifled slug might fill the bill. I gather there were no witnesses."

"Not a one. The store clerk thought he might have heard something but he couldn't be sure. He was listening to heavy metal and has the tats to prove it."

"Did you talk to the gunny's family?"

"The local dicks did. Thing is, he and his wife had been separated for a while and she and the kids live in San Diego. I listened to a recording of the phone interview. It didn't seem worth backtracking out there."

"We can always do that later," I said. "We've got better leads here. What about physical evidence?"

"There wasn't any. No shell casings, no bullet, no trace evidence. This killer was very careful, Jazz." This told me Dee suspected we might be dealing with a professional, too. "So how about you?"

I filled him in on all I'd learned. "We need to run down James Mills, to find out what he's been up to all this time. I want to take a close look at Daniella, too. Something's not quite kosher with her."

"Well, she is an odd duck, all right," Dee allowed. "I wouldn't put her that high on the list but you've had a lot more contact with her than I have. You done a background check on her?"

I explained the problems I saw looking at the company files and running a normal check. "I think I'm going to ask Sam to do a deeper background check on her and on Nigel, too. He can do it without alerting anyone. I'll run them through NCIC myself."

"Daniella, I understand, but why Nigel? He doesn't make sense. He's the one who hired us. You have a hunch?"

"No, but I try to check out a client first. I didn't this time since I'm working for Nordwald. There may be something back there in Nigel's history we need to know. Call it due diligence."

"I thought we left that crap behind when we retired," Dee grumbled.

"The difference is that I'm doing it for us, not someone else. Then, too, this is anything but a normal case."

"Are you kidding?" Dee snorted. "None of our cases are normal these days, Jazz. I don't think I'd know normal if it bit me in the ass. I don't think you would, either."

"You have a point there, partner," I replied. "Anything else?"

"No, you and Nicole have a good flight home." Something in the way Dee said this told me he had turned a corner in how he looked at Nicole. Like many other policemen of our generation he believed premeditated homicide deserved punishment. While we would never talk about this, I sensed that he now considered what Nicole had done as a public service.

I thought about Daniella Cooper on the final leg of our flight home that afternoon. When I did, I had an interesting thought. What if the conspiracy was wider than just Daniella and the killer? What if Daniella, James Spradley, and John Mills were in cahoots? Or what if it was limited to Daniella and Spradley? John Mills could then be a red herring Daniella used to divert team Jazz. Yet why does Daniella continue to kill after the death of her accomplice? it could be simple resentment. 'If James and I cannot have the million bucks, then nobody else will live to enjoy their prize.'Her goal might then be to take them all out.

Somehow, Daniella was the key. Or so I thought, but what if I was wrong? What if she was simply a tortured soul who didn't know how to be a normal human being? There were lots of those around and being troubled is not a crime. Or what if it is, I thought, and spaceship Earth is just one vast prison?

At the thought, I laughed aloud and Nicole gave me an odd look. When I explained why I laughed she rolled her eyes and shook her head. "There are times I believe you think too much, husband," she said. "I like your idea that this is purgatory better. At least, that way there is hope."

"Hope?" I replied. "Hope is a city in Arkansas."

"Actually, there are 26 places called Hope in the United States," she informed me. "There are 50 such places in the world."

"Somebody has been searching the Internet, hasn't she?"

"So it appears," she replied, looking pleased with herself.

"And you have been just waiting to tell me this, haven't you?"

"Ever since the last time we had this conversation," she smiled. "So what is bothering you, Jazzbeau?"

When I explained, Nicole nodded. "I think Daniella has been driving your investigation," she told me. "You seem fixated on her. How would things be if you could take her off your list of suspects? Where else could you look?"

I was stupefied. "I don't know," I admitted. "It would be a whole new ball game. I'll have to think about that."

"You do that," she replied, smiling. She gave me a gentle kiss to take any sting out of her words.

I kissed her back and settled into my seat for a nap. My bride was right, as she normally was when it came to me. Sufficient unto the day is the stewing thereof. I had done enough thinking for the moment. So I turned my thoughts to our children and how happy I would be to see them.

Troubled Waters

16 When I got into the office Wednesday morning, the first thing I did was to call Willard Nordwald and bring him up to date. When he heard that we had been to Seattle to question Trudy, who was on leave, Willard insisted that I put our expenses on the Jolly Good Times tab. "You went there on business, didn't you? I assume that in your judgment the interview needed to be in person and that your wife participated. So at least put your flight expenses on the bill. That includes your wife's seat, too."

When I tried to argue that Nicole was along for the ride, Willard cut me off. "She helped you with the interrogation, didn't she, Jazz? What is the difference between her assisting you and Steve Dirado doing so?

"She's a lot easier on the eyes," I replied. "Not to mention, smarter than both of us put together."

Willard chuckled. "Look, Jazz, you've done a good job keeping the lid on expenses for this investigation. You're also doing a great job in a highly fluid and ambiguous situation. So enjoy the collateral perks when you can. Where do you go next, if you don't mind my asking?"

"I've got to rule out any connection between what is going on now and Susan Pleyer's death. I would have done that first had I known about her murder. There may not be any connection but there is a good possibility there may be, too. I would be negligent not to look at it. Most people are never even indirectly involved in a homicide investigation. This the second one for Nigel and there is a direct connection."

Willard sighed and shook his head. "This whole situation is a real can of worms, isn't it?"

"Given how deadly it is, I'd call it a kettle of vipers. By the way, do you happen to know Susan Player's maiden name?

"It's Ford," he replied. "Like the car. Or the former First Lady."

The next thing on my list was talking to the detectives that handled Susan Pleyer's murder in New Jersey. This is not something I particularly wanted to do. No one likes a Monday morning quarterback, particularly with a closed case. My first job would be to convince the detectives that I was not finding fault in any way. What I was after was to find out why the detectives thought Nigel had hired a contract killer. Even though their perpetrator had confessed, there was a slight chance someone else might have been involved.

To put it another way, it was possible Nigel had gone through a broker who actually hired the killer. This was not very likely but I felt I needed to rule the possibility out. I would prefer to talk to the killer face-to-face if I possibly could. This would allow me to make my own assessment of the killer and whether he had an accomplice. It would be much easier to do this if I had the goodwill of the investigating officers.

Of course, I could go through Willard and subpoena copies of the case files. The problem is that there is a lot of information that does not get into the case book. This includes impressions the detectives developed while working the case. Most effective investigators develop an intuitive sense that picks up on things that may not be immediately apparent. This is the information I was after and the only way to get it was to talk directly to the officers in person and to coax it out of them.

Since I had been the director of a law enforcement agency, I thought it might be better to use the chain of command. That is what I would prefer as the head of a large police department. It was a simple matter of courtesy that cost nothing but which could reap a large harvest of goodwill.

I decided it would be better to go in with as much background as I could. So I started with the victim and did a search on Susan

Ford Pleyer. This got immediate results with a simple Google search. Ford is a common name and there were millions of hits. Yet the first five were exactly what I needed.

The murder of Susan Ford created more of a sensation in the UK than it did here in the States. While the UK is infamous for its tabloids, there are some quite responsible papers there. The the *Guardian, the Independent* and the *Telegraph* all ran sober accounts based on solid information from the AP news service. Later I learned that Susan Ford's godfather was quite prominent in the British publishing industry and her death had generated a lot of sympathy for her family.

There was also a lot of sympathy generated for Nigel, her bereaved husband. Their wedding four years before her death had been a major social event attended by a great many important people. It was remembered as a joyful event with lots of food, plenty of wine, and live entertainment put together by Nigel's people. Of course, it was Susan's mother who was given credit for bringing it off without a flaw.

As I followed the story, I found out that Susan's remains were returned to England for burial. This took place at a quiet service in the cemetery that surrounded a small church used by generations of Fords. Reading this I thought, trust Nigel to do the right thing. I had done the same when I buried Nelly, the bride of my youth, in a country cemetery with several generations of her family.

Armed with this information, I called the borough police department in Chatham, New Jersey. The chief was not in but his assistant told me he would be available the next day and I set up an appointment for half past two that afternoon. When the assistant asked what the call was about I told her I was working on a case that might be tied to a homicide there.

"Oh, you must be talking about the Pleyer homicide," she said.

"As a matter of fact, I am," I answered. "How did you know?

"Oh, that's easy. Thus the only homicide we have had here in longer than I can remember. People around here are still talking about it."

After hanging up, I sat there thinking about what I needed to do next. Nothing came to mind, so I decided to jog my memory with an infusion of frozen yogurt. Sometimes I think that Sam McKee's internal clock is set in sync with mine. Sam was standing at the yogurt machine when I walked into the canteen.

"I am told the white chocolate macadamia nut is particularly good this morning," he said. "So is the vanilla bean." I was in the mood for simplicity so I went with vanilla bean on a waffle cone.

When we sat down, Sam asked how the case was going and I filled him in. "Do you ever get a simple case, Jazz?" he asked.

"Yes, I did. It was back in the 1970s, as I recall," I answered him. "I caught a kid assaulting a vending machine."

"How did that turn out?" McKee asked, smiling.

"He pled guilty. Then the next week his mother appealed the case and got him off. It seems I had not read him his rights correctly."

"My condolences," Sam said dryly.

"The saddest thing about it was that a year later he was in prison for assault and battery during a home invasion," I said, shaking my head sadly.

"For real?" Sam asked. "That's awful."

"Gottcha," I told him, smiling. "Hook line and stinker. Of course not. But he did get caught assaulting a parking meter. Believe it or not, it was a felony. That time I read him his rights correctly."

"Now I don't know whether to believe you or not," McKee said, raising a laconic eyebrow.

"I don't, either, half the time," I replied. Lifting my waffle cone, I said, "So here's to good friends and great yogurt."

"And to mud in your eye!" He looked at me intently. "You're in a funny mood this morning. Something happen?"

"It's this case, Sam. It's driving me bonkers. Nothing seems to be coming together. We seem to be generating lots of leads. Yet we don't seem to be resolving many at all."

"Well, maybe you're trying to hard. Maybe you need to relax and do something different."

"I'm in the middle of the case, Sam. I can't just bail out any time I like. Who else is going to carry the ball if I don't?"

"Don't you have two other people working with you? Why can't they pick up the slack? What would happen if you had a burst appendix or fell down a flight of stairs and broke a leg? I bet either of them could run this investigation almost as well as you."

"For goodness sake, man! Don't tell Dee that! I'll never hear the end of it if you do."

McKee chuckled. "What's it worth to you?" he asked.

"The next round of yogurt," I told him, and he grinned.

"Seriously, Jazz, I haven't seen you strung this tight a long time. This is the perfect time of year to grab your camera and head for the woods for a day."

"And would you be coming with me?" I challenged.

"Touché!" Sam laughed. "On second thought, are you offering Maine or New Hampshire?"

"Well, I hate to admit it but I have no idea," I told him. "We've lived here all this time and haven't ever explored this area that much. Heading for the woods means going to Arkansas or Wyoming. There's something wrong with that, isn't there?"

"Not really. At least, not to me. There are too damned many people in this part of the world, and some of them are always around. There's not enough elbow room for me."

We talked about that for a while, our favorite places. Neither of us had been to Shenandoah National Park and we agreed that was a shame. It was less fifty miles away but somehow it never came to mind. Sam chuckled. "All we have to do is to mention it to our wives and we'll get there for sure."

Having satisfied my yearning for yogurt I returned to my desk and sat there wondering what to do next. All I could think of was busy work. So I stuck my head into McKee's office to ask him if he would care to join me in the Cathedral for the midday service. He was not there, so I called my bride and told her I felt an urgent need to chase light and that I might be late for supper. Since my camera case was still in the car, I grabbed it and headed for the National Cathedral. On the way there, I decided that if anyone asked what I was doing I would tell them I was taking pictures of persons of interest.

When I talked to the Chief of Emergency Services in Chatham the following day, I learned that neither of the detectives involved in the Susan Pleyer murder investigation were part of his department. "We are far too small to afford one full-time detective, much less two. The whole borough has less than ten thousand people. I'm a good friend of the police chief in Newark and we contract with them for any major investigations. That means anything bigger than stolen cars or simple burglary, usually by latchkey kids with too much time on their hands and not enough supervision."

I also learned the lead detective had retired several years back. He moved to a cabin he had bought many years earlier near Grand Meadows, New Jersey. Looking this up on the computer later, I learned that this was not far from the infamous Valley of the Shadow of Death Road. No one knew for sure why the road was named that but it was a constant source of irritation for local people. The name attracted lots of macabre visitors, some of whom kept stealing the road signs. I wondered if it never occurred to anyone to simply change the name of the road. Or make it into a cash cow with speed traps.

The chief also gave me the phone number for the lead detective. I called and told him who I was and what I needed. Since it was so late in the week and I did not want to spend the weekend in the Big Apple, he agreed to meet me at his place on Monday afternoon. I thanked him and asked if he had the phone number for his former partner, but he did not.

"That may sound strange, Jazz, but Winton and I were never that close. Aside from the job, we never had much in common. He was my partner and I would cover for him as much as I could. Thank God he never committed a felony to my knowledge, and he was smart enough to walk the line when I was around. He knew I would never lie for him on the stand. Even so, he damn near crossed the line several times and I did hear about several times he did cross it. I was stuck with him because nobody else would work with the man. I only did so as a favor to the big boss. He rewarded me with a desk job during my last six months. Eight to five and no bloody crime scenes at three in the morning."

The lead detective's name was Alpin MacIntosh but he went by Al. He was a spare Scottish soul, native to Inverness, with a severe countenance and a mellow burr. Underneath this austere appearance, however, lay a keen sense of dry humor. I also sensed a great deal of kindness. "You know how the job is," he told me, "When I retired, I wanted to get away from police work completely. Most of the mates I worked with seemed to be moving to Arizona or Florida. So I more or less stayed put. You won't find a lot of retired cops in my neck of the woods and that's just fine with me."

"Well, obviously, I never quit police work," I told him. "I officially retired early from the Arkansas CID and spent a year chasing light. The job damned near killed me but after a few months my wife got tired of having me underfoot and this was all I knew how to do well. There were only so many things around the house I could fix for the handyman to repair. So I started consulting. Now I'm tearing my hair trying to catch another serial killer and wondering why I am."

"Another serial? I thought I recognized your name. So you think the earlier Pleyer case might be connected to the one you're looking at now?"

"Yes, I do, though it may not be a significant one. Still, I don't believe in coincidence, not when some of the people are the same. From what I've been told, you thought that Nigel killed his wife or had her killed."

"I did, but I thought a lot about the case over the years. Now I'm not so damned sure. Maybe he was guilty and maybe he wasn't. I would give it thirty-seventy in his favor now. All I know is, his alibi was rock solid and we never turned up any connection to a hit man. The thing is, I just didn't like the bloody *sassenach*. I wanted it to be him and my partner, Winton, wanted it to be that, too. So we were not all that objective. The victim, Susan, reminded me too much of my own daughter. She married a real piece of work, too."

"I understand Susan was having an affair. Was there any hard evidence of that?"

"Aye, there was, but nothing we could put with a last name. All we had was the initial J from some love letters we found." He smiled. "The chances are the first name was John, which probably would make the last name Doe."

I nodded. "You have to start somewhere. I don't suppose there were any fingerprints on the letters, where there?"

"Only from Susan. Everything else was smudges that were absolutely useless. You know what that means." He shrugged.

"Well, in my book that means that they were probably blotted out with a household iron or a little cornstarch."

"That's what my book says, too. We're damned lucky most criminals aren't very smart."

"Or flunk out of professional crime school."

MacIntosh liked that one. "Yes, there's a high dropout rate from those, isn't there? Of course, there are also those we never catch. It could be your man is one of those."

"It certainly would seem that way," I replied. "But it looks like our leading candidate got himself assassinated eighteen months ago."

"Assassinated, is it?" MacIntosh asked. I could see his interest had been piqued.

I told him about the murder of James Mill, who we also knew as Jaques Auden Michon *et al.* When I was done, he nodded. "That sounds like a professional, all right. A damned good shot, too. I'm glad it's your case and not mine. The big question is who shot him and how all this ties in with the Susan Pleyer murder. That's the key question."

"What about the one who confessed?" I asked. "How confident are you that he was for real?"

"Oh, he was the one who did it, all right. He knew too many details not to have been there. The thing is, when we asked him if there was anyone else involved, he denied it. Winton accepted that at face value but I was a bit uneasy about it. There was something in the man's eyes that told me he was lying. I would have pushed it but the local jurisdiction said no. They had a confession and that's all they wanted. Case closed."

"I need to talk to him. Any idea where I could find him?"

Al gave me a lupine grin. "Yes, in a grave at one of our fine prisons. What goes around comes around. He got himself shanked."

I had the feeling MacIntosh was not done so I waited. After two long minutes, he chuckled and looked at me with amusement. "You are very good at this, Doctor Phillips. But then, I suppose you've had a lot of experience."

I allowed that was true and he nodded. "It occurs to me I am being a bit of an arse giving your man, Nigel, a full thirty. When I look myself in the eye, I have to say I think he is innocent. The man may be a bloody Englishman, but he did not kill his wife."

"So here we are, back to square one," I replied. "Who killed Susan?"

"I wish I could help you, lad," he said. From what I could see he was not that much older than me. In fact, he was probably younger. Yet I shrugged it off. There was no offense intended. It was probably how Scotsman normally talk to one another, an expression of acceptance like Australians use the word "mate" or the way Americans use "buddy."

"Actually you have," I replied. "You've given me a lot more grist for the mill. Thank you for your honesty. I really appreciate it."

Driving back to Newark I thought about what Macintosh said, about how his judgment was affected by his dislike of Nigel. This made me wonder how my dislike of Daniella was affecting my judgment in the case. I had no doubt that it was. Like Macintosh, I wanted her to be the perpetrator and I remembered something my grandfather used to say: if wishes were horses then beggars would ride. So I asked myself a critical question. What other suspects did we have?

Who came to mind immediately was our missing Marine. I had to think hard for a moment to remember his name. Yet even that didn't work so I pulled off the side of the road to look at my case notebook. It took me a couple of minutes but I found it, Sergeant Hailey Beck. When I saw his name it jogged my memory of what Dee had told me. I wondered how I could have been so obtuse. Sergeant Beck stood out like a sore thumb. He was a sniper who had gone missing a long time ago and I moved him to the top of our list.

Then I remembered something else and I took out the list of players Trudy had given me. She had listed the names alphabetically and it only took a moment to find Hailey Beck. He had been a participant on one of the earliest Last One Left events but did not come away a winner. I looked at the list of events Daniella had attended and discovered she had been the security director for the event where Hailey was a player.

I noticed that Leon Spitz had worked that event, too, and I gave him a call. I expected to go directly to his voicemail but Leon answered in person. When I explained what I needed, Leon laughed. "Man, that's a long time ago. Which event that you said was?"

I gave him the dates of the event and what information I had about Sergeant Hailey Beck. "Oh, hell yes, the jarhead! Yeah, I remember him. He was a sore loser and a real dipshit and he didn't make it very far. They were working two-man teams on that event, as I recall, and nobody wanted to team up with him. He got cut from the cast real quick, the first one as I recall. I'm surprised he was ever accepted as a player in the first place."

"How did he respond to getting cut?" I asked.

"Oh, he got sore as a boil. Cussed everybody in sight and even made some threats. Not that anything came of them. He was all wind and no sail and they flew him home right away. Do not pass Go. Come to think, there weren't any Marines on any of the events I worked after that. Not that I remember. I guess one was enough."

"It sounds like it," I replied. "That's too bad. It must have hurt the show."

"Are you kidding? It turned out to be pure gold. The viewing public ate it up, him stalking off the set shaking his fist and every other word a bleep. Our ratings went through the bleepin' roof."

Then I remembered something Dee had pointed out. "Wait a minute, Leon. There was at least one other Marine on the show, Ron Henly. He was a million dollar winner."

Spitz laughed. "You're right. How could I have forgotten him? He was one of the best."

"It's called old-timers syndrome, Leon. It's hell to pay."

It was only after I had hung up that things came together in my mind and the full implications struck me. The Atlanta police thought Ronald Henly was brought down by a single shot from a sawed off shotgun at forty yards. Who better to make such a shot at a running target in poor light than a trained sniper? We had a strong suspect.

When I called Dee to tell him what I had figured out, he laughed. "I wondered how long it would take you," he said. "The thing is, how in the hell do we find the peckerwood?"

"We may not have to," I replied. "Let me check with Willard. That may be someone else's job."

"Wouldn't that be nice for a change."

My next call was to Willard Norwald. As luck would have it, his secretary told me that Willard was in New York for a meeting. She gave me his hotel room number and suggested that I call him on his cell. I did so and was sent directly to voicemail. I left my name and number and said that I needed to talk to him somewhat urgently. "It is not, I repeat, not an emergency," I said. "We do need to talk today or tomorrow, if possible."

Since there was little I could do before I talked to Willard, I called my bride. She was working at home and we talked a while before my phone told me I had another call coming in. It was Willard and I explained briefly what was going on. He suggested that I meet him at this hotel and have lunch with him. I reminded him it would be more like supper, and he laughed. "I've been inside all day working in a room without windows," he told me. "We just broke up but I need to be here tomorrow, too. Shall we say in an hour? I need to shower and wash off the lawyer grime."

When we were seated and had ordered our meal, I said, "Are you in a hurry? I would prefer to wait until after we finished eating to talk."

Willard smiled. "That's right. I believe you told me that the first time we broke bread. Or do I misremember? How is your family?"

We took our time with our food, talking about this and that. I don't remember exactly what subjects we covered, but I do remember having a wonderful conversation. We both seemed reluctant to get down to business but after a while Willard said, "I think it's time to talk. What do you recommend?"

"I've given it some thought this afternoon," I answered. "We are at the point we are pretty well convinced Hailey Beck is our killer. Working as a police investigator, the next step would be to gather evidence. In this case, it would also be a hell of a job and very expensive. I simply don't have the resources to do the job quickly and thoroughly. Nor do I have the time to devote to it. I have other commitments coming up. So what I would recommend is one of two things. One would be to bring in the FBI at this point and I would be glad to help sell them, if need be. The other option is to turn the case over to Steve DiRado and Robert Delgado and let them gather enough evidence to compel the FBI to take the case. Doing so would mean generating a lot of publicity, but I believe it could be used to advantage for Jolly Good Times."

I paused and Willard waited patiently. "What I am telling you is that there is no way to avoid publicity. Nigel must make a decision which way he wants to go. I believe I am legally bound as a peace officer to inform the Atlanta police who killed Ronald Henley and why. I also believe I need to inform the Chief of Police in Bethlehem, Pennsylvania, who we believe killed Jaques Auden Michon, also known as John Mills and various aliases."

Willard nodded and sighed. "I was afraid it might come to this. Nigel may not like it but I don't see any alternatives. Our firm would be in a real ethical bind not giving what we now have to the police. I would certainly vote against such a course of action."

"I believe you need to be the one who tells him," I said. "I will certainly make myself available to go with you."

Willard agreed to set the meeting up with Nigel and I placed a call to the Chief of Detectives in Newark. I had never met the lady, but she was familiar with my work and told me she had been meaning to call me. "We would like for you to do a seminar on investigative technique," she told me. "I understand you're based on the East Coast now."

"We live in Washington and I do a lot of consulting out of there," I replied. "When were you planning to do this?" I took out my planner.

We found dates that worked for both of us. She thanked me and asked, "So what can I do for you, Jazz?"

"I'm looking for a detective named Winton," I told her. "He worked a homicide in Chatham a number of years ago. His partner was named Macintosh and I need to talk to Winton about the case."

"Al MacIntosh would be a better source of information," she replied and I told her I had already talked to him. "Winton left this department not long after he worked that case," she told me. "He left under a cloud. He never said anything but I think Al was glad to see him go."

"That was the impression I got, but I still need to see him. You know how it is, Chief. Winton may mention something I didn't think to ask Al, and that detail might break the case."

The Chief chuckled. "That's what I drill into my people. The devil is in the details." I heard a drawer open and paper rustling and a moment later she read off a phone number. "That's the most recent number I have, but it's three or four years old. I doubt it's any good. Leroy Winton is something else."

I thanked the chief and tried the number she had given me. There was an immediate intercept. The number was no longer in service. So I phoned Nicole and after we visited for a moment, I asked her to run a trace on Leroy Winton. She called me back in twelve minutes.

"You hang out with some real sleaze balls, Jazzbeau," she observed.

"That's better than hanging with them," I replied and she chuckled. It was a sound I never tire of hearing.

Nicole read off a list of phone numbers and addresses. "This slime bucket keeps on the move," she said. "Those numbers are arranged from newest to the oldest. It would be a stupid thing to do but he just might go back to an old hideout or use an old phone number."

"You're talking about the man like he's a criminal. What did you find?"

"He is a criminal. He's just not been convicted yet." She read off a list of offenses. "I'm surprised Internal Affairs hasn't nailed him."

"Did I hear you right? Suborning homicide? He must have left Dodge just ahead of the posse."

Nicole told me I was correct on both counts.

"Thanks, sweetheart, that's very helpful. I think we're getting very close to breaking the case wide open."

I called Dee let him know what was happening and was surprised when Karin answered the phone. She sounded cheerful as she told me, "Dee and Bobby are out fishing. Bobby really reminds me of you, Jazz. I haven't seen Dee so cheerful in a long time. They even go to AA meetings together."

I felt a pang of jealousy and chided myself for it. I was glad Bobby and Dee hit it off so well and when I talked to my partner, I knew why. Dee now had a protégé, someone with whom to share the rich knowledge of criminal investigation he had accumulated over a lifetime.

"The kid is a natural!" he told me when he called a couple of hours later. "You don't have to tell him twice. I wish you could put him on full time."

"So do I but McKee has already hired him. I think Sam's going to put him on the Kwan Tea project. He and Akio should work well together."

"Do you ever regret becoming a spook, Jazz?" Dee asked.

"I'm not a spook, Dee. I'm still a policeman and I think Sam prefers me to remain just that. The difference now is that I'm mostly working white collar crime, corporate crime, and I really like that. So does Bobby."

I told Dee what I had learned. "I think we need to run down Hailey Beck," he told me.

"That may be a whole lot easier said than done," I told him. "The Marine Corps has written him off. I don't think anyone is still looking for him. I imagine he feels fairly safe now."

"All the better. He may not see us coming."

"I have no idea where to start," I told him. "The assassination of John Mill is the latest activity we know. Even that is only a maybe and it's over eighteen months old. It's been quite a while since he took out a winner, too. Apparently he has the money to get by and it would be quite easy for him to lie low."

"Yeah, unless his demon is working on him. If it is, it doesn't matter how much money he has. It's an itch he can't scratch. It will only grow worse until he kills again. You know that as well as I do."

"So why don't we set up a trap?" I asked. "Surely there is some way we can draw him in. I'm sure he's aware we are after him but I don't think he knows that we are aware of who he is."

My partner looked troubled. "I don't know, Jazz. This strikes me as a pretty smart perp. He might turn the tables on us. Do we even know what he looks like? The Marine Corps wasn't very forthcoming when I asked for a picture."

"We can always fall back on the Jolly Good Times event photos. I'll go by their office tomorrow and see what they have. I'll email you wherever I can come up with."

"Why don't you just send it to my phone?" Dee asked.

"Because I don't know how," I told him and he laughed.

It was late that afternoon before I managed to get to get to the Jolly Good Times office. I was surprised to see Trudy there. "Hello there, stranger," I said. "I'm surprised to see you back."

There were other people around so I didn't offer a hug.

"Billie was driving me crazy," she declared. "I remember now why we didn't encourage her to stay on the East Coast. We are such different people and I don't like her hovering. I get a little lonely here sometimes but it is better than being bossed around by my own child. Grandchildren are a whole different ball game."

"Oh, I get bossed around by my kids all the time," I told her. "I am the one who spoils them."

"Meeting Nicole in person, I see why. She reminds me of a jaguar I saw in the zoo. I would hate to have her on my trail."

"I know what you mean. She's very intense but she's also incredibly gentle and she doesn't hold a grudge. I am surprised and very grateful she lets me hang around."

Trudy laughed. "I'm not. Why don't we catch up over dinner at our place? Or have you already eaten? I was thinking deep dish pizza." She smiled and there was a festive note in her voice. "My desk looks like a recycling station but it can wait until tomorrow."

My telephone interrupted us just then. It was Willard Nordwald calling to ask if I would be available for a meeting with Nigel in his office at three the following afternoon. "Yes, that would be good. I'm already in New Jersey running down a lead. I'll see you then."

When I got to Trudy's place, she greeted me with a hug. She was wearing a soft caftan that reached almost to the floor and I could tell there was nothing but her underneath. "I really miss you," she murmured as we sat looking into the fireplace. "I know it's only been a few days but I couldn't help thinking about you. The time we had in Seattle was simply not enough. What am I going to do when you leave for good?"

"I think we need to live in the now," I told her. "That's all we have. I think we need to enjoy it to the fullest. *Carpe diem!*"

We had abandoned the trappings of civilization and were seizing the day enthusiastically when the doorbell rang. "That must be the pizza guy," Trudy said, pulling on the caftan.

I grabbed my clothes and headed to the bedroom. "Check who it is before you open the door!" I told her.

"Who is it?" she asked, looking out the peephole.

"Special delivery!" a muffled voice answered. I drew my pistol and waved Trudy away from the door. I crouched and moved to the door, picking up a magazine as I went. When I got to the door I held the magazine up to cover the peephole. A moment later a bullet tore through the peephole, knocking the magazine from my hand. This was immediately followed by another bullet six inches lower.

"Dial 911," I whispered hoarsely and Trudy grabbed the phone. I waved her over behind me and began to dress. Then I whispered, "Move my stuff to the guest bedroom, please."

I could see she was quite frightened, but she smiled and wiped some lipstick off my lips. Then she grabbed my bag and my laptop and carried them down the hall. A few moments later she was right behind me again. "My goodness, Doctor Phillips, life is never dull with you around."

The response time of the Newark police was very good. There was a uniformed officer at the door inside of three minutes and two detectives showed up five minutes later. Then the pizza guy showed up fifteen minutes after that.

It took a while to explain things to the detectives. The lead insisted on having a crime scene tech extract the bullets from the wall opposite the door. She also had a hard time believing me when she asked who I thought might want to harm me. I told her I was after a serial killer. "How do you know that?" she asked.

"It's my job to know," I told her. "I have a whole team going after this guy."

It went back and forth like that for a while and finally I had enough. "Look, Sergeant. If you don't believe me call your chief of detectives and ask her who Jazz Phillips is. I was just talking to her this afternoon."

"Yeah? What's her name?"

I looked the Sergeant directly in the eye. "Her first name is Chief and your name is about to be Mud if you give us me any more crap." The sergeant glared at me but I saw her partner dialing his phone. He spoke into it and a moment or two later he handed the phone to me."

"Jazz, what's going on?" she asked.

"The perp I'm after just took a shot at me, Chief," I answered. "Nobody is hurt but the Sergeant doesn't believe me. I am sorry to bother you."

"It goes with the turf," she told me. "Jen just made Detective Sergeant. She is a very good officer. Let me talk to her."

"I am sure she is. She is certainly tenacious." I handed the phone to the detective.

It was pushing midnight when the police left and our pizza was cold. "Are you sure you want me to stay?" I asked Trudy.

"Are you kidding, Jazz? Isn't that the same person who was trying to poison me?" I shrugged and nodded and she kissed me lightly on the lips. "You're not going to get off that easily," she declared. "Besides, I can't eat all that pizza by myself and I'm way too wound up to go to sleep."

I allowed as all that was quite true and we needed to do some unwinding. So we put the pizza in the microwave and took up where we left off when the doorbell rang. Even so, we were both keyed up from the attack and tore at each other like there would be no tomorrow.

Afterward, when we were lying quietly in one another's arms, Trudy giggled. "That was awesome. You don't suppose we could hire the man to come back and shoot the door again the next time we're together?"

I called Nicole the first thing the next morning. I dreaded calling her because I knew how she would react to the attack. Nor was I wrong. There was an ominous silence after I finished telling her, so long I thought we had lost the connection. Then I heard something that made my hair stand on end. It was a feral growl so deep I would never have guessed it came from a human throat. It sounded like the roar of a lion, only deeper and far more fierce. Not much frightens me, but that growl did. I knew exactly what it meant and I was glad our killer was not in the same room with her. She would have torn him to pieces with her bare hands.

"Sweetheart!" I said, speaking in what Nelly called my command voice.

It hung in the balance for a long moment before I heard her sigh. Then I heard her choking, trying not to cry. After a few moments she cleared her throat and spoke in an almost normal voice. "I'll be all right now," she told me. "How is Trudy?"

"Scared out of her wits at first, but she'll be all right. Neither of us was hit. She seemed to be in fairly good shape this morning. She was even able to laugh about it a little."

"She's a tough lady," Nicole replied. "That's the second time this shit-heel has come after her." Her use of profanity reminded me just how disturbed she was. She doesn't use Anglo-Saxon expression much these days except when we are alone. Little ears learn fast and she normally uses Brazilian Portuguese. Of course, the little ears learned that quickly, though not the meaning. One of their schoolmates, the child of an Angolan embassy employee, was shocked to hear Jack demonstrating his fluency one day.

"It's a good thing you were there," she added. I started to point out that if I had not been there the attack probably would not have happened. Then I bit my tongue. No one can accurately predict what a serial killer will or will not do. "I assume you will be staying there again tonight," Nicole said. "Tomorrow night, too," she added. It was almost surrealistic to hear her assume this.

"I was planning to drive home tomorrow afternoon. There is nothing I need to do here."

"No, you need to stay with Trudy. I'll call her and let her know." Again I was struck by how strange this was by conventional standards and how easily we both had come to accept it.

It was as if Nicole was reading my mind. "You've come a long way, baby,'" she said dryly, quoting a very old commercial. "Us girls seem to adapt a lot easier than you guys."

After the call was ended, I sat there thinking about what I needed to do next. Then my phone rang and the ringtone told me it was important but not an emergency. Neither the caller's name or number was given and I started to let the call go to voice mail. Then something prompted me to take it and I did.

"Yeah, this is Leroy Winton," a surly voice told me. "You the guy who left the message?"

"Yes, this is Jazz Phillips. I'd like to talk to you about the Susan Pleyer case. Could we get together?"

"Might could. What's it worth to you?"

"Well, I could buy you lunch at place you choose," I suggested.

"Should be worth more than that," he replied. It was almost a snarl.

"That depends on how good your information is. I'm a fair man and I will treat you right. At the very least, you'll get a good lunch and a few dollars. Hobson's choice."

"What the hell does that mean?" Winton asked.

"It means take it or leave it. You in or out?"

Leroy grumbled a bit but he took my offer. I was surprised when he gave me the name and address of a sports bar in downtown Newark. We agreed to meet there at 11:30 to beat the lunch crowd. That gave me over an hour to find the place and I decided to take a cab.

The place we met was named Harley's there was a sign on the front door that said, "No Rice Burners Allowed!" I was about ten minutes early and I grabbed a table and ordered a cup of cappuccino. I told the waiter that someone would be joining soon and we would order then. I asked him what the specialty of the place was and he told me it was Harley's Honest-to-God Hoagie. This came with special fries and a piece of pie.

I recognized Leroy Winton immediately when he walked in. He looked like a bitter soul and his face matched his voice perfectly. I tried to put him at ease after we ordered but he was not having any. Nor did he want to enjoy our food and visit before we got down to business. "I'm surprised the Chief of Ds gave you my number. She always liked my partner more than she did me. Of course, he was a real goody-two-shoes ass kisser. Wouldn't butter melt in his mouth. You talk to him? I bet he gave you an earful about me."

I allowed as I had visited Macintosh, but he had not run his partner down at all. "All he told me was that the two of you were not that close. He also said that you and he were in agreement about Nigel Pleyer, but that the jurisdiction shut you down."

"You damn sure got that one right!" he declared. "Did he tell you that someone else copped to her murder later on?" I nodded and Leroy went on. "That stuck in my craw. I think that guy was lying. You know what I mean? Lots of people waste our time copping to things they no way could have done. Murder seems to draw them like flies."

It went like that for over an hour and I didn't learn anything I didn't know. That's the way investigation goes, sifting through a lot of muck to find the gold. It has to be done but I was glad when the time came for my appointment at Jolly Good Times. I paid for our lunch and handed Leroy a fifty dollar bill. "What the hell is this?" he demanded, looking even more sour than when we first met.

"That's a perfectly good bill," I said, knowing he would have complained no matter how much I offered. "I know because I was there when it was printed." He was not amused and I held out another fifty. "So was this one. Hobson's choice."

Taille Haut!

17 The meeting at Nigel's office went as well as could be expected. He had heard about the attack at Trudy's and that took some careful explaining. I told him I happened to be there for supper and had taken Trudy to the visiting fireman's apartment after the attack was over. "I didn't think it was safe for her to stay there," I told him. "He might have come back. Particularly since the first attack."

"The first attack?" Nigel asked, shocked.

"Yes, when someone broke into her apartment and poisoned some of her food. That's why she was in the hospital in Seattle. They thought it was a stroke, at first, but her blood test showed it was methamphetamine. That can exhibit the same symptoms as a stroke."

"Why was I not informed?" Nigel demanded.

"That's on me," Willard interjected. "Jazz did report it to me, but we decided to keep it under wraps until we could tell you in person."

"Why didn't you tell Daniella? She could have passed it on to me."

"We decided that the fewer people they knew about it, the better," I said. "I did not want the killer to know we were aware of his attack. The more we can keep him in the dark, the better."

Nigel was not satisfied. "Daniella is my head of security. Surely you could have informed her."

I decided it was time to take off the gloves. "I don't think you want to know the truth, Nigel. Or maybe you don't want to knowledge it. Daniella has been at the top of our list of suspects from the get-go."

"How can you say that?" he demanded. "She has been with our company from the first. She is the most loyal employee I have."

I sighed. "My partner, Dee, will tell you the same. The first sign was that she tried to commandeer the investigation. You were not at the meeting. It was myself, my partner, Willard, and Daniella. One of the first things she did was to try to fire us for asking an awkward question. Since then, she has tried to impede our inquiry and get us out of the home office. Once I caught her trying to break into my computer."

"So Daniella is your chief suspect?" Nigel asked. I could see he was not about to accept this.

"No, she no longer is. However, we have not cleared her from being a possible accomplice. We are almost certain the killer has been getting help from inside the company. At the very least, he has been receiving inside information. No one else we have looked at has a motive we can see. Of course, we may be wrong. We often are. Our primary effort has been toward protecting you. I would very much like to be mistaken, but wishful thinking can cost lives. The stakes are simply too high."

I could see that my attempt to mollify Nigel had failed. It was as if he had not heard a word I said. So I decided to plunge ahead. "We have also come to believe that the perpetrator of the winner murders may be tied to the death of your wife, Susan. It's all here in my report." I handed Willard two copies of the report and he handed one to Nigel, who glanced at the top page and tossed the report aside. It was quite obvious that man was very angry with me.

"I need to speak with my attorney," Nigel told me, nodding toward Willard. "Alone."

"I'll wait in the canteen," I told Willard and left the executive office. I made a quick pit stop at the washroom on the way and got myself a cup of designer coffee. I had just seated myself when Trudy entered the canteen. She walked over to the seat at my table.

"You may not want to sit too close," I told her. "There is lightning in the air and I am ground zero."

"What happened?" she asked, quite concerned.

"I just told your boss the truth as I see it now. He didn't like it at all."

"Oh, dear. What did you tell him?"

"I cannot be specific without violating client confidentiality," I told her. "I can tell you I reported things as Dee and I see them. I also told him about the first attack on you. I tried to keep you as far out off the line of fire as I could. I hope I have not poisoned the well for you here. I told him what we told the police. I was there for dinner and took you to the company apartment with me in case there was another attack."

"I hope you didn't say anything against Susan," she said. Seeing the answer in my eyes she added, "Oh, dear."

Dom walked up and join us. "There are a lot of strange vibes around here today," he observed. "Any idea why?"

"Jazz just told Nigel some things he didn't want to hear," Trudy said.

"About the…?" Dom left the question unfinished.

"Among other things," she answered. "He cannot be specific. You know, client confidentiality. The point is the boss didn't like what he heard."

"Ah," Dom nodded sagely. "Well, that would do it, all right," he said. "I guess the more left unsaid, the better." Looking at Trudy he said, "I heard about last night. I hope you're all right. That must have been scary."

"Terrifying is the word," she said. "Jazz was kind enough to put me up his guest bedroom."

"From what I hear, the guy ran off without trying to get in," Dom said and I nodded. "That's strange. Did you shoot back?"

"No, it was too risky. A bystander could have been hurt. Like someone in another apartment."

Willard approached the table and my company left. "Nigel wants to talk to you," he said. "I convinced him it would not be wise to kill the messenger and he agreed. So please be gentle, Jazz. I'm not saying you did the wrong thing by confronting him, but he's feeling pretty bruised."

"I know. The truth can be nasty and he's a nice guy. I'll use kid gloves."

"Thanks for telling me the truth, Jazz," Nigel said when we were seated. "I'm sorry I got so angry. I hope you're wrong, but it's best to not sugar coat the facts, is it?"

"I hope I'm wrong, too," I answered. "Our prime suspect is Hailey Beck, one of your contestants. The only evidence we have is circumstantial, but he fits the bill very well. We have suspected from the beginning that the killer may have had inside help. There is no solid evidence who this might have been. The attack last night does clear Jaques Michon, unless he was an accomplice earlier in the game."

I paused and Nigel waited patiently. "Despite what you may think, I respect Daniella's capability and her personal loyalty to you. Everything she has done can be explained by that. Keeping you in the dark could well be motivated by her desire to protect you."

Nigel nodded and I went on. "Even so, I have to follow my experience and intuition. I would appreciate it if you read over my report and make notes of questions you have. You are the only principal figure in the company I have not spoken with. You may have a critical piece of information you don't realize you have. So we do need to talk."

"How about now?" Nigel suggested. "We could get something to eat at the bakery. There is a quiet corner there where we can talk."

"Are you aware there is a bug in that table?" I asked.

"There is? I had no idea. That is not acceptable! I'll have a word with the owner about that!"

"I would prefer you did not," I told him. "We might be able to use that to catch our killer."

"I started to ask if you thought it might be one of our people," Nigel said. He looked like he had just bitten into something extremely sour.

"It might be. Or it might be the killer. Either way we can use it to pass along misinformation."

Nigel's face brightened slightly. "Like Operation Mincemeat the Allies used to fool the Germans about the invasion of Sicily."

"Exactly. We might be able to catch the killer or his accomplice inside the company. If nothing else, we stand a good chance of finding out who planted the bug." I paused, unsure of whether to share the next thought.

Nigel sensed my hesitation. "Go ahead, Jazz. No holds barred. I'll try not to take anything you say personally."

"Well, you don't suppose…"

Nigel started to say something but changed his mind. "No, that couldn't be right."

"What cannot be right?" I asked but Nigel shook his head.

"It's not necessarily bad," I said. "It might be Daniella keeping tabs on loose lips. To protect you and the company."

Nigel nodded. "It might be. She sometimes augments my instructions a bit more than I might like. Tell me more about this fellow you think may be our killer."

"His name is Hailey Beck and there was a little confusion about him at first. He was a contestant that Leon Spitz told me was very unhappy. He was on one of the early events and was apparently sent home early in the game. Leon tells me nobody liked him and that he was a sore loser. He apparently made a real scene leaving. The point is that he has plenty of motive to kill, resentment and revenge, and he has the skills to make it happen. What's missing is any hard evidence and that is going to be hard to get. We don't even know for sure where he is or even that he was the one who attacked us last night."

Nigel nodded. "So how do we go about catching him?" he asked.

"We don't. That's not our job. What we need to do is call in the professionals. With all the jurisdictions involved, that means the FBI."

"No," Nigel insisted. "If we do it will be in all the papers. That's exactly what I want to avoid."

"What other options do we have?" I asked. "We don't have the resources or the authority to bring the man in. At some point the story is going to hit the news. I am afraid that if you wait, someone else may die and you may be painted as the bad guy. We need to at least let the FBI know what we suspect. That way any consequences fall on them."

"Why can't you track him down yourself?" Nigel asked.

"That could take years," I replied. "I simply don't have the time. You would probably be better off having someone else to do your security and putting Daniella on his trail. She seems to be quite resourceful and I'd bet she has the determination to get it done."

"So you are refusing to finish the job?"

"No, I am telling you I have done what you hired me to do, which was to determine what lay behind the death of your winners and to identify who the killer is if there was one. I am also telling you that I have other commitments, among which are my family and my consulting."

Nigel thought about this. "Is it a matter of money, Jazz?"

"No, Nigel, it is not. Were I twenty years younger it might be different. I am aging and I have a young family. My children need me. As does their mother. Had I not been on my toes last night, I might not be here today."

"Jazz is right, Nigel," Willard said, speaking for the first time. "That is how I laid it out for him, and that is what he has done. Nor does he have the necessary authority to do what you would like him to do. As your legal advisor I recommend that you bring in the FBI immediately. I think that if you manage the spin as I know you can, the publicity you get will be an asset, not a liability."

Nigel sighed. "I suppose you're right, but I would like Jazz to be available to consult about this. Could you do that, Jazz?"

"Yes, I can, on a very limited basis. I think, for your protection, I need to work under the legal umbrella Willard provides."

That's the way we left it and I felt very lighthearted as I drove home two days later. Nicole had insisted that I stay in Newark until Trudy's new security door had been installed. It would have been simpler to patch the existing door but Trudy didn't trust it. She wanted a steel door mounted on a steel frame and a police lock installed inside. It took a day to get the steel door ordered and delivered and a second day to get it installed. So Trudy and I played tourist in New York after the door was ordered. I had never been to the top of the Empire State building or to the Guggenheim Museum. Nor had I spent much time in Central Park. I came away with a better understanding of why New Yorkers love their city so much.

When the workmen were done the next day it was late and I knew the weekend traffic would be atrocious. There were two major events going on and the freeways would be overloaded, coming and going.

Trudy was not disappointed by this, of course. "I know you're anxious to get home to your family, Jazz, but it's been so wonderful having you here. I need to write Nicole a thank you note."

"Well, you know the police motto, to serve and protect," I told her with a grin. "I am glad you got the security door. You may want to get your landlord to reinforce the hallway walls, too."

"Speaking of service…" she said, raising an eyebrow and giving me a sweet smile. "I ordered in some barbecue ribs from a place that claims to do them Southern style and I have two quarts of New York's best frozen yogurt. They should be here soon. Would you like a beer or a glass of wine while we wait?"

I opted for beer, especially since she kept Sam Adams cold for me in the fridge. Trudy lit the gas log and we sat there quietly like an old couple snuggling on the couch. I was still disturbed by how natural this felt, but not enough to do anything about it. After a while our cuddling evolved into necking and then into something more. As usual, the doorbell left us scrambling. Nor was the delivery man fooled. When I turned to set the food on the kitchen counter, Trudy laughed. Somehow I had not got my shirttails tucked in and my buttons were one hole off.

The next morning I managed to get out of the city very early. Traffic was not that bad and once I was out of the urban area I was able to make good time. Rather than stop by the house, I went directly to the school gym where Jack's team was playing.

Marie was all over me and insisted on sitting in my lap but I did manage to greet my bride with a kiss.

"I missed you," I said, talking to Marie but looking into Nicole's eyes. She seemed very amused.

"You're very chipper this morning," she said with a smile that bordered on a grin. "You must have had a...successful...week."

"I had a ball...in a 'Sixties sort of way."

Nicole laughed. Hanging around with me she had picked the patois of the aging Aquarians. "That's good. I'd hate for you to get out of practice."

Nicole's mood changed when we talked about the attack on Trudy's. "This shit-heel is getting to be a real pain in the ass," she said. "I think we need to do something about it."

"I do, too, but we don't have any evidence to back up our suspicion. All we have is a highly suspicious disappearance, professional level shooting, and what we suspect as a motive. None of this is admissible in court."

"I wasn't thinking about arresting him, Jazz. Or due process. I'm only concerned about stopping him. I don't want anyone else hurt."

"I don't either, my love, but we have to do it right. Otherwise we are no better than him. The first thing is to make sure Hailey Beck is alive."

"Didn't the Marine Corps investigate?" She asked. "Or would it be the Navy?"

"It would be the Navy, the NCIS, in fact."

"That was who you used to work for, wasn't it? Don't you know someone there who could help?"

"Yes, I worked for them back when they were still the NIS. That was during Vietnam. My contacts there are forty years old. No one there would even remember me. There is probably a record of my service somewhere but it's probably in a dusty box in a warehouse."

"Well I'm sure Sam has the contacts," Nicole reminded me. "Why don't you ask him? In the meantime, I'll do some digging, myself."

What my bride did not say was that her digging would most likely be illegal. Don't ask, don't tell, I told myself. "Just be very careful, sweetheart," I told her. "Your husband worries about you. He likes having you around so he can grab you at moments like this."

That was the end of that conversation. We found other things that needed doing and saying to one another, and I spent the next few days running things down for Sam. At one point, I gave Trudy a call to see how she was doing. "You'll never guess what I've been doing," she told me. "I decided to stand my ground with this crackpot, so I am taking the firearms safety course. I should have my license for a pistol within the next two weeks, and I visit the range every other day."

A chill ran up my back when I heard this. "Please be very careful, Trudy. Believe me, it is better to put yourself in a safe situation. Even if you are justified shooting someone, you are in for a world of legal grief. That may seem ridiculous, but it is true. Accidents do happen, too. It would be less trouble to get yourself a big dog."

Trudy sounded disappointed when she replied. "I thought you would be proud of me," she said. "I thought I was being proactive."

"I am very proud to know you, Trudy, packing a pistol or not. The problem is that the guys who run the firearms safety programs tend to emphasize protecting yourself from physical harm. What they don't tell you about is the world of legal caca that goes along with exercising your right to do so. The other thing they don't tell you is how taking another person's life makes you feel. It's not fun, I assure you. Even when that's what they deserve and you have no other choice."

I was a little hypocritical telling her this because I had only shot and killed a suspect once. Then it was by accident and I am lucky I didn't kill anyone else. What I was telling Trudy was true, but I only knew this by observing what happened to other officers when they had to kill in the line of duty. At the time I killed Wally Keller I wondered what was wrong with me not feeling any remorse. It was my partner, Dee, who helped me sort this out. His exact words escape me, but he asked me how I felt about killing a poison snake that was about to strike while I was changing a tire on our patrol car. The truth is I never lost any sleep over Wally Keller.

I was surprised when I got a call from the NCIS a few days later. The investigator had been there a long time and was familiar with my books. Everyone we knew in common was retired or dead but he had looked me up in the NCIS records. "You did some damn good work, Phillips," he told me. "I read your report on that case they made you stand down. That was a friggin' shame. Seems to me you had the bastards nailed."

I allowed that it seemed that way to me, too. "On the other hand, things turned out well for me back home in Arkansas. Not least was the fact I got to spend almost every night at home with my wife."

"You got that right," he told me. Then he got down to business. "I'm told you're looking for one of our missing Marines," he said. "Sergeant Hailey Beck, as a matter of fact. What's your take on him?"

"I think he's our killer. We don't have anything like proof but there are a number of things that point toward him." I quickly summarized what we had and what we were guessing. "Of course, any second year law student could punch a dozen holes through that. This guy is good. He doesn't leave any physical evidence we can find. All we have there are two ten-millimeter slugs. We don't even have the cases to go with them. On the other hand, there are only two of us on the case, three now, and it's spread all over more than a dozen jurisdictions. Some of those are international."

"So how come it's you, not the FBI, who is involved?"

"Who I am working for is a law firm representing a client. So I am not allowed to tell you much more than I have. Attorney client privilege. As it is, I am probably bending the rules a little even telling you what I have."

"I see." Somehow my caller managed to put forty degrees of frost into those two words. "So you've gone over to the dark side," he replied. It was a statement, a judgment, not a question.

"Not at all," I declared in the same tone. "Unless you call national security the dark side. Most of my work is in international corporate crime. The people I work for took down Kwan Tea and I was part of the team that did it. So don't talk to me about working for the Dark Side. It exists and I fight it every day."

"No need to get huffy," he said. "You know how it is, Doctor Phillips. The frigging lawyers jam us up at every turn."

"Aforesaid lawyers keep us honest," I reminded him. "Good intentions are no substitute for competent police work. I know how the frustration can tempt an investigator. Letting it get to you is not professional and I apologize if I'm preaching to the choir."

The investigator at the other end of the line laughed. "You must have been hell on wheels in Arkansas," he said. "By the way, the name is Donovan, first name George."

"It's good to meet you, George. I go by Jazz. That's what most people call me."

"Not the Beast Buster?" he asked, testing.

"That sounds like the name of a grade B cop show sponsored by a low grade snake oil company."

"Fearless leader of the Headhunter Team," he added, probing my limits.

"You've been talking to Trina, haven't you?" I asked.

Donovan allowed as much. "Sorry for the wise ass," he said. "You just sounded too good to be true."

"Yeah, well, you know how it is. I can walk on water in North Dakota in January, too," I told him. "On the other hand, I have been known to try to switch TV channels with the garage door opener."

Donovan chuckled. "Fair enough, Jazz. Let's talk about Beck. What do you need to know?"

"A good recent photo would really help. All we've been able to come up with are snapshots several years old. Those show the sergeant with a military haircut and no facial hair, but we have software that can add that. What would help most is a good, high definition face on and profile. Like a booking mug shot with high-definition detail. I would also like to see any personal papers he left behind and a set of fingerprints. Your own assessment would help, too."

"That's easy enough," he replied. "Where would you like me to send them?"

I gave him the address the agency used for mail and told him to mark what he sent for me. "I really appreciate your calling," I told him. "Getting in touch with NCIS was on my list but I didn't know who to ask for."

After I hung up, I called a number at the Agency and asked for a trace on the most recent call made to my cell phone. Six minutes later I got a call back telling me the call had originated at the NCIS field office in the District. The number was for a Special Agent George Donovan.

This was reassuring. I could have been talking to our killer. I didn't really think so while we were talking and I had not given that much away. Even so, it was reassuring to know I had not.

Taking out the steno notebook I had been using for the case, I began to think about what we needed to know about Sergeant Beck. Since he was in the military, his movements across the country should be easy to track. I flagged that one for Donovan. He had the access and resources to do that fairly quickly. It was also part of his job.

I was in the middle of a thought when my computer bleeped, telling me I had an urgent message. When I opened my email there was a message from Donovan telling me he enjoyed our conversation. It also said there were photos of Hailey Beck attached and I was glad to see he had sent high definition RAW files. While these took longer to download, there were only two of them and they would give Michael Angelino more data to massage if need be.

When I opened the files the images were superb. What I was looking at was a middle aged man with bland features and salt-and-pepper hair. It was a face that could be easily forgotten. It was also a face I found disturbing. What troubled me was the complete lack of affect. Were this our killer, there was no sign in the features of the terrible state of mind which had to be driving the man. Or his complete lack of empathy.

What I found most disturbing, however, was a strong sense I had seen this face recently. Try as I might I could not remember the context. It could have been someone in the elevator or walking down the street, or even a store clerk. My sense of it was that I had never spoken to the man, but I couldn't even say that for sure. He was a man never seen, one whose first line of defense was the ability to fade into the background like a copperhead. From there he could strike, quickly and deadly, like he had at Trudy's door. Only when he had complete mastery over his victim would he reveal himself.

I was thinking about this as I went through the mental exercises I use to jog my memory. Sometimes these work and sometimes they don't, and this was one of those days they didn't. Strain as I might, I simply could not recall when and where I had seen Beck.

It was almost a relief when my phone rang again. When I answered, I recognized the voice on the other end but I couldn't place the name, Adam Smith. The accent was that melodious way of speaking sand-lappers, the natives of coastal South Carolina, use to charm the rest of us.

"You may not remember me, Doctor Phillips, but I am the night doorman at Ms Howard's apartment building."

"Yes, of course I remember you, Adam. My mind was a thousand miles away. What can I do for you?"

"Well, I don't want to get into no trouble but I got something you might like to see. Thing is, I like my job here and I don't want to lose it. I guess I could give it to the police, but I thought you might like to see it first. It was from that night Ms Howard's door got shot."

"Can you give me some idea what it is, Adam. What you tell me will stay between us."

"It's a tape I took, only it isn't a tape. It's a recording and I've got it on one of those little thumb drives. It shows time and date, and I took it with my own camera. I do that in case we get robbed or something."

"Why didn't you give it to the police, Adam?" I asked.

"I didn't want to get in any trouble. I wasn't sure if it was legal to take pictures like that."

"I've seen the surveillance recording," I told him. "It shows a man coming in but you can't make out his face."

"You can on mine. I sat it low down so you can see the faces, for sure."

I found myself getting excited. "Here is what I want you to do, Adam. Make two copies of the recording on thumb drives. I will reimburse you for them. Make sure they are both good copies and then give one to the police on the other one to Ms Howard. Tell the police exactly what you told me. I would rather you did not mention the fact that you made a copy for me. It's okay if you do, but it would be simpler for me if you did not. I promise you your efforts will be rewarded."

I told myself I needed to calm down after I hung up, but it was hard to do. Assuming the face on Adam's video matched the one Donovan sent me, we could place Beck in Trudy's apartment building at the time the shots were fired into her door. That would be enough for the Newark police to get a warrant for Beck's arrest and to put out and an APB for him. We could also make sure there was a copy of his picture in every police cruiser in Newark and possibly New York.

The next call I made was to Trudy. I told her what the situation was and to ask Adam for the flash drive he was making for her. "When you get it, please ask Dom to make another copy and to email the best picture directly to me. Then, if you wouldn't mind, drop a copy in the mail to me and keep one for yourself. Adam will be giving a copy to the Newark police."

Trudy and I visited for a few minutes until she had to get back to work. I called Nicole to let her know what was going on and told her I had pictures of Hailey Beck for her to see. I was surprised when she laughed. "I've already seen them, lover man. But don't ask and don't tell. You really don't want to know."

"You totally amaze me, wife. Have I ever told you that?"

"Only a few dozen times, but I never tire of hearing it. Stud Muffin," she added, knowing the effect the sobriquet would have on me.

"I have an idea," I told her. "Is your husband out of town?"

"Funny you should ask, sweet man. As a matter of fact, he is. How soon can you get here? I'll fix us some lunch."

When I got to the office the next morning I had an email from Dom waiting. It had a couple of attachments and when I downloaded these and opened the files, I found myself looking into the empty eyes of Hailey Beck. "Gottcha!" I declared.

"Got who?" a familiar voice asked from the doorway. I looked up and saw Willie Dill smiling at me.

"Good morning, Willie," I greeted him. "I was just talking to myself."

"Work around here long enough and that happens," he replied. "I haven't seen you around lately. You doing all right?"

I told him I had been working on a case in New Jersey. "My deepest condolences," he answered, with a wry smile. "It sounds like you just broke the case."

"Not completely but I can place my primary suspect at the scene of an assault. So we have probable cause to get warrants. Assuming we can find him and where he lives."

"Well I am glad it's you who has to fool with that and not me. That's the one thing I disliked most about the military, all the damned paperwork."

"Due process is what keeps us all safe from the abuse of power," I told him with a shrug. I smiled. "I have a full lecture about that on tap if you care to imbibe."

"It's a little early in the day for hard spirits," he chuckled. "I'll leave you to your rat killing."

I picked up my phone and called Dom to thank him for sending the photos. "I hope you're close to an arrest," he said. "This whole business has people in the office pretty uptight. Everybody will be glad when it's over."

"Not the least of whom is me," I assured him. "Getting shot at makes it all way too real. I'm damned glad to get back to the District. Soccer games are all the excitement I need these days."

"So when will you be back here?"

"I'm not sure. Pretty soon. I need to talk to the Newark police and that's best done in person."

That reminded me of the photos and I called the number on the card the lead detective had given me. "You're lucky you caught me," he said. "I was just about to head out. We caught a nasty one. Gang-related, three shooters down and two bystanders dead. I haven't even checked my email yet. Just a minute." A moment later he was back. "Yup, it got through. He's a sweet-looking asshole isn't he? We're still waiting on the Pentagon for what they have. How did you get this so fast?"

"I've got good friends in low places," I told him. "Actually, I used to work for the Navy as an NIS investigator. That's been forty years ago but I guess it still makes a difference." I didn't mention that I worked for the Agency and had high level Pass Go clearance from Homeland Security. Or a wife who was a world-class hacker.

"Any idea where this guy lives?"

"Somewhere he can fade into the background, like a transition area. A cheap SRO hotel would do it. I don't know how he's fixed for money. Or where he gets it. It could be savings. The only suspicious thing we've come across is that he was moving odd sums of money slowly out of his regular savings account. It was almost empty when he disappeared."

"What you mean by slowly?" he asked.

"Between 2,000 dollars to just under 8,000 every few weeks. He was trying to fly under the 10,000 dollar IRS tripwire. What he apparently didn't know was that the tripwire was moved back to 5,000 dollars some time back. I think the reason he was moving odd amounts was to keep from attracting attention."

"So he's careful and he is also good. I still haven't figured out how he got out about apartment house without anyone seeing him."

"The easiest way would be to hide out somewhere in the building, maybe a vacant apartment or one where the owners are out of town."

"My lieutenant's flagging me," the detective said. "I've got to go."

I sat there for a moment, trying to figure out what to do next. Nothing suggested itself but I realized I had not heard from Dee for a while. So I punched in his number and he answered on the first ring.

"How did you do that?" he wanted to know. "I had my phone in my hand and was just about to call you. Bobby and I have been showing the picture you sent all over Atlanta. We didn't get much except from the river run but we can place him in Atlanta on the day Henley was shot. It's a popular trail to run. It was a nice day and we must have talked to three hundred runners. We got seven who recognized his picture."

"What picture?" I asked. "I just got it this morning, myself."

"It was that lady from the office," he told me. "You know, your friend the HR lady. It really helped. She emailed it around midnight and I got it on my phone. I forwarded it to Bobby and we went out early this morning showing it around."

"Which picture are you talking about? The one from NCIS?"

"Yeah, that's the one we were using. The new one your friend sent was better. It was a candid and our perp has aged a lot since the first one was taken. Why, is something wrong?"

"No, Dee, just the same old senility. I forgot I had sent you the one from NCIS and you're right, the new one is better."

Dee laughed and I heard him talking to Delgado. Then they both laughed. When Dee came back on the line I asked him to head for Washington and meet me there. "How about Bobby?" he asked and I told him to bring Delgado, too.

When I hung up I sat there for a moment going back over our conversation. The mistake with the pictures really bothered me and I wondered if I was getting too old for this. There were plenty of other things I could do to fill my time, not least was my family. I wondered if it was time to hang up my badge and move to Wyoming permanently.

Then I thought about the kids. The way things were they had the best of both worlds. I wasn't sure how the cultural poverty of ranch life in rural Wyoming ranch life would affect them. There was no reason to take such a drastic step. I could retire and spend my time chasing light around the District and there were things like the Great Smokies or the Chesapeake Bay to explore with my camera. Nicole could continue her work for Sam if she wished and I could take over getting the kids wherever they needed to go. I could even do odd jobs for Sam now and then, limiting myself to the analysis of documents.

The only question in my mind was whether I had what it would take to make the change. Nor did I feel competent to make the evaluation. So I did what wise men have done throughout the ages. I cleared my desk and called my wife. She was surprised to hear from me at that hour but thought a midweek date was a wonderful idea.

"May I ask what prompted this?" she inquired.

"I need to talk through a career issue," I told her. I started to add that it was no big deal but I stopped. It was, in fact, a major decision affecting all of us and I needed her levelheaded assessment. At the moment, my own thoughts and feelings were in shambles.

When we met at the restaurant, Nicole and I enjoyed our food first before getting down to cases. When the coffee arrived and I told her what I needed to discuss, she smiled. "You've been restless for months," she told me. "I didn't know what was going on and you didn't seem to know there was anything going on. Which is why we had that strange conversation about fidelity. I didn't want anything to come between us, and I didn't want you tearing yourself apart with guilt."

"I admit it took me by surprise," I allowed. "On the other hand, you often do. So what do you think?"

"I think you need to chase light. I am not saying you should but that you need to, like a writer needs to write or a tenor needs to sing. Aside from our family life, that's the one thing that seems to fulfill you most."

I couldn't deny the truth of what Nicole was saying. Yet it would be a big change, one that was a little frightening. I said as much to my bride and she laughed. "Of course, it is. But I have no doubt you'll come through it fine. Look at what you've already had to survive and come to terms with. You have been widowed twice and have lost a partner who saved your life. I think Sofya would tell you there is a lot of survivor's guilt in that. On top of that, you have been forced to retire. Even though you agreed it was necessary for your health, stepping down from the CID was major stress. I would be surprised – no – worried if you are not a little frightened looking at retiring again. Hunting bad guys has defined who you are, the Beast Buster from Little Rock. I was scared to death having you on my trail. That's how good you are at what you do."

"I could say the same about you, my love. In fact, you turned my life upside down. Not that I'm complaining. The life we have now is so much richer than anything I've known before."

I saw tears form in Nicole's eyes when I said this and when she answered it was in Portuguese, our language of love. "Be careful, my sweet man, or you'll have to carry me out of here in a sponge." She reached out and took my hand, intertwining our fingers.

"We are getting rather serious, sweetheart," I answered in Portuguese. "Does one of us need to fart or something?"

Nicole burst out laughing, a deep belly laugh that turned heads in the restaurant. "Somehow that sounds even more vulgar than in English." She gave me a look that could get us arrested in Arkansas. "I know you need to talk about all this, but I'm having trouble restraining myself until we get home."

I looked at the ticket and laid some bills under my wine glass. "I think we need to get out of here!"

An hour later we were lying peacefully in one another's arms. "Do you need to talk, sweet husband?" She asked in Portuguese.

"I think we just did, my love," I answered. "The decision seems rather obvious now. It's time to hang up my badge. Once this case is done, I will be available to Sam for thirty-minute consults and a fresh look at things that puzzle him. Other than that, I am out of the field. I would like to have Thanksgiving with our friends here in the District and Christmas at the ranch. Just to underline my retirement, I'd like to winter in Wyoming and not come back here until after Easter."

"Thanksgiving and Christmas sound great," she answered. "Maybe we need to talk a little more about where we winter. I'm thinking about the kids. They seem to be doing well the way we're doing things now. I'd hate to disrupt that."

"You're right, of course. We can work it out as we go."

I took my time getting to the office the next morning. When I called in, Sam's secretary told me he would not be in until just before noon. "I can get you in for a half hour at 11:30, but he needs to leave for the airport by noon. Is it urgent?"

I told her it was not but that I did want to see him before he left town. "Why don't you ride to the airport with him," she asked. "The car will be coming straight back here."

"Let me try for 11:30," I said. "Thirty minutes should be more than enough."

I was sitting on my desk thinking about what I needed to do next when my phone rang. It was the lead detective from Newark calling to let me know Hailey Beck had been spotted there. "We got really lucky, Jazz. One of our uniform officers was taking pictures of an accident site and spotted him in one of her shots. We sent a couple of plainclothes officers out to look around and they spotted him a couple of blocks away. He was going into a SRO hotel and one of the officers had a quiet word with the clerk. We have warrants and a plainclothes team has been keeping and eye on the place. Beck hasn't come out and we have people positioned at both ends of his hallway."

"This guy is extremely dangerous," I told him. "I would strongly advise against going in without SWAT. He is probably armed with grenades and SEMTEX, too. Have you read his file?"

"I can't say that I have," he answered me. "I think you're

overreacting a bit. We know how to do this."

"I'm sure you do, but going after this guy I'm after and going after a drug dealer are two different things. This guy is hard-core Marine Corps and highly trained in urban warfare." I wasn't sure about that last, but I didn't want anyone to get shot. Body armor covers a multitude of mistakes.

"We really don't have time to wait," the detective told me. "We need to go in now. Don't worry, Jazz. We'll be all right."

Those turned out to be famous last words. The detective followed legal protocol and knocked on the door. Unfortunately the officers handling the door ram were not wearing body armor. A double-barreled blast from a sawed off 12-gauge killed both of them as they were moving into position. They never got a chance to swing the ram.

At that point the operation turned into a full-fledged firefight. Four other officers were shot, three of them almost fatally. The lead detective took a round through the head. It was his sergeant who called in SWAT and even then, it was touch and go. The firefight almost ended when Beck lobbed a fragmentation grenade into the hallway. One of the SWAT team was also a Marine and was just back from the Middle East. He was able to grab the grenade and toss it back into the room just before it exploded, shredding the hallway wall with shrapnel. Three more of the SWAT team officers might have died if they had not worn armor. They were peppered with shell fragments.

The body they found in the room was wearing armor and had survived all of the bullets that struck him. It was the grenade that killed him, exploding almost in his face. The result was that Beck's features were too badly damaged to be able to identify him from his photo and this had to be done by DNA and fingerprints. Yet there was never any question that the body was Sergeant Hailey Beck and there was enough stolen explosives in the room to have leveled the hotel. It was a miracle that didn't happen.

Loose Ends

18 That was the end of the case. Our investigation ended with the death of Hailey Beck. This was an anti-climax for Team Jazz. We did the work and others made the bust. That didn't bother me at all. I have always believed that the bottom line was bringing the bad guys to justice. Personalities and turf games are irrelevant. They waste valuable time and energy better spent detecting. Given human nature I doubt they will ever go away. The limelight of celebrity simply too seductive.

It was never established if Hailey Beck was Susan Pleyer's killer. Yet that was just one of many loose ends left drying in the wind. That's the way it is in the life of an investigator. There is never time to run down all the loose ends. The case load is demanding and a detective can only give so much time any one case. There is always another one on the front burner and there is always pressure to close a case as quickly as one can.

As to motive, no one will ever know what was in Hailey Beck's heart and mind. The most apparent motive we could see was revenge for how he was treated as an event player. His attitude seemed to be that if he could not be the winner, no one who did win deserved to enjoy their victory. His mission was to make sure their time on earth was cut short as a punishment for lack of respect. This theory seemed to be substantiated by papers found in his blasted room. Among these was a list of all the winners with the ones he had killed crossed out.

Even so we were never able to figure out why he went after Trudy, or if he was responsible for lacing her sweetener with meth. It could have been Daniella who did this and I who was the target. Dee doesn't agree. "Jazz, as far as you are concerned, Daniella is the wicked witch of the West. She can do no right."

I started to differ but my long time partner stopped me with a raised eyebrow. "You may be right, Dee," I allowed. "I still wouldn't put it past her." Nor did it help that Nicole agreed with him. There are times a man just can't win. Yet they didn't rub it in. Not much.

As a courtesy, I wired a copy of Hailey Beck's mug shots to the Chief of Police in Bethlehem, PA. He called me back a couple of weeks later to thank me. While they never got proof that Beck pulled the trigger, they were able to establish that he was in the city at the right time.

I also gave Macintosh a call to thank him for his help. He had seen the news article about the firefight and told me it was glad he had missed that party. He also told me the death of the officers had hit him hard. He had been the training officer and a mentor to the lead detective.

Macintosh also told me that Leroy Winton, his former partner came to a sad end. He was killed a couple of weeks after we closed the case and it was in a drug deal gone bad. Nor was Winton on the right side of the law. He was the buyer and was carrying a briefcase stuffed with hundred dollar bills. The sad irony was that there was no cocaine in the case allegedly full of drugs. What it held was a mixture of other white powders and the suppliers intended to rip Winton off from the get-go. What they didn't know was that the cash Leroy was carrying was counterfeit. Nor did they know the Newark police had caught wind of the deal and were there waiting for them. Fortunately there were no police officers killed or wounded in the ensuing firefight. The supplier and his bodyguards were not so lucky.

We also never discovered who the inside person was at Jolly Good Times or if there even was one. The microphone in the bakery table remains a mystery. My theory is that it was put there by Daniella to monitor table talk by the employees at Jolly Good Times, but that is only a guess. As Dee pointed out, I have trouble seeing much good in her. To me she remains an enigma. Nor is it one I care to clarify.

The James Spradley crash remains a mystery, as well. Yet I find it easy to accept the conclusion that it was, indeed, an accident. Nor did I ever find out for sure if Daniella was James Mills,

Junior's, lover or if she persisted in sidetracking that investigation. It simply does not matter. Nor am I sure it ever did.

Trudy Howard retired from Jolly Good Times and moved herself and her husband to Seattle. Her take on things, after surviving two attacks that could've been lethal, is that life is simply too short to deal with things that don't matter. The reason she gave Nigel, however, was that she wanted to be close to her daughter and grandchild. She told me that he suggested she continued to work for Jolly Good Times and offered to set her up in an office there. She told him she would consider it but not to hold his breath. She said it was time for her to sit on the beach and watch the waves.

I was relieved when she told me this, as was Nicole, I think. I told my bride that I was not going to do that sort of thing anymore, not even if she ordered me. I went on to tell her that she was all the woman any man in his right mind could ever want. This inspired her to show me exactly how abundantly I am blessed.

I was surprised a month after the investigation ended to get a letter from Nigel. In it was a check and a single sheet of paper with a short message, "Thank You, Jazz! You did a marvelous job!" It was signed with a large capital N, complete with a nineteenth century flourish. When I called to tell him I had already been well paid he laughed. "I don't suppose they give bonuses in Cop World," he said. "However, you were working in the private sector, and we do."

I was talking with Dee a couple of months after that and he told me he had come up with an idea for a new Jolly Good Times event. It was inspired by our investigation and was called Killer. The point of the game was to find the designated "killer" of other players in the game. This killer slays one or two other players during each television episode. The kicker is that if someone makes an accusation that's false, they are disqualified and sent home. When it gets down to the final three contestants, each of them is required to accuse one of themselves or one of the contestants who has previously been eliminated. The one who names the killer then wins the million dollars. If none of them identifies the correct killer, the killer gets the million even if he or she has previously been eliminated.

When he asked me what I thought, I told him to have at it. Maybe he could sell the concept to Nigel. "However," I said, "you might want to give it some time and refine it before you spring it on him."

"Nah," he replied. "I don't think so. The poor guy has probably had enough murder. Maybe I can think of something else."

"Now wouldn't that be nice?" I asked him. "To think of something besides murder?"

From the Author

This is the twelfth Jazz Phillips mystery and I am as tired of murder as Jazz is. We've had a good run, the Beast Buster and I, and we've dealt with an amazing number of issues besides those involved in catching very sick people. I say sick rather than bad because I am not wise enough, smart enough, or compassionate enough to judge or condemn another human being. The most I can do is to judge their actions and whether or not these require us to put them away in a place where they cannot hurt themselves or any other human being. I don't think it is possible to have any chance at restorative justice with them, but we do need to treat these individuals with the same compassion and kindness we could wish for ourselves.

Turning to another question, people often ask me which of the characters in the series is me. The answer is none of them and all of them. Jazz Phillips is the man I wish I was, as are Sam McKee and Willie Dill. The single character who comes closest to me in flesh and blood is Forster, the cranky old Anglican padre Jazz goes to from time to time when he is troubled.

Before I bring this to an end, I would like to thank all of you for reading the Jazz Phillips series. And if any of you are inspired to keep the series going, have at it. All I ask is that you treat your characters and mine with respect. Among other things, this means allowing them to tell you the stories. Listen to them and they will show you wonderful things about being human.

So merry Christmas to all, and to all a good night!

Jazz Phillips Mysteries
Approximate Case Chronology

Sep 1987   Murder on the Run

Oct 1997   Jazz in the Cross-hair

Mar 1998   Jazz Plays the Big Easy Blues

Sep 1999   Jazz in the Golden Light

Dec 2000   Jazz and the Black Widow

Oct 2000   Murder in the Choir

Mar 2001   Murder by the Board

May 2002   Jazz Draws a Wild Card

Oct 2003   Murder in the Kirk

Mar 2004   Murder was a Blast

Sep 2006   Murder by the Queen

Sep 2010   Jazz and the Last One Left

www.ingramcontent.com/pod-product-compliance
Lightning Source LLC
Chambersburg PA
CBHW070900250626
47159CB00003B/1134